Pru Blum's life hasn't been easy, but working as a cellist with the Lower Georgia Symphonic Orchestra is her solace. She depends on her friends and uncle for support, but she's resolved to become stronger and more independent. However, avoiding her abusive ex, Cliff, isn't easy . . . especially since he's a member of the orchestra too. His overbearing personality and unwanted attention stop her in her tracks each time she tries to move forward.

Shawn Levinson's life seems disjointed, almost as though it's someone else's. His parents adore and expect him to marry his girlfriend, Helena, and for him to work for her father's corporation. Deep down, he knows their relationship is a sham. Besides, sitting at a desk and wearing a tie forever isn't his dream. Whenever he tries to follow his own path, though, everyone dismisses his hopes as foolish. He doesn't have the strength to oppose two families, so he escapes to Georgia to work on his parents' retirement home and look for some clarity.

When these two lost souls literally collide, sparks fly, but neither wants the complication of a relationship. And Shawn hasn't mentioned anything to Pru about Helena. No matter how hard they try to distance themselves, they can't seem to keep away from each other. By the time they're ready to admit their feelings, their pasts and secrets are poised to blow up in their faces. Falling in love may be exactly what they need . . . if they can each get out of their own way.

Dear Prudence
Copyright © 2023 Karen Janowsky
ISBN: 978-1-4874-3924-8
Cover art by Martine Jardin

Published by eXtasy Books Inc

Extasy
BOOKS

Look for us online at:
www.eXtasybooks.com

DEAR PRUDENCE

BY

KAREN JANOWSKY

DEDICATION

For Richard

CHAPTER ONE

Pru planned to have her panic attack tomorrow. For now, she unfurled herself along the bed, spine uncoiling from having slept in a tight little ball of anxiety. Sunrise was imminent, and the symphony of frogs and crickets outside welcomed her to the calm before the storm. The Lower Georgia Symphonic Orchestra's conductor, Martin, was planning for the whole orchestra to sight-read a brand-new piece today. She fully expected his frustration to quickly build into a gale-force squall.

Rolling over, Pru gazed, bleary from sleep, out the window, watching the black early morning turn dark blue, then periwinkle. In her periphery, she spotted the chain-link fence, the same kind that separated all the houses in the neighborhood. Wisteria twisted its way through the links, impossibly enormous purple blooms fighting for sunlight.

She swung her legs over the edge of the bed, pushed aside the tangle of blonde hair that obscured her vision, and stood. "C'mon, Matilda."

Matilda lifted her boxy head, thumped her tail a few times, and resumed snoring.

Pru stepped over the yellow lab and grabbed her pink kimono from where it was draped over the spindle-backed chair she used for cello practice. She closed it tightly enough to cover her breasts, which she'd long felt were too ample in proportion to her tiny waist. She had to wrap the tie around twice.

She made her way into her apartment's square kitchen

where the vinyl flooring curled up from the floorboards in one corner in its battle with humidity. Pru filled and set the electric kettle, then craned her head back toward the bedroom. "Mattie, wake up."

A still-groggy Matilda loped into view, propelled by slow wagging, and parked herself by the sliding door in the living room. When Pru opened the door, the dog came alive and barreled outside before sliding to a stop halfway across the yard and sniffing around. Large mosquitoes hovered over a puddle a few feet ahead, and an ominous-looking wasp nest took up real estate on the beam separating Pru's side of the cracked concrete duplex patio from Tommy's. The strong, citrusy smell of the blooming magnolia tree in the middle of the yard blended with the heady, cloying wisteria, leaving a thick, velvety texture that coated her tongue. Sunlight radiated its pink, then orange glow across the scraggly lawn. It shone through the blossoms and branches, still wet from last night's rain. Birds began to call to each other.

If things could stay just like this, Pru thought she'd be okay with being alone. And after today, she would be.

In the patchy Bermuda grass, no-see-ums pricked at her ankles as she headed to the fence full of wisteria. She admired the plant's insistence. Once it dug in its roots, the twining, woody vine was there forever, expanding its claim on the land and fighting back when anyone tried to rein it in or kill it. It always found its way back, bigger and more deeply colored than before. Pru worked her fingers around a couple of stems and pulled them off, her mind wandering to her possible plans to leave the Lower Georgia Symphonic Orchestra once and for all.

However, leaving would mean searching for some other state orchestra to play in, which would mean auditions and the expense of moving. She'd also be that much farther away from Uncle Barney down in Florida, as well as her only three friends in the world.

Joe kept saying she should go to mixers and ladies' nights at Rooster's Liquor Lounge, but crowds and cacophony were panic triggers, and bringing Matilda along in her orange service dog vest would scream "Defective, needy woman seeks loving relationship." Besides, if a man came home with her, he'd just run away when he saw her body. What was it like to be comfortable in one's own skin and with one's own company?

Her goal this summer would be to find out.

CHAPTER TWO

Shawn leaned on the kitchen counter and finished the last of his soggy Frosted Flakes. The wall unit blew cold-ish air at full blast but did nothing whatsoever to alleviate the humidity in the room. At least he wouldn't be late with the rent for this shithole of an apartment, thanks to today's much-needed job. The pay for simply putting a bunch of furniture away in an air-conditioned room was disproportionate to the labor but worked in his favor.

As he washed his bowl, the drug dealer in the apartment above him and her boyfriend were already screaming at each other. The only time Shawn had asked them to keep things down, he'd earned a black eye in exchange.

He reached up, yanked open a warped, woodgrain cabinet, and shelved his breakfast things. As Shawn pulled off his T-shirt and headed toward the bathroom, his phone sounded. He hit the speaker button and continued the ten or so steps to go shower. "Hey, Helena."

"Good morning, my dear." Her voice was treacly ooze. He pictured her smoothing one of the lacy silk nighties she liked to wear over her flat, tight stomach. She'd be making the pouty face that usually accompanied that particular tone of voice. Her performance was all theater—still, his cock twitched.

"I'm getting ready to go to work. Did you need something?" He noticed his reflection in the mirror over the sink and turned away. Shaving had been too much to bother with this week, and the beard he was sprouting needed a trim. He shoved down his boxer briefs, kicked them away, and turned on the water. The pipes moaned before water came out in a few strong, short spurts, and then the stream began.

"I woke up thinking about you." Again, that voice—thick as cough syrup dripping from a spoon. "I hear the shower. Are you undressed yet, Shawn?"

"Helena, I don't have time for this right now." His body clearly disagreed. "Is there something in particular you need from me?" Steam started to rise from around the gray plastic shower curtain. He reached in and lowered the water temperature.

"Only you." Her voice caught as her breath quickened. "You know what I was thinking of this morning? The first few months we were together, and how sometimes you'd wake me up with your fingers inside me. I would wake up having an orgasm." There were a few seconds of ragged breathing. "Tell me you miss me."

Shawn took a steadying breath, but he could almost feel the silk in his hands when he pulled down her short pajama bottoms—the ones that hardly covered enough to warrant wearing in the first place—and the way she would grip around his fingers when she came. He could feel the firmness of her breasts through the fabric when he crawled up and helped pull her top off. Helena's head would tilt back, exposing the hollow of her throat, and her auburn hair would be spread on the pillow, mussed from sleep. This woman was the epitome of every teenage fantasy he'd ever had, and she wanted him.

How was that possible?

He looked into the sink, resenting her for all of it, including the automatic reaction she elicited from him.

"I want your cock in my mouth."

His fist, of its own volition, wrapped around his dick. As if she were Pavlov, and he her trained dog. This was one of the main reasons why Shawn was more than 900 miles away from home. He needed to think things through with his brain instead of his libido.

He reached over and turned the hot spigot off altogether. "That's enough."

She moaned in that same liquidy tone — one that made him want to jump into the shower and scrub himself raw even as his hand started to pump. "Shawn."

Shawn braced his hands over the counter and willed himself not to get sucked into this stupid mini-porn. Medium brown wavy hair stuck to his face as the room grew more humid. His face was reddening in the mirror, and he was as hard as ever. "I'm late. I can't do this." His increasingly shaky breath betrayed him, though. His hips were moving already. "I've really got to go."

He fumbled to hang up before she could reply, then hurried into the shower, nearly missing the step over the edge of the tub. He only caught himself by pressing a hand on the wall before slipping. The water hit like an icy slap, but the shock was exactly what he needed.

CHAPTER THREE

Pru shivered in the even-more-frigid-than-usual church where the LGSO rehearsed. From her fifth-position seat in the cello section's room, Pru half-listened to the fourth-chair sight-read and half-studied the most difficult solo section of Prokofiev's *Sinfonia Concertante in E Minor op. 125*. They'd been instructed to play the piece one by one in front of each other. The thought hadn't even occurred to her to practice. The torrent of thirty-second notes began to blur beneath the bright fluorescent lights, so she stared at the ripped posters of string instruments lining the acoustic foam walls.

As Sandy, the orchestra's draconian concertmaster, stepped in front of her, the woman's shadow darkened the sheet music. Between her black shirt and pants and her nearly white skin, her looks projected "undead." Her pale blonde hair was pulled into a tight ponytail, making her narrow face and sharp features practically skeletal. Pru sometimes wondered whether, in the sunlight, Sandy sparkled like the vampires in the *Twilight* books.

The concertmaster's arms were folded. "Your turn. Go."

"Just fair warning, I—"

"Didn't practice it. Understood. Begin."

Shaking, Pru picked up her bow and skated it across the first few wrong notes. She wasn't supposed to start over. Over the course of about thirty seconds, she'd already made herself look incompetent in front of her colleagues. Her face was hot. She loosened her hold on the bow, fumbled, and dropped it. Pru tried to avoid eye contact with everyone as she ducked to retrieve it.

Sandy drew her eyebrows forward and down. "Again."

Pru wasn't even sure she felt the heavy strings against her fingers as she moved her hand up and down the neck of her instrument. She skidded the bow a few times and plowed through, shutting her eyes and wincing when she finally made it to the end. Her heart pounded, her arms ached, and she was sweating from the feat of endurance involved in playing the passage. There was a reason a lot of people considered this one of the hardest classical pieces for cello ever written.

When everyone had had their turn, they gave her obvious sideways, assessing glances before rising and carrying their instruments back to the stage.

Pru trudged across the pitted, scratched floor to her seat in the theater. The forest-green stage curtains resembled drooping leaves, and the air conditioning froze the sweat on her face. Scarlett O'Hara might have been onto something about using drapery as a layer of warm clothing. She thought of the old Carol Burnett sketch. She imagined a curtain rod balanced over her shoulders, heavy velvet curtains and gold tassels hanging over her as she feigned dignity and grace. She couldn't help letting out an inappropriate giggle as Martin Johnson, the conductor, opened his mouth to say something. The short, balding man wearing his standard argyle cardigan and perfectly ironed khaki cargo pants stared at her, somehow managing to slice through her amusement with the precision of a knife thrower. Pru straightened in her seat.

Scriabin's *Mysterium*, after nearly three hours of sightreading, was a nightmare. Everyone looked miserable, including Cliff on the other side of the stage in the primary seat of first-row violinists. His blond head and broad shoulders rose several inches above most of the other violinists, even seated. When he noticed Pru, he winked. She rolled her eyes and looked away, pretending to concentrate on whatever red-faced Martin was shouting at the clarinet players for the third or fourth time. There was a collective sigh of relief when he announced, "Make sure you know this piece when we reconvene in September."

The din of conversation, well-wishes for the summer break, and instrument cases being shut washed over Pru as she dropped her head back and closed her eyes.

"Pru? Are you in?"

She opened them again. Violet, a middle-aged woman with umber skin and bright blue streaks in her gray hair, was holding her flute case and smiling at her.

"Sorry, what was your question?"

"Are you coming to O'Malley's?" Violet was one of the few people there who went out of her way to be nice to everyone. Pru almost wanted to say yes.

"I think—"

A heavy hand landed on her shoulder. "We'd love to join you," Cliff proclaimed. Violet's smile vanished.

His grip was tight. His sharp, musky cologne curled through Pru's windpipe. She pulled forward in a short coughing fit. As she doubled over, the man let go and whacked her back so hard she pitched forward, but Violet shot a hand out to steady her.

"Thanks, but I think I'm going to go home and relax," Pru wheezed. Her back and shoulders tightened, her throat scratchy from Cliff's scent. She rose and wove her way toward her instrument case.

"Pru, come back here." Cliff would have made a great drum major in a high school or college band—his command echoed through the room. She moved faster. The chairs and stands were too close together to navigate with that big instrument, though. When Pru swerved to let an oboist named Steve pass, she stumbled back into a music stand. The stand rocked and fell over with a clang, the others in its path echoing as they dropped like dominos.

The whole room quieted. Everyone stared as Pru's face burned. "Sorry." She looked down, apologizing more to the toppled pile of stands rather than any particular person.

One hand gripping her cello, she bent to pick up the first stand. "Leave them." Sandy stood next to her, scowling. She jutted her pointy chin and narrowed her eyes. "Just go. We've got this."

"I'm really sorry."

"I *said* leave."

Pru nodded once. "Right. Have a good summer." She found and zipped up her case, then headed backstage. This area was almost devoid of props and equipment. The board of directors always hired someone to clean up the stage and rehearsal rooms once the season was over. She headed across the dark, scuffed floors and past a wall of cubbies overstuffed with sheet music.

When she got to the exit, which led to the foyer, she turned around. She knew she ought to go socialize with everyone. However, Cliff would consider that a victory. Pru texted Edie. *What are you doing tonight?*

Pru watched the three dots on her phone wave as Edie responded. *Proofreading my paralegal's civil complaint and preparing a few pleadings. Don't forget you have a lunch date tomorrow.*

She did? *I didn't forget. I'll meet you in the park to talk about it afterward.*

Sounds good. See you at High Hill Park by the old benches around one-thirty on my lunch break. Pru noticed Cliff by the stage entrance. He was flirting with a trombonist whose name she'd forgotten. He'd raised his hand to lean against the threshold, allowing his Bulldogs shirt sleeve to pull back and reveal bulky biceps. The trombonist had short red hair. She stared up at him, smiling and wide-eyed as Cliff looked down her shirt. Pru was pretty sure he'd slept with at least half the women in the orchestra over the course of the season—not that she cared.

She turned to leave, but Cliff saw her and headed in her direction. His violin case butted against the backs of her legs as he followed her through the foyer.

Pru stopped and turned around. The man towered over her. He was smiling, but his cornflower blue eyes were narrow, and there was a menace to the set of his artificially whitened teeth. His caramel-blond hair was darker in here, adding to his shadowy presence. The strong jaw, along with the perfectly symmetrical balance of a straight nose and wide-set eyes, reminded her of an evil Ken doll. Underneath the alcohol and citrus of his cologne, he smelled like American cheese and a Slim Jim.

She focused on the chickenpox scar on his forehead. "Cliff, I don't want to go to the pub with you." Her heart began to race.

His eyes crinkled. He relaxed his shoulders and laughed. "We can just have fun somewhere else then. You mentioned your place." He stepped forward and reached for her.

"*No.*" Pru took a step back but tripped over her own feet and stumbled. She turned and picked up her pace toward the door.

The temperature changed from thin and icy inside to hot and soupy outside as he kept up with her all the way to the parking lot. The humidity was so heavy that her breath was labored by the time she stopped by her trunk and dug for her key, her back to him.

When she found the key and opened the hatchback, Cliff grabbed the cello case. "I've got it for you, babe." He stood so close that his hips almost touched her butt. Then he took a step back, lifted the cello into the car, and slammed the door shut. "See how good we are together?"

Pru whipped around and bumped into the back of the car. Heat blasted through the thin cotton of her skirt and into the backs of her legs. Standing against the metal bumper was like sitting on a hot stove, but better to immolate on her ancient Escort than throw herself into Cliff's arms. "We're not."

He leaned his hands on the rear window, caging her between his arms. As her skin seared against the car, her insides went cold. "Where's your mongrel?" he asked. She'd thought about bringing her today, but most of the time orchestra practice was, all things considered, a safe place. Matilda had never liked Cliff. That should've been a red flag from the beginning.

"She's home. Waiting for me and *not* for you."

"Listen, Pru." His muscles softened, but he still had her pinned to the car. "We've had some rocky moments, but overall, think of how happy you were with me. I want you back. Let's try again this summer."

Pru wasn't sure her body could stiffen any more than it already had. His eyes widened, and his lips loosened into a sad puppy face. Still, her heart pounded. "Get out of my way, Cliff."

Their chests were a couple of inches from touching. "Babe, think about it." His eyes narrowed as he half-smiled. That was the look he got just before he was about to deliver an insult in the most loving terms possible. "I care about you. You're obviously lonely. And have you met anyone while we were apart?" He didn't wait for an answer. "No one else wants you. Anyone else who gets close enough to you will see a sad little girl who still cries for her dead mommy and daddy in her sleep." He put his hand on her cheek.

Pru's fight, flight, or freeze response usually started and stayed with freeze, so it was a surprise even to her when she swiped his hand away and shoved his chest. He almost lost his footing as he took a half step back. His mouth twisted into a frown.

Fast as she could, she ducked and slipped out from under him, slid into her car and shut the door hard. Cliff was still standing behind the vehicle. "We're not finished here." His voice boomed.

She cracked the window open and twisted around to look at him. "You'd better move if you don't want to get run over." Then she hit the gas hard and peeled out of the parking spot so quickly the tires squealed. Cliff jumped aside. Pru slammed on her brakes a second before she crashed into someone's oncoming car. The driver swerved as she waved in apology and sped away.

Chapter Four

Shawn shot up his middle finger as a dark blue Escort tore out of its parking space, nearly T-boning his car before driving off. Oddly, that same driver had now slowed to a stop by the parking lot entrance. The car yielded to five other vehicles, then flashed its turn signal and exited.

Backing into a space, Shawn turned to Joe. "Are you waiting here in the air-conditioned car, or are you going to help me move stuff?"

Joe's Braves cap was lowered past his forehead. He hadn't bothered to shave, and the only visible parts of his face were the sunburned tip of his nose and the red-brown stubble covering a bourgeoning double chin. His hands rested on his belly, which was just shy of hanging over his belt. "You're the one getting paid. I think you've got this." His Southern accent, with its slow, elongated vowels and stresses on the first syllable of most words, was thicker than it had been when they were undergraduates at SUNY Buffalo.

"The faster I work, the sooner we can get to our day drinking."

Joe tilted his visor up a notch, let out an exaggerated sigh, and unstrapped.

The asphalt of the rapidly emptying parking lot was shiny and black amidst the heat. All the pavement in Georgia so far resembled the La Brea tar pits. Shawn imagined his feet stuck and his body pulled into the gooey mess until he was sucked below the surface of the earth. His and Joe's sunglasses fogged the moment the car doors opened. Shawn pulled his down the bridge of his nose. "How the hell do people live like this?"

Joe shrugged. "The answer's in your question. Summer in landlocked Georgia is hell."

A shadow crossed them as they made their way through the scorching parking lot. They halted when the darkness expanded over them. "Joey! Long time, my friend!"

In front of them was a linebacker of a man who could have been the result if Cary Grant and Robert Redford were combined into a new creature under the direction of Victor Frankenstein. The man had the most punchable mouth Shawn had ever laid eyes on. The moment the thought arose, guilt lassoed his brain and reined him in. Maybe he was an okay guy who just made an obnoxious first impression. Still, he reeked of artificial oranges and cheese.

Joe gave him a closed-mouthed smile. "How's it going, Cliff? Did you get my invitation?"

"Sure did." Cliff was holding a violin case. "I'm heading out to O'Malley's with some of the musicians. You and your friend can join us if you want." There was a familiar, haughty tone of entitlement in his voice that was made worse by the Georgia accent.

"Shawn Levinson." Shawn put out his hand. Cliff looked at it but didn't take it.

Well, screw you too.

"I'm here for the summer," Shawn said. "I'm a plumber. Joe and I got to be friends the day I was snaking an enormous turd out of his mom's bathroom." He and Joe used to play this game all the time when they were in college, just to see how far they could go before someone called bullshit.

Joe grinned. "Yup. My mom took one look at his plumber's crack and ratty Kiss T-shirt, and she was a goner. His port-a-potty stench was like catnip to her. I walked in on her riding him like a bronco." He grimaced.

Shawn suppressed a laugh. "We were so into it that we

didn't even notice him. Gotta say, for a woman in her sixties, she's got some stamina."

Joe pretended to gag. "Anyhow, I needed a drink after witnessing the debauchery. Shawn and I ran into each other at a bar that evening. We've been buddies ever since."

Cliff blinked and cocked his head. "I see. At any rate, O'Malley's."

Joe gave a tight smile. "Too much to do today. I'll catch y'all later."

The other man flashed a used car salesman-style grin and walked farther into the lot.

Once inside, Shawn and Joe collapsed into a laughing fit. "You think he believed us?" Shawn asked as he leaned against the wall and wiped his eyes.

"Who cares?" Joe said, out of breath.

Shawn grinned. "So, who is Cliff, *Joey*?"

His friend rolled his eyes. "He's the only one who calls me that, and it's because he knows it used to annoy me. He's a childhood frenemy—a trust fund baby who thinks his money and looks are all he needs to get by. My parents and his go back a long way as business associates, so I was *asked* to invite him to my party in a few weeks."

"Nice." They headed through the wide foyer lined with fliers for tutoring, summer Bible camp, and a production of *Jesus Christ Superstar*.

"He's probably annoyed that I make more money as a professor than he does as a principal violinist with the Georgia Philharmonic's poorer, red-headed cousin, even with his shit-ton of family money." Joe pointed to a T-intersection. "Over there."

Directly around the corner were the double doors to backstage. They reached the stage and started to pick up folding chairs and music stands. "I'd have introduced you formally, but he's a prick."

Shawn laughed. "So I gathered." He grabbed two chairs under each arm and headed backstage.

"I meant to ask, how's Helena?"

"Don't ask." Shawn propped the chairs against the wall. "The less I think about that whole situation, the better." He'd begged his parents to let him fix up the property they'd bought to retire in — that would mean getting away from everyone. Plus they'd be paying him. He strode toward the far end of the stage, grabbed four more chairs, and went backstage again.

Joe had put down his music stands and was tapping his foot, arms folded. Ever since he'd seen some of Helena's pictures on social media, most of them selfies in bikinis, Joe had been incredulous that Shawn hadn't taken the next step. Shawn and Joe had been friends since they shared a dorm in college. It was nice to have a friend who knew him well and didn't judge that much. However, Joe also could see right through him sometimes.

Shawn put his hands on his hips. "Don't give me that English professor stare. I don't have to turn in a report for you."

"She's hot, she's rich, and she wants to marry you. What's there to think about?" Joe followed Shawn out again.

"I just need some space from her." He sucked his lips behind his teeth and his arms tensed. Over the past month or so he'd been away, he'd noticed that the less he thought about Helena, the better he felt about life. His phone buzzed with a text.

Joe pointed at the phone. "Her?"

Looking down, Shawn saw the message. *Has the tile for the master bathroom come yet?*

Shawn shook his head. "Mom." He texted back. *It's in the house, waiting for me to lay it.* He inhaled. Here it comes.

Why haven't you returned Helena's calls?

And there it was. He took a moment to figure out what to say. *I've been busy working.*

We miss you up here, honey. I can't wait to hug my boy. And I know Helena is dying to see you. She loves you too.

Shawn sighed. *Miss you too, Mom. On a job. Gotta run. Love to Dad.*

Closing out the texting app, Shawn mumbled, "Fuck my life." He turned off the sound on his phone and scanned the room. There was more to do, but now it was easy to see how badly the back wall needed repainting. He thought about contacting the building's manager to ask if he could work on it. Anything to drag his feet before deciding what to do with his life. "At least Cliff told us what bar *not* to go to."

Joe raised an imaginary drink. "Hear, hear."

The floorboards squeaked for the next half hour as they arranged stands, chairs, a podium, and a bunch of other stuff lying around, getting everything into its proper place.

Shawn sat on the last chair onstage and looked around. This wasn't much of an auditorium—maybe a hundred or so seats with threadbare olive fabric and dark armrests that needed to be sanded and restained. Maybe he could propose fixing those too.

During the last phone call with his dad, Shawn had asked for an advance on his payment. The car had needed several replacement hoses, and his electricity was on the verge of being cut off. The air conditioner in his apartment sucked, and it cost a small fortune not to swelter to death. Shawn had stammered through the whole conversation, his head hanging and eyes averted from his father's imaginary presence.

Beyond the stage lights, he imagined an audience of his family and Helena's. He was putting on a one-man show where he was the *schlimazel*. Helena would have been wasting her time all these years if he didn't do what he was supposed to do, and his parents would be crushed.

Joe's elongated shadow crossed him. "Your ass is the one thing between me and a couple of beers before I finish grading sixty exams on *Hamlet*. C'mon. I'll buy."

Hamlet's line—"I am pigeon-livered and lack gall"—crossed Shawn's mind. *Hamlet* used to be his favorite tragedy. Outside, the blacktop appeared wavy in the afternoon steam. The steering wheel was almost too hot to touch, like a metaphor for something whose meaning Shawn couldn't quite identify.

CHAPTER FIVE

Pru walked through the entrance to the park, a steel gate that had been made to resemble old wrought iron. The entry opened to an expanse of soft grass of a shade of green she was sure didn't exist in nature. She passed the sloping sidewalk to her left, which led to a chaotic playground full of children in brightly colored shorts and T-shirts. Early May and school was already out for some kids. The high-pitched squeals and shouts sounded like an unrosined bow pulled across a too-tightly strung piccolo violin.

She headed right, down another concrete sidewalk that turned into cracked asphalt. The path wound around the renovated tennis court and past the not yet renovated basketball court, where the moldy nets sagged in the humidity. From that point, the paved trail ended. Pru hopped over the pebbles and broken pieces of pavement, upsetting a small lizard hiding beneath them. The brown creature lifted its head. Pru hadn't thought a reptile could give someone a dirty look, but its eyes seemed to narrow at her before it turned and ran into the woods.

Edie was sitting on a wooden bench along the original walking trail. The trail used to be an easy-to-walk dirt path. Now, though, the overgrown roots that jutted from the ground resembled gnarled hands reaching through the leaf litter. The overgrown trees created a shadowy canopy, the sharp shadows of their branches completing the Hitchcockian feel of the path.

One of Edie's arms was extended across the back of the

bench. She was making circles in the dirt with one of her blue flats.

Pru sat next to her. "Hey."

Edie glanced over. "Hey, yourself. How did it go?" She turned her head to face the trees opposite the bench, and they listened to the trill of birds calling to each other, punctuated by the thwap of a tennis ball hitting the court's pavement a few yards away.

"Sid was nice," Pru said. "He told me about his sisters up in Atlanta, and his brothers and parents in South Korea, and some of the stuff they used to do as little kids."

She studied Edie's profile and waited. The woman's skin was even and brown except for a nearly heart-shaped patch of vitiligo on her temple, and another patch by her ear. The tiny bits of sunlight through the trees highlighted her sloping nose and smooth, wide forehead.

The woman narrowed her eyes at Pru. "You messed up again. I can hear it in your voice. What happened this time?"

"And that's why you're a trial lawyer." Pru forced her mouth to twitch upward. Edie was an attorney in a large law office not far from there.

"You told him that story."

"It wasn't the gory version."

When Pru was almost nine and her little brother was seven, her family had been in a car accident. Her parents had died, along with her brother. Pru had lived with her grandmother after that. When Grandma Esther died, she went to live with Uncle Barney. Her stomach had twisted once again as she told the story. It almost always did no matter how many times she repeated the tale. She couldn't remember exactly what else she'd said to Sid, but halfway through their meal he'd announced that he had to go, put a handful of bills on the table, and left in a hurry.

Edie sighed and patted Pru's hand. "Stand up, Miss Blum."

She straightened and pointed ahead.

"Why?"

"Stand up." Edie snapped her fingers. She had on what Tommy half-jokingly called her "Law and Order" face. Pru couldn't help imagining the *bah-dum* sound from the TV show. She got up and stood in the middle of the walkway.

Edie leaned back. "You are five-foot-three and weigh, what, about a hundred fifteen pounds? You're twenty-six but you look like a teenager in that sundress and that long pony-tail. Spin around for me."

"This is my lucky dress." She lifted her chin. "It's got pock-ets." The green spaghetti-strap garment brushed the middle of Pru's calves as she turned.

"It should be, showing off that hourglass figure of yours." Edie grinned. "You're a cross between a wide-eyed, pink-cheeked kewpie doll and a pinup girl. Your whole body prac-tically screams *fuck me.*"

"Does it?" She looked down. The dress wasn't especially revealing. Her cleavage wasn't visible at all, which was an-other reason she loved it. Pru clasped her hands behind her back and paced in front of the bench. "It's been just under a year since Cliff. I think my brain's screaming too, but Edie—"

"How do you somehow manage to scare off every man I set you up with the minute you open your mouth?" Edie tapped a rounded, yellow nail with a tiny rhinestone flower glued into it. She looked straight ahead. "I don't think I know any more single men in the firm I can talk into meeting you."

Pru knelt to pick up a discarded tennis ball on the path and tossed it in the direction of the courts. "I don't think I'm cut out for dating." She turned to her friend. "I think I should just learn to be alone from now on."

"Only if that's what you want, and I don't think you do. But how intense of a relationship do you want with BOB for the rest of your life?"

"Battery Operated Boyfriend and I are doing well, thanks very much. He's very intuitive about my needs. And his soothing, midnight-blue color is attractive to me," Pru replied.

Edie snorted a laugh. Pru grinned, then stopped pacing and sighed. "Maybe Cliff was right though," she continued. "Maybe I'm too damaged to be in a relationship if it isn't with him." She sat again.

Her friend whipped around. "Do *not* go there. Do *not* go back to him or so help me—"

"Not a chance." They'd talked the subject into the ground for months. Cliff claimed she was frigid, except for the times when she managed to put her inhibitions aside. At those times, she was a slut. Pru suppressed a shudder when she remembered yesterday afternoon. "I do wish he'd leave me alone."

"Is he bothering you again?" Edie straightened. "I'll slap him with a restraining order so hard he'll be limping for a month."

"I blew him off." Pru grinned again. "I almost ran him over."

Edie grinned back. "Good girl. If you ever really do it, you'll have an attorney at your service, *pro bono*." Across from them, a couple of squirrels quibbled over half of a browning apple someone had tossed into the woods. "Did you get Joe's invitation to his birthday bash in July?"

"I'm part of the entertainment," Pru told her. "But this weekend I've got another function. Remember Geoff Reid?"

"Is that this weekend?" Edie tilted her head and tapped her finger again. "Do you have any idea why he's having a formal party?"

"I think it's a business thing. I heard there are going to be some important corporate connections, and that a few politicians are going too." Pru hated those parties. Uncle Barney had dragged Grandma Esther and her to those kinds of functions all the time when he was still working in the upper echelons of corporate America.

"I'm glad I dodged that bullet," Edie said. "A couple of my bosses are going though. I'll give you a tip. I mostly get through those things by quietly judging people and focusing on not rolling my eyes all night."

"I will heed your sage advice, counselor." A corner of Pru's mouth lifted. "At least I don't have to stay after I finish."

"Maybe you should. Maybe Prince Charming will be around." Edie elbowed her and winked. "You'll be wearing makeup and formal clothes. You won't look like a kid for a change. Wear glass slippers—or at least acetate ones."

Pru chuckled. "I'll rummage through my closet and try harder to behave immaturely."

Edie glanced at her watch and smirked. "My lunch break is over. I gotta go. We'll talk more later."

Reaching into her pocket, Pru pulled out some cash. "When you see Sid, can you give this to him, for lunch?"

Her friend took the money and sighed. The women hugged, and Pru watched her make her way up the path. Her friend was tall and lean—a runner—and her gait was all precision and surety. The oak moss hanging from the branches she passed was limp and heavy. Pru shook the dirt and pebbles from her sandals and stood.

Prince Charming. Sure.

CHAPTER SIX

The path was still and quiet enough for Pru to close her eyes and hum Dvořák's *American Quartet* as she strolled through the shade while she conducted the imaginary music. The sound and vibrations filled her, almost as if her pulse and breath synched to its rhythm. Dvořák had finished writing the whole ensemble in something like thirteen days. The *lento* part with the cello solo was a joy. She especially loved playing in minor keys. In this one, her whole body quivered with the strings of her instrument at the violin and viola accompaniments.

Without warning, a hard thud reverberated through Pru's chest and down her spine. She gasped. Time seemed to slow as she fell. Strong hands yanked her up by the armpits before she hit the ground. Her nose and forehead thumped against someone's chest. Her eyes opened to a blur of gray fabric. The man who'd caught her was solidly athletic and somewhat sweaty.

"Are you okay, miss?" He kept his hand on her arm while she steadied herself, then let go.

"Sorry." Pru looked from the man's chest, which sported the SUNY Buffalo logo, to his face. His wavy, medium brown hair was damp and stuck to his forehead, and he had one of those half-stubbly beards that were so popular right now. His lips were sunburned and his reflective sunglasses made her face look egg-shaped in their reflection.

The man pulled his lips back with his mouth closed. "You looked like you were having a seizure or something. Should I call for help?" He had a hint of a northern accent, with rounded vowels and dropped r's.

Pru narrowed her eyes and put her hands on her hips. "I was conducting." Neither of them moved for a few seconds, and then he laughed. His teeth were straight and even, with a slight overbite.

"No offense. Sorry." He dropped his shoulders. "Are you a conductor?" He raised his eyebrows and cocked his head — he had an open, curious expression, as opposed to the predatory or condescending ways Cliff often regarded her.

"No, I'm a cellist with the LGSO. I'm doing a private function this weekend and another in June, and I have a piece of music in my head. Sorry I was in your way." They both stepped in the same direction to get around one another, stopped short, tried again a few times, and laughed.

"Since we seem destined to dance today, I'm Shawn Levinson." He pursed his lips. "I'm not trying to be creepy, but out of curiosity, where's the gig this weekend? I'm doing some setup for a couple of parties this summer. They both feature live classical music, and one's this Saturday evening."

"The one this weekend is for someone associated with Gordon Community College, and the other's a friend's thirtieth birthday party. Do you know Joe Schulman or Geoff Reid?"

Shawn tilted his head. "Joe and I were roommates in college. I'll be helping set up tables and stuff at Geoff's event, and for Joe's thing later on."

"Joe was my freshman comp TA in college. I guess I'll see you there."

"Cool." He took a step to move this time, and Pru shuffled to let him pass. On his next step, his foot hit a large, exposed root. He stumbled forward and stopped short. She staggered backward into a thick, overturned tree trunk behind her, lost her balance, and plunked onto the hard wood. She caught herself just before pitching over the trunk and onto her back. A shock of pain burst behind her knees.

Shawn cringed. "Oh, jeez. Are you hurt?" He pushed his sunglasses on top of his head. His eyes were dark brown, his irises circled by a faint, almost gold ring. Out of nowhere, at the sight of this disheveled stranger Pru's hands started to sweat.

She crossed her foot over her thigh to take off her shoe again. "It's fine." As she dumped some pebbles out, she looked up. He was watching her, lips tight and brow wrinkled. Sweat dripped from his brow, past his eyes, and down his neck.

"Excuse me. Sorry." He grabbed the hem of his T-shirt, turned partially away from her and wiped his face with it. Shawn's torso was all lean muscle. Pru tried not to stare at the trail of dark hair that disappeared past the center of the V-line of his abs and beneath the visible waistband of his underwear. Dropping the hem, he cleared his throat and she looked back at her feet.

A cool breeze swept down the trail. The shadows deepened and thunder cracked. "Must be time for the daily downpour. I'd better go before I miss the bus," Pru said. Just as she stood, the skies swelled and burst open. Within seconds, they were both soaked. The path was a muddy, green blur. "I guess I'll see you soon. I'd better hurry," she said loud enough to be heard over the downpour.

They began to walk. Shawn raised his voice as well. "Does the bus take you straight home? Do you have a way to stay out of the rain if it drops you off in town?"

"I walked a couple of miles into town to meet someone and took the bus here afterward to see another friend. I'll probably have to grab a cup of tea or something and wait out the rain on Main Street." She quickened her pace up the trail, looking down to avoid big puddles.

Shawn jogged to catch up. They rounded the tennis courts

and onto the more even sidewalk. The sky had turned gray-black, the rain falling even harder. "I can give you a lift," he shouted.

Pausing, she shivered. Just hopping into the car of a complete stranger would be stupid . . . even if his oval face had a sharp, sloping jawline and soft, prominent cheekbones to go with pretty eyes and a kind smile.

She shook her head. "No, but thanks."

Shawn must have sensed her apprehension, even as they were yelling. He held up his hand. "Scout's honor, I'm just a good Samaritan."

Ahead of them, the loud hiss and grinding of the bus's motor kicked in as it drove away. Pru's shoulders became heavy. "You're not a serial killer or anything, are you?"

Tossing his head back, he laughed. Then he sputtered when water got into his mouth and up his nose. "I promise I'm not." He coughed. "I teach yoga. I try to take non-harming seriously."

"Okay." As they made a run for it, her feet slid on the inner soles of her sandals. She was still only a few paces behind him, but a slew of shouting kids and parents surged in the same direction and bottlenecked at the intersection before the gate, separating her from Shawn. She watched the crowd push along like an enormous, lumbering animal.

Pru's hair was so heavy that the tip of her ponytail settled at the top of her ass and tickled. She reached behind, ineffectually wrung it out, and flopped it over her shoulder like a scarf. Shawn wasn't visible anymore. Stepping onto the grass, she stood on tiptoes, using her hand as a visor to peer around the slowly diminishing crowd.

As soon as she shifted her weight, the ground displaced, her feet slid, and her shoes went flying. Pru waved her arms a few times, fell, and made a long, muddy gash through the turf as she skidded backward. The impact pulsed along her spine. Her dirty clothes were like a rope net catching every-where, pulling her back as she stood. One shoe was sticking out from some upended turf and the other was nowhere in sight. She retrieved the one she could find. Her bare foot squelched in the ground, while the back of the single shoe thwapped against her heel as she staggered ahead. She couldn't see much, but judging by the waning sound of kids yelling, almost everyone had left. Probably Shawn, like Sid, had changed his mind.

Sinking into the spongy grass, she hugged her knees to her chest and lowered her head against them. The downpour pounded against her bare shoulders and her back. She rocked back and forth, pretending that she was shaking because she was cold and that the water on her face was only from the rain.

CHAPTER SEVEN

"Looking for this?"

Pru jerked her head up in the direction of Shawn's voice. He was standing a few feet from her, a living, blurry Monet holding her missing shoe. "Here, let me help." He approached, knelt to slip it onto her foot, and offered his hand to help her stand.

As he led her toward a green-and-brown, older-model Outback, she noticed a long tattoo of something on the underside of his forearm.

Shawn hurried past her, splashing through a puddle and immersing a foot in order to open the door for her. She looked down at the worn, beige seat. Before she could get in, he said, "One sec." He reached into the back, spread a towel over the passenger seat, and gestured for her to sit. "Your chariot awaits," he shouted over the thunder.

Small, vinyl flakes fluttered to the floor from beneath the towel as she sat, and the faint scent of pine air freshener clung to the upholstery. Shawn got behind the wheel, reaching once more into the back seat for a loosely woven blanket checkered in gray and red. He leaned in and tucked it over Pru as the windows steamed. "I'm turning on the heat and the defroster, but you're going to get cold first."

He turned the ignition and indeed, freezing air blasted Pru's neck and chest while the car's carriage rumbled beneath them. She hugged the blanket more tightly.

"Sorry about that," he said. "I'm just going to idle here and wait for the window fog to clear up." The word "fog" had a subtle "aw" sound to it.

Shawn's hair stuck in straight clumps to the back of his neck. Pru noticed his slightly curved nose and long eyelashes. He rubbed his palms over his face and pushed his hair back. "I don't understand how people drive in this weather."

"You're not from around here, are you?"

"How did you know?" He chuckled. "I'm from New York, near Tarrytown."

"Oh, okay."

"It's where Ichabod Crane lived," he explained. Pru's expression must have been as blank as her memory of that reference because he added, "From the story." The way he said it—"stawry"—made his voice sound warm rather than corrective.

Playing with the edge of the blanket, she tried to remember whether she'd read that book and hoped she didn't look as stupid as she felt.

Tapping his fingers on his armrest, Shawn stared ahead at the opaque windshield. Then he turned to her again, leaning his elbow on the steering wheel. "I'm setting up my folks' new house down here. My dad's retiring this fall, and they want to live in warmer climes. It's the least I could do after I got a degree in English instead of business like they'd hoped."

"I took a couple of English electives." Pru wondered what she could say that wouldn't make her sound imbecilic. "I once read this book for my American Literature class where this family moves their dead mother in her coffin to another town in Mississippi, and all kinds of bad stuff happens, and the siblings all hate each other, and they lose the coffin a few times, drill holes in it, and by the time they get where they're going the corpse smells really bad. I think one of the siblings got arrested, and one of them tried to get an abortion but her brother stole the money she had for it to get dentures or something."

Silence.

"I didn't like it much. I never quite got the point of the book." She still couldn't remember the name of the one he'd been talking about earlier.

His closed-mouthed expression was hard to read. "Not a Faulkner fan?"

"Was he the author? Didn't he also write a story about this old lady who dragged her fiancé's corpse into her attic and had sex with him all the time?"

Shawn chuckled. "Yes, that's the same guy."

They watched the rain come down in sheets, completely obscuring the windshield. Pru focused on not making her cuticles bleed as she pushed them back. After a moment, Shawn cleared his throat. He felt sorry for her, she was certain. She wasn't as well-read as him, and she looked like a child who'd gotten pushed into a puddle and missed the school bus.

Shifting, she turned to face him more directly. "When I was about six or so, my great-grandmother died. I didn't like her much as a kid." Pru knew she should stop, but it was as if her brain was watching her mouth's impending train wreck. "When she babysat, we had to watch soap operas with her all afternoon. I felt kind of bad because she was my grandmother's mother, and Grandma was my favorite person in the world. Grandma Esther *got* me, y'know?" She took a short breath. "I probably might've dragged my grandma's coffin to somewhere else if it was her last wish." She closed her mouth abruptly, unsure of where she was going with any of this.

Shawn cleared his throat. "*As I Lay Dying.*"

Pru's eyes widened. "Oh, no, I'm so sorry. What from, if you don't mind my asking?"

He stared at the sheets of rain falling over his windshield. She'd offended him. She shouldn't have asked. A few seconds passed.

Widening his eyes, he lifted his chin slightly. His stomach

tightened and released with his breath as he smiled. "No. That's the name of the Faulkner novel."

She wound the end of her ponytail around her hand. "I used to read all the time. At my great-grandmother's, we weren't even allowed to go play in another room or anything, so I'd bring a book into the den. I read a lot after she died too."

For the love of everything, shut up, Pru.

Of course, she just continued. "Great-Grandma Ilana lived in a small apartment and kept the TV volume loud because she was mostly deaf but she wouldn't admit it. That made it harder to concentrate. After the funeral, when she was lowered into the ground and everyone else was busy crying and chanting along with the rabbi in Hebrew, my little brother Sammy and I got up close to the edge of the hole and he shoved me in. He *claimed* it was an accident, but I never believed him. He was kind of a jerk sometimes."

Shawn didn't respond.

"I hit my head pretty hard," she went on. "And I thought all the broken-up tree roots around the coffin were arms. Some scraped against me as I fell. The gravediggers who jumped in to get me out, they said I kept fighting. For a long time, I dreamed about yelling for her to let me go, but she couldn't hear me because, y'know, she was almost deaf—and she was dead."

He wrinkled his brow and seemed to assess her. Pru's breath shook as a few quiet moments passed.

Then his eyes and jaw softened. "That must've been terrifying for you. I'm sorry all those things happened."

Pru's muscles stiffened. Her mind was voiceless static for a second or two. Only Tommy and Edie had ever tolerated her babbling nonsense when she was nervous. "Yeah, it was. And thanks." *Change the subject before you sound even weirder.* "What's that tattoo of on your arm?"

"It's Sanskrit." He revolved his arm for her. Green foreign letters were woven around some bright sapphire blue-and-white lotus flowers. "The words spell out *om mani padme hum*. It means *the jewel is in the lotus*. The lotus is a symbol for en-lightenment, but its roots grow in the mud."

Pru nodded. "I see." At this point, it didn't even pay to pre-tend she wasn't an idiot relative to him.

Shawn continued. "So, real wisdom resides deep within the petals of a flower that looks like it's lifting from out of the mud. The swampy muck symbolizes our ordinary, recursive minds." He looked down then lifted his eyes to her. Their eyes met. He looked down again as he extended his hand. As she lifted her own to take it, he rested his palm over the gear shift handle.

She exhaled.

"I'm nowhere near that point, mind you," he said. "My brain's lotus flower is wound up pretty tightly."

Pru's gaze wandered to a rearview mirror ornament—seven small, rainbow-colored crystals stacked from red, at the bottom, to violet at the top.

His eyes followed her trajectory. "Those are the colors of the chakras. They symbolize the different kinds of energy eve-ryone contains. The red one at the bottom is for feeling grounded and secure, that dark blue one near the top is for intuition, and the purple one above it represents our connec-tion with the rest of the universe." He shrugged. "I don't think there are colored circles of energy all around us, but I do like the reminders that we're all multifaceted."

Pru put her hand to her chest and felt the blood drain from her face. "Oh, no."

He straightened. "What's wrong?"

"My little silver *chai* is gone. It's a Hebrew letter that means—"

"Wait here."

"Don't. It's okay. Really—"

Before she could finish protesting, Shawn was out of the

car and into the wet onslaught. The windows fogged again. She made a circle on the glass with her hand, but the rain was coming down too hard for her to see. How was he going to find it? How would he even know what he was looking for?

A few minutes went by.

Maybe he'd slipped too? Had he hurt himself? Maybe she should get out and look for him. Should she call 911? She should have turned down his offer to drive. He could have been dry and at home by now. She should at least buy him a coffee or something for his trouble when he returned. She shouldn't have said anything about the necklace. Main Street Bistro closed after lunch. What time was it now? What if he'd fallen and was unconscious or something?

Pru winced. She imagined a pinball pinging around in her head, ricocheting and setting off buzzers and bells.

Eventually, Shawn's soggy form approached the car. The muscles of his torso and the slant of his waist were in clear relief when he got close. He got back into the car, pale and blue-lipped. "I'm so sorry. I went all the way back to where we started out and I couldn't find it."

"Thank you for looking." She couldn't keep the wonderment out of her voice. "I don't want you to go back out there, but um, did you know what you were looking for? It's shaped sort of like a little table with one leg unattached. It's a Jewish symbol for life. Grandma gave it to me on my bat mitzvah." Her voice cracked and she cleared her throat. "That was so nice of you."

Shawn angled his fob toward her from the ignition. A small gold Star of David pendant hung from the key ring. "My grandparents gave me this as a necklace when I was bar mitzvahed. I never wear it anyway, but I heard it wasn't a fantastic idea to advertise that you aren't Christian in this part of the country, especially the farther out from the city you get."

She lifted her eyes to him. "That's true, unfortunately. I

mean, a lot of people around here aren't overtly anti-Semitic. At least, not intentionally. But the sentiment is pretty obvious in their attitudes." Her shaking subsided by a fraction. When the subject came up—usually when she was asked what church she belonged to—people tended to take a half step back and look her over, possibly to find the fabled horns on her head. She was always relieved to find someone who understood.

"I get it. The prejudice is more *sub rosa* in the North, but it's there too." One corner of his mouth lifted. "Incidentally, what's your name?"

She cringed. "Oh, it's Pru Blum. It's spelled B-l -u-m, but it's pronounced *Bloom.* "

"Short for Prudence?"

She nodded as something niggled just past her consciousness. Then she brightened. "The Headless Hunter."

"What?" He squinted.

"I couldn't remember the name of that story about your hometown."

Shawn leaned back and chuckled. Tiny creases spread past his eyes. "Why didn't you just ask? It's the Headless Horseman. He's a character in a story called *The Legend of Sleepy Hollow.* "

As she looked out the window, Pru wrung the fabric of her dress through the blanket. Water seeped between her fingers.

He leaned around to see her. Their faces were inches apart. His breath smelled like cinnamon. This close up, she could see the small flecks of gold in his eyes against the dark brown, and the honey-colored hair mixed with the brown in his beard. She sucked in her lips as he settled in his seat and turned on the windshield wipers.

"If you feel safe enough, let's brave this," he said.

"Okay."

Fastening his seatbelt, he asked, "Where to, Pru?"

CHAPTER EIGHT

Shawn turned into the driveway of a lemon-yellow duplex with a black Honda and an ancient-looking blue Ford Escort under a wide, white carport. The neighborhood reminded him of the kind that students often rented. The houses in this area were better-kept, at least. There were no cars lined up at the curbs, and all of the homes had neat, green lawns and flower beds. The chain link fences separating the homes had been overtaken by purple, flowering vines, creating the illusion of walls of blooms between the homes. In the pouring rain, everything blurred a little as water rushed from roofs and downspouts, creating waterfalls from the houses and small pools in the grass. The overall effect was a fairytale-like gestalt.

He parked behind the Escort, and they stood under the carport. The heady scent of wisteria hung in the thick air, even in the storm. Pru turned to Shawn and smiled as they shivered, a tableau framed in purple flowers.

"Ready?" she asked.

"Ready as I'll ever be." He rolled back his shoulders and took a big step into the rain. Their shoes squelched, submerged by a half-inch as they half-jogged along the short walkway to a few stairs that led to a covered cement porch with a black railing.

"You're going to meet my roommate," she warned. Like many of the people he'd met so far down here, Pru's vowels were elongated, making one-syllable words sound like two. Her accent was more subtle and less edgy than Joe's, though.

She might be the first person I've met down here on whom it's absolutely adorable.

When Pru smiled, her cheeks colored, revealing a few light freckles. She had big blue eyes, a delicate, gracefully sloping nose, soft-looking lips, and perfect, seashell-shaped ears, all set off by the soaked Rapunzel hair and a wet dress revealing a Marilyn Monroe figure.

She pulled open the screened storm door and unlocked the faded blue front door. Shawn tried to keep his gaze between the top of her head and the brass door knocker, rather than on her long ponytail, which reminded him of a brand-new pencil, just sharpened and tapering to the top of her ass.

Knock it off, Shawn.

"She's prettier and a lot smarter than me. Everyone who meets her loves her," Pru was saying. When they were inside, she told him, "I'll grab some towels." She whistled more of the tune she'd been humming earlier as she disappeared around a corner.

Before Shawn could notice anything about his surroundings, heavy, galloping thuds sounded from ahead. A stocky yellow lab launched itself at him, thumped its paws on his shoulders, and gave his cheek a few slobbery licks. He patted the dog's sides. "Okay, it's nice to meet you, too," he said with a laugh as it panted hot breath into his face.

He tried to scan the room and get his bearings, but the dog was having none of it. Scrunching his eyes and sucking in his lips, Shawn tried to avoid the worst of the tongue.

"I see my roommate's introduced herself," Pru said. Less than a minute had passed, and with his new friend blinding him with affection, it was hard to get the layout of the place aside from noticing that the walls were painted a faded, mossy green. She was standing behind the dog, towel tucked under her arm. Her free hand was on her hip, and she looked like she was trying not to laugh.

Then she snapped her fingers and pointed down. "Matilda,

off." The dog dropped onto all four feet and sat, looking up with her tongue lolling to one side.

Pru had changed into a pair of denim cutoff shorts and an REM T-shirt and had clipped her hair up off her neck. She looked down and scratched behind her dog's ears. "Go lie down." Matilda trotted a few paces to a cushion in a corner between the couch and the sliding glass door and plunked down with a *rumpf.*

Shawn grinned. "You're right. She's very good-looking, and I like her already. But there's no contest about your being prettier." Their eyes locked as he said that, and she bit her lip as she looked away.

She handed him the towel. "I should've asked if you were allergic first. I'm making some tea. Can I get you anything? Are you hungry? You can sit if you want." The couch was a queen-sized futon whose wide brown armrests were scratched in places, revealing the natural wood beneath. The futon was covered with a brown flat sheet with a faded rose pattern. In front of it sat a thick oak coffee table with rings where people had left their mugs.

Above the futon hung a large, framed print of art-nouveau-style string instruments on a flowery background of green, blue, and yellow. Next to that was an Alphonse Mucha print of a woman. Daisies were woven into her blonde hair like a crown, and she looked straight ahead, a hint of amusement playing over her face. A bouquet of wildflowers filled her arms. "Just take the sheet off. That's so the couch doesn't get covered in dog hair." Pru took a breath as he started to towel off. "You must be freezing."

"I'm fine. I wasn't going to stay—"

"Oh, I have an idea." Pru leaned over the sofa and banged on the wall. "Hey, Tommy, can you come over for a minute?" she yelled.

There was no reply, but the door opened within a few

seconds. A stocky man of about Shawn's height, with dark brown skin and short dreadlocks, walked in as if he were about to speak to a large audience at a podium—tall posture and shoulders back. He'd gone for a *Sopranos* look, with a beige track suit zipped all the way up.

"Nope. Nobody's home. This is his ghost. Please leave a message." Tommy's accent was similar to Pru's. His voice was a low-range tenor that belied his round, unlined face. He could have been the adult version of the Gerber baby.

"Tommy, this is my soaked friend, Shawn."

They reached out and shook hands. Tommy was a lot more muscular than he'd seemed at first glance.

"I don't suppose you can loan him some dry clothes?" Pru asked.

"Hmm . . . maybe." Tommy stepped back, put his hands on his hips, and looked Shawn up and down. Small crystal stud earrings glinted as he moved his head.

Shawn was sure he'd gone pale. "Oh, no, I couldn't—"

"Gimme a sec. I think Andrew has stuff that will fit you. I'll see if he has anything left in his drawer." He hurried out.

"Pru, this is nice of you, but I—"

Somehow she wasn't behind him anymore. Instead, she was on the other side of a half wall with a pass-through, her back to him.

Shawn remembered an Arthur Rackham print of *Undine* that he'd seen in an art book years ago. The girl in the picture was sweet, buzzing with energy, wisps of hair seeming to float and settle as though she'd just moved. He couldn't get the image of Pru in that wet dress out of his head as he made the association.

She hoisted herself onto the counter and opened a cabinet. Shawn squinted at the faded denim hugging her butt, and the space where her back and shorts met. He shook his head and blinked a few times.

"I've got rooibos, lavender, chamomile, mint, or ginger lemon," Pru said, twisting around. "Or if you like coffee, I can make that too. Do you want a snack? I'll take out some cookies. I've got some CDs over by the bookcase if you want to listen to something other than the air conditioner and the rain."

What must it be like to live in a brain that constantly darted all over the place like that? It was hard not to compare Helena's rehearsed veneer with Pru's unguarded stream of consciousness.

"Do you want some help with that top shelf?" he asked.

Pru pulled out a few boxes of tea and swung her legs over the counter. "I've got it. Thanks, though." She looked down, cheeks reddening, then hopped onto her feet and started running water into an electric kettle.

You are currently with Helena.

The door rattled open again. "These should sort of fit." Tommy held out a red polo shirt and a pair of jeans.

Thank them, turn them down, and get out of here before you get any more comfortable – or any hornier.

"Are you sure?"

The other man nodded. "They may be a little short on you." He pointed toward where Pru had come from earlier. "Bedroom's down there."

After passing through a short hallway with a partially open linen closet, Shawn opened the door to Pru's bedroom. The walls were a faded sky-blue. Her bed was a full-sized futon, similar to the couch except folded out, covered with a thin, crumpled kantha quilt. The quilt was patchwork, with mismatched designs in well-washed and faded jewel-tones. Next to the bed was a plain, white wooden table, with a drawer that had a small half-moon cut at the top. A black cello case rested next to a music stand in the far corner on the other side of the bed, just past a large window with semi-sheer, pale green curtains. On the wall opposite the bed was a desk covered in envelopes and papers. A closed laptop kept them from falling on the floor.

What caught his eye most, though, was the sole decoration — a heavy, glazed clay tile about the size of a poster on the wall next to her closet.

Shawn took a few steps closer. The tile featured a relief of a tree, a red bird perched on one of its branches. Along the top border in raised yellow letters was the phrase *To Everything There Is a Season*. The bird and letters were deep and bright in contrast to the earthy browns and greens of the tree and the dusky blue backdrop.

Tommy had sandwiched a fresh pair of plaid boxers between the jeans and shirt, as well as a travel-sized stick of deodorant and a plastic bag for Shawn's wet things. As he pulled on the dry clothing, he heard the man say from down the hallway, "You didn't launch into one of your bizarre stories, did you?"

"I literally just met him today." Pru's voice rose as she spoke.

"That's not what I asked."

"I did, but he didn't act like I was a weirdo, so maybe you and Edie are wrong. Maybe my stories aren't as off-putting as you say they are."

"Countless failed interactions beg to differ." Tommy chuckled. "Maybe he didn't kick you out of the car because he seems like a decent guy."

Pru said something that sounded defensive, but Shawn couldn't quite hear what it was.

Tommy guffawed. "Okay, maybe he realized you're insane and he was treading carefully since you were in his car."

She mumbled something else, softer this time.

"Get over here," Tommy said. "I'm kidding."

"All he has to do is check out the medicine cabinet." Pru's voice quavered now, and she said something else that Shawn couldn't hear clearly.

"In all seriousness, you should probably start taking your meds again now that summer's starting."

Shawn glanced at his reflection in the full-length mirror on the bathroom door. The jeans were an inch or so short. Still, he was dry and didn't smell like a wet dog. Besides, at five foot ten, it was nice to feel relatively tall.

He headed into the bathroom to pee. When he finished, he noticed that the bathroom's beige tile-patterned vinyl flooring was peeling from the corners. He could offer to repair it—it would only take him a couple of hours. The toilet and pedestal sink were avocado green. Above the sink was a fake wood-grain medicine cabinet. Thinking on what he'd overheard, he wondered what the medications were for.

ADHD, maybe?

Hating himself a little, he reached toward the cabinet.

"Give him some credit. Why would he go snooping around your personal stuff? C'mon, Pru. I've got a sixth sense about people." Tommy's voice was clearer through this wall.

Shawn exhaled, dropped his hand, and headed out to join them again, finding them in the kitchen. Pru had her arms wrapped around Tommy's waist, her head buried against his chest, and he was rocking her. He planted a kiss on the top of her head.

"Oh, sorry." Shawn's shoulders dropped, and his chest contracted a little.

Tommy looked up as Pru turned. "You didn't interrupt anything," he said. "But if I were single, I'd want *your* number. The only girl for me is snoring and farting in the corner by the couch." He let go of Pru and went back into the living room to open the door. "It was good to meet you. Hope to see you around, Shawn."

Pru had removed the sheet and put a tarnished silver tray with a teapot and two cups on the coffee table, as well as a chipped china plate with red-and-gold embellishments around its edges with a few vanilla wafers on it. The actual futon was plain, off-white apart from a few faded paw print stains.

"You don't keep kosher, do you?" she asked. "These have tons of lard in them."

Shawn chuckled as they sat on opposite ends of the couch. "No, I'm not even a little religious."

Pru shifted to face him with one leg folded beneath her. She made a quiet slurping sound as she sipped her own tea, while he looked around the room again. An air-conditioning unit took up most of the front-facing window. Through the sliding glass door on the other end of the room, sunlight strained to push past the rain and storm clouds. There was a small TV on a low, narrow table beneath the pass-through, a floor lamp like the kind you could get at Walmart, and a short bookcase with a few CDs and some books. The books were mostly about musical theory.

"Music major?"

She nodded. "Tommy and I both were. We both went straight from our undergrad degrees and pulled each other through our comp exams when I was finishing my doctorate and he was finishing his master's. He's the band director at Gorge View High." She looked around, as if trying to take everything in through Shawn's eyes. "The duplex is his. I want to pay rent, but he won't let me, so instead I just donate what he could have charged me to his favorite charities every month."

His eyes widened. "Wow."

She shrugged. "I know. Tommy and my uncle keep telling me to stop giving so much of my salary away."

"No, I mean wow, a doctoral degree." But the wow was also for her generosity. She obviously didn't have a lot of money by the looks of things — if he could live rent-free, he'd take the extra cash and run. Shame flashed through him. He'd lived rent-free with Helena for the past year, and mostly was disgusted with himself for choosing a comfortable lifestyle over being truthful with her — or himself.

"So, what do you do for work aside from teach yoga?" Pru put her cup down and bit into a cookie.

Warmth crept up his neck. "It's a little undignified."

Tilting her head, Pru pursed her lips. "You don't dance for women and let them stuff money into your G-string, do you?"

"What? No, I . . ." Her lips were pressed together, and one corner hitched up. He leaned back and rolled his eyes. "Very funny." He lowered his chin and raised his eyes. "No. With a bachelor's degree in English, I'm qualified to teach yoga and do handyman work. And some carpentry if it's basic stuff." He pushed his fingers through his hair. "I'm not that good of a dancer, even when I've had a few too many. And I don't own a G-string."

She bent forward and laughed — a real, honest-to-God belly laugh. How long had it been since he'd heard Helena do that? Shawn was pretty sure the answer was never.

"Why would you be embarrassed about that?" Pru's cheeks were pink from that short outburst. "Will you teach me yoga? I can't pay much, but I've always wanted to learn." She leaned in, all earnestness. Dark blue bands surrounded her pupils, sending lighter blue rays through dove-gray irises that darkened around the outer rims. She didn't seem to realize she was crushing half of a vanilla wafer into tiny crumbs onto her plate and lap.

He tried to pay attention to the small voice telling him to say no and stop staring at her thighs. "Yeah, of course I will." He looked around again. Those piles of papers on her desk were probably bills. "Don't worry about paying. Having someone to keep me practicing without a class in front of me would be great."

Hadn't he come all the way down here to stop thinking

with his dick?

A smile lit up her face as she destroyed what was left of her cookie along with several layers of his defenses. His knees felt like they'd loosened themselves from his legs. Shawn was torn between asking her on a date and making an excuse to leave but he couldn't think of a reason to go. He didn't need a reason. He also didn't need this complication in his life.

"Let's start next week, once we're done with Saturday's party."

"Yay." She clapped once, giving a little bounce in her seat. But there was a layer of agitation in her voice. He noticed the tightness in her jaw that kept returning when she didn't let her guard down. He'd been too busy refereeing the fight between an impending hard-on and his common sense to pay attention before. He was an asshole.

Pru leaned in and extended her arm, but it was shaking. Fumbling with the seat of the futon to steady herself, she lost her balance, grasped Shawn's thigh and fell into his unready arms.

She smelled like the musky lilac of the wisteria vines growing outside. The thing Shawn had discovered about those flowers was that once you inhaled, the scent seemed to enter your bloodstream for a while.

From behind Pru, Matilda struggled and stumbled as she rose. The lab crammed herself between the table and couch and wedged her huge head between them. That was a good thing too, because Shawn's hard-on was close to winning the argument. He let go of Pru and scratched the dog's head.

Pru's ears turned pink. "That was meant to be a handshake."

"It's all good." He cleared his throat. "Are you okay? You're shaking."

She shook her head. "I do that sometimes. It's just a thing that happens. Thanks, though." Backing away, she shooed

Matilda from the tight space. The sun had won its battle with the storm and overpowered the clouds. Wet light surrounded Pru from behind the sliding glass door at the other end of the room.

Shawn knew he was absolutely hosed.

CHAPTER NINE

Pru shivered as the air conditioner in the window kicked in and the glass above it fogged.

"I should get going. Let me get your number before I go so we can set up yoga." Shawn held out his phone.

A few seconds must have gone by before Pru responded. How long had she been gawking at him? She accepted the phone. Her fingers trembled so much that it took a few tries to get her number typed in as he watched. "It's the AC." She pretended to shiver again then handed it back to him.

He immediately called her. "Now you've got my number too." He lowered his head, took a breath, and then raised his eyes to her. They reminded her of the last golden-brown sky of dusk just before the fade to nighttime. Cliff's eyes were icy blue, even when he was being sweet. Shawn's eyes made her think about sinking into them.

I don't want a relationship to fill in all my broken pieces.

"Thanks for letting me dry off—and for the snack and loaner clothes." He stood.

"It was the least I could do." Pru followed him out the door. "Thanks for bringing me home. And for going out in that miserableness to try to find my necklace."

They alternately stared at each other and the porch, arms dangling at their sides. Her hands were still shaking—her legs too, for that matter. She chewed on her bottom lip then licked it and smiled up at him.

Standing still, he blinked at her as uncertainty spread across his face and then he looked away.

"I'll see you soon for yoga," she said.

Shawn snapped his gaze from the porch railing up to her. "Absolutely." The corners of his mouth turned up by a tiny fraction. "I'll, uh . . ." He pointed toward the street. "I'll get going."

Pru watched from her door as he got into his car. He waved before driving off.

When she shut the door, the floor wasn't quite steady beneath her. Her lungs thought they were running a marathon and her rib cage was in their way. Matilda trotted over and licked her hand.

"G-go get Tommy." Matilda prodded Pru to the couch, then turned and unlatched the door. She pawed at the knob until it opened. A few seconds later, Pru heard her barking at Tommy's door. The dog returned with him in tow.

Tommy patted the dog's head and sat close to hug Pru. Matilda watched for a moment then pawed her leg.

"Okay, Mattie. It's okay now. Good girl." Pru was still trembling, but the world was less wobbly when she was curled up in a ball on Tommy's lap. Meanwhile, Matilda had helped herself to the other cookies and sprawled on the floor. "I survived a stranger in my house."

"And a handsome one at that." Tommy stroked her head. "He's into you."

"No, he's not. Even if he were, I shouldn't. I haven't even had my yearly post-season meltdown yet. And I want to be on my own the rest of the summer instead of pining for love like last year."

"I think you're having your panic attack as we speak."

Pru clenched the side of his shirt as she sat up. "You, Joe, and Edie can't keep dropping everything when I need someone. I want to know how to need myself. I feel so small sometimes."

And yet I'm clinging to my best friend for dear life.

Tommy, with an arm around her, looked down and tapped

his finger on his thigh a few times. "Being self-sufficient is important." He faced her. "But you don't have to be isolated or lonely. It's not one or the other. As for feeling small—well, I hate to be the bearer of bad news, but you're petite."

That made her giggle. She unwound from him and Matilda trotted over, thrashing her "demolition tail," as Edie had once dubbed it. The tray and pot landed with a crash. Crumbs, tea, and glass spilled and scattered on the floor.

"Dammit." Pru started to push herself up.

"I've got this. You sit there with the Yellow Destructress. Do you need your rescue meds?"

Tommy rose and Matilda jumped up to take his place. She laid her paws over Pru's shoulders and nuzzled her, then lowered her head and licked her arm. Pru rubbed the white fur around the dog's muzzle. "My girl." She leaned over and kissed her between the eyes. "No, I should be okay."

After he'd cleaned up, Tommy sat on the coffee table across from them. "He's not going to be a stranger. I can feel it. You just gotta get out of your own head and calm down."

"Not likely. For either."

Tommy cocked his head and pouted.

"I can't focus on anything but Uncle Barney and Matilda right now." Pru pushed back a cuticle, but Tommy swatted her hand away because she was making it bleed.

"Stop it." He frowned. "Listen to me, my dear Prudence. You need to come out and play more."

She pretended to yawn at the Lennon joke. "Really, Tommy?"

"I mean it." His tone softened. "Matilda is seven. She's got a few more good years left, and you're taking super good care of her. If she needs the other hip replaced, we'll find a way to make it happen, I promise." He moved to the couch. "And Barney has told you over and over to stop sending cancer treatment money and to stop asking to come down every other weekend. He wants you to enjoy your life."

Tears stung in her eyes. "No. I'm not going to lose them. I won't let it happen."

"Baby girl." Tommy leaned in and grasped her hand.

"Stay and watch a dumb rom-com with me."

"Sounds good." He grabbed the remote from a side table and sat on the other end of the couch. Matilda bounced her tail on his lap as he scratched her butt. He chuckled. "As usual, I get the exhaust fumes side." Flipping through the Netflix menu, he glanced at her. "Maybe you should at least use the clonazepam when it gets bad. Just take half of one."

"Maybe." She knew that he knew that was a "no," and that he knew better than to push the point. Tommy picked a movie — small decisions were too much when the symptoms became this pronounced.

Pru focused on the opening credits. Matilda was still hanging in there, doing her job. The dog, Uncle Barney, her friends, and music were enough. They had to be. Pru reached over Matilda, and Tommy grabbed her hand. This was enough.

CHAPTER TEN

Shawn tried to get rid of the fog on his windows by rolling them down. He drove, white-knuckled, past the rows of old houses, down the parkway with its grocery stores, and past a shopping mall whose sign was so faded he couldn't tell what it was called.

He came to a side road lined with grass that looked as if it had been colored in with green Day-Glo markers. Reducing his speed, he passed through the security gate of the well-manicured community that contained his parents' new house and forced himself to relax as he wound through its Stepford Wives, cookie-cutter streets.

The open car windows helped him see better, but the humidity nearly sealed his borrowed shirt to his body. Something that smelled cloyingly sweet hovered around him. Maybe it was the wisteria scent clinging to his skin in the wet summer air. Now, wisteria was Pru's scent—a stranger he should have cut ties with after dropping her home. By the time he got to the right street, long after the heavy floral scent had faded, he still sensed her.

It was ten at night by the time Shawn returned home from installing the last of the kitchen appliances. He toed off his shoes and plunked onto the couch with a beer. There was almost no give in the cushions, and the shock of hitting the frame shot through him. In the house he and Helena shared, there was a large, comfortable leather sectional and a fifty-inch smart TV over the fireplace. She never let him screw her by the fireplace because of the expensive Persian rug.

It was, after all, Helena's place, and she couldn't seem to let him forget that. He just lived there. They knew each other's bodies well enough to synchronize their orgasms. The image of her perfect, firm ass in the air as he fucked her over the couch popped into his head and his cock twitched.

She takes care of me. She says it's because she loves me.

Shawn drank half his beer down without stopping for a breath. Then he leaned his head back against the cushion.

He opened his eyes twenty minutes later because the phone was vibrating on the particleboard coffee table. "Mom?" he said as he picked up.

"Hi, sweetie. I was going to leave a message, but I'm glad you're still awake. I have some things we need to talk about."

Last time she'd called this late, Dad had been admitted to the tachycardia unit of the hospital with a heart attack. That was what had prompted his decision to retire earlier than planned. "Are you and Dad all right?"

"We're fine, honey. We're just so concerned we can't sleep."

If they wanted to discuss what he thought they did, calling in the middle of the night was next level. An invisible rock started to push its way down to Shawn's stomach. "Okay, what's going on?"

He heard the phone switch to speaker. "We've been thinking about what happens when we sell the house and move down to Georgia," his mother continued. "We've been talking to Doug and Candace about this too."

Shawn took another big swallow of his drink. Doug and Candace were Helena's parents. "We agreed that you've been waffling about committing to Helena and getting a real job for too long," his dad said. "We can't support you forever. It's time for you to do the right thing for all our sakes."

The rock continued its descent. "And that would be what,

exactly?" Shawn already knew the answer. He finished off his beer and stood to rinse it and toss it into the recycling bin.

"Doug had your father look at a job contract he's drawn up," his mother replied. "You've got a good career at Jupitelligence waiting for you, as well as a soon-to-be fiancée. Helena's so good for you."

"This was your emergency?" Shawn's jaw tightened. "I was afraid something happened to one of you." He started to pace from the kitchen to the end of the couch. There wasn't enough room, though, so he half stomped in circles around the living room instead.

His mom whispered something to his dad, who started in again. "Shawn, listen to me. It's time to grow up and be a responsible adult. Enough is enough. Everyone went through all this trouble for you, and you will *not* turn this down. Are we clear?"

Said the people calling at a ridiculous hour, assuming he'd be up for a chat. A few answers vied for a response, but all were immature and inappropriate. "Noted. Goodnight, Dad."

His father's voice hardened. "You are twenty-nine years old. Everyone's patience is running thin. It's time to do as you're told and act like an adult."

Shawn grabbed some of his hair and pulled at it as he paced faster. "Think about that sentence. You just told me to do what you say and act like a grownup all in the same statement. Which is it?" He took a second to slow his breathing so he wouldn't yell. "And I'll give you a hint—the right answer is the one about making decisions as a grown man, which I'm pretty sure I'm doing anyway."

"Then act like a grown man, Shawn." His father's voice was almost a yell. Shawn could picture the angry glare that accompanied it.

"Dad, let's not fight about this. We should have a conversation during the day instead of now, late as it is."

In the background, Mom said, "Fred, your blood pressure."

"Ellen, I'm fine." His voice was soft and loving for her. Then he returned to Shawn and adopted his previous tone. Shawn was tempted to hang up on him, childish or not. "We aren't finished with this conversation. Get some sleep and think about what we've discussed." When his voice was low and stern like this, the automatic response was for Shawn to hang his head and feel like he'd shrunk a few inches. His parents ended the call.

Retreating to the bedroom, Shawn tossed his clothes into the plastic laundry basket. Then he tugged the dresser drawer to unstick it so he could dig around for a T-shirt.

Even knowing that Shawn had grown up in suburbia and had a college degree, Helena's parents had originally thought he was too unpolished for their daughter. That was, of course, until they realized he'd grown up in the upper middle class and his dad was a sought-after political wonk with a lot of connections in Albany and Washington, DC. The difference was that his family had always lived modestly compared to Doug and Candace's huge estate.

He shoved off his shorts and lowered himself onto the air mattress on the floor. He couldn't remember whether he'd even been all that interested in Helena the first few times he'd seen her. The relationship had just kind of happened.

Closing his eyes, he breathed and thought back. How long was he happy when they started seeing each other? Now that he had some space, he wasn't sure he ever had been, aside from the lifestyle and sex.

He pictured himself and Helena together as he drifted off, but her height had lessened by a few inches, and her hair had turned blonde.

CHAPTER ELEVEN

Shawn finished straightening a tablecloth and glanced around. The ballroom of Evermore Plantation featured huge domed floor-to-ceiling windows with thick royal-blue drapes lined with gold. Guests filed in, shaking each other's hands as Shawn wound his way around them to the other side of the room.

He'd been forced to go to these corporate networking parties by his father ever since he was a teenager. As was typical, half the people there were impressed with themselves and preening while the other half fawned over the first, hoping to be noticed. Every time he was at one of these events, he pictured the guests as characters on *The Muppet Show*. Their skin had felt-like textures in all manner of color and species. He imagined them dancing and telling groan-worthy jokes all night.

If only they were that much fun.

Between the windows were huge, ornate portraits of what must have been the place's original owners, and landscapes of the grounds as they once had been. He began to wander along the perimeter. There were oil paintings of orchards laden with figs and pears, horses grazing in a lush field, and women holding parasols—he couldn't help picturing Miss Piggy. One painting showed a stern, bearded man in a stuffy suit who reminded him of Sam the Owl, and an equally stern woman dressed up in so many layers of lace and silk that Shawn needed a few seconds to find her face. She was Miss Piggy in a different costume.

He tugged at the sleeves of his suit—a tan jacket with matching slacks, a light blue button-down shirt, and a dark blue tie. His mother had insisted he bring two suits down with him, "just in case." Shoving his hands in his pockets, he found himself wishing he could leave. He was supposed to stay at least through the performance, though, until his replacement came to take the equipment away.

Everything the quartet needed was ready to go, including the stands for each of the instruments. Pru's cello rested by the seat closest to the tables and chairs. Waitstaff threaded their way through groups of guests, expertly carrying trays of hors d'oeuvres and champagne glasses with just one hand. Without warning, a violent bang broke through the room. Shattered glass rocketed past his feet, with a few stuffed mushrooms rolling behind at top speed like tiny, fungal NASCAR racers. Everyone turned toward ground zero.

Pru was squatting in the middle of a pool of champagne, covering her face with her hands. The floor was littered with shattered glass and smashed mushrooms. Shawn picked up his pace to head over to her.

"It's my fault. I should've been paying attention." Her apology was muffled through her hands. Her shoulders hunched forward and her head dipped toward her chest as she shook.

"Please, let us," a couple of bus people said. When Pru noticed Shawn, the color in her face drained.

He took a few steps and knelt next to her. "Are you okay?" She took his outstretched hand and stood with him. He kept his hand on her mid-back as he ushered her toward the door where the musicians were supposed to enter the room later.

"I was just about to make sure my music stand was the right height," Pru said. Her cheeks, neck, and chest were bright red.

As soon as the door shut behind them, they found

themselves in a wide, gray hallway. Pru slumped against the wall. Her hair hung in a loose braid, and she wore a long, simple, dark blue dress with no embellishments—not even jewelry. The dress bared her shoulders and showed just a hint of cleavage—which, Shawn remembered, he shouldn't be staring at.

He stood by the wall, facing her. "Take a few deep breaths, Pru." Subtle, pale suntan lines striped her shoulders. He watched her collarbones and the hollow of her throat as her breath lengthened bit by bit. Her forehead and mouth smoothed and softened. Dry and styled, her hair was on the yellow side of light golden, and a few strands had slipped from the braid and skimmed behind her ear.

"You're going to be fine," he reiterated, both to himself and to her.

"You are one of the few truly kind people I've ever met. Thank you, Shawn." She chewed her bottom lip, dipped her chin, and lifted her eyes to him. "I'd better join the other musicians—we're on in a couple of minutes. Are you going to stay and listen?"

"Absolutely." He pinched his lips together and lifted them at the corners. She probably had no idea about the effect she was having on him.

Thank God for that, at least.

Rocking on his heels, he watched her walk toward the rear hallway. She probably thought his motivations were completely altruistic. They were, for the most part. If she had been a man, or wasn't as intriguing, though, he wouldn't have been this invested. He turned to head back out to the ballroom, unable to sort out what his intentions were when it came to this person he shouldn't be thinking about so much. Sighing, he returned to the room.

Once she was playing, Pru's demeanor was nothing like the bundle of nerves Shawn had just witnessed earlier. With her cello between her legs, she took on a weightless, dreamy expression as her head moved with her bow. He stepped closer and watched her long, precise fingers on the neck of her instrument. He couldn't resist inching even closer. There was some more color to her complexion. It was hard not to sway along as she played.

As he watched, he registered someone coming his way, and a firm hand landed on his shoulder. "Well, you're a familiar face. It's Shawn, right?" He turned to find Cliff standing next to him, impeccable in a dark blue tux. "Looks like my girlfriend and I inadvertently coordinated our outfits." He pointed to Pru.

Shawn looked from her then back to him, trying not to gape. "How long have you two been together?"

Cliff smiled. "Just under three years, depending on which of us you ask. She broke up with me last year, but her head's in the clouds most of the time and she doesn't know what she's doing. She's mine."

For the second time, the image of sending a fist through the man's teeth popped into Shawn's head. "All right."

Pru, meanwhile, looked blissful — as if the music had carried her to a different place.

"Isn't she beautiful?" Cliff gripped Shawn's shoulder until the hard pinch shot partway down his back. Without taking his hand away, the man looked down at him. Cliff was about three inches taller to begin with, but in this moment, he seemed freakishly enormous. "I just need to remind her that she belongs to me."

Shawn shuddered. They were standing at a posh gathering in what had once been a large plantation mansion. Whoever had lived here had had slaves, and Cliff had just claimed ownership of someone. His tone was forcibly light, and his body was rigid. Shawn noticed a few women watching them. From a distance, he was sure Cliff appeared friendly and handsome.

Shawn pulled away, almost colliding with a server laden with wine glasses. "Excuse me," he apologized, then turned back to Cliff. "I need to go check on something." He took one last glance at Pru and wound his way to the open bar before remembering he'd planned on driving himself home soon.

The more distance he put between himself and the ever-expanding circle of insanity surrounding this woman the better.

The stench of several colognes and perfumes combined into a mildly toxic cloud throughout the room. Shawn kept his head low and tried to hold his breath as he wove toward the swinging kitchen doors. The odor was marginally less nauseating in there. The hot, tangy, boiled crawfish smell settled on the back of his tongue, making his throat tighten as he rushed past servers and cooks, around the corner, and opened the door that led to the basement.

The basement door closed behind him with a loud click.

Crap. Really?

Shawn tested the handle, but the door didn't open. He checked his phone to call for help only to discover the battery was at two percent. A second later it turned itself off. Hopefully there was another exit in here.

After waiting for his eyes to adjust to the dark he descended, a modern Dante escaping the fiery eighth circle of hell where the politicians, hypocrites, and deceivers spent their eternal damnation. It seemed like there was no way forward except down.

CHAPTER TWELVE

Pru didn't feel as though thirty minutes had passed before the quartet was standing, bowing, and heading to the locker room with their instruments.

The other three soon waved to Pru and left, but she sat for a few seconds, staring at the blue metal lockers. She didn't really notice them, though, still high on the music. The perfect pitch of the instruments lingered in Pru's head. The sound was so pure that it almost sparkled. She closed her eyes until terra firma slowly solidified around her.

She wished it hadn't as she opened them to find Cliff staring down her dress. "Come out to the party with me." He didn't wait for Pru to refuse, just grabbed her arm so quickly that she almost fell as he pulled her to stand.

"Ow."

He loosened his grip.

Jerking her arm away, she said, "I don't want to. I'm going home."

He gripped her hand and led her out the door.

"I *said* I don't want to go out there. I also don't want to stay in here — or be *any*where with you."

Their steps clicked along the hallway as he propelled her forward. Every time she tried to veer away from him, he moved with her. "Just for a few minutes. Then we can go home."

Pru stopped moving her feet and he slid her along for a few steps until they stopped just in front of the door to the ballroom. "No, not *we*, Cliff. Just me. You're not listening. I'm not going *anywhere* with you."

His fingers dug into her arm again as he steered her into the party. "Let's socialize." He smiled the way she'd seen parents did with children, along with an admonishment of, "Look at how much fun we're having." Pru never could understand how he kept his composure when he was like this. As soon as they got through the door, his gregarious, public persona was on full display, and he began chatting with people as he slid an arm around her waist.

"Let go of me," she muttered.

Bending in closer, his lids lowered halfway, and he ran the index finger of his free hand from her wrist to her inner elbow. "Do you remember when we went to a function like this in Atlanta? You were so tired at the end of the night that I had to carry you into the elevator." He kissed behind Pru's ear and didn't give her room to pull away as she grimaced. "I'd had the staff spread rose petals all over the room, and we made love in what smelled like a flower garden. I'll never forget how you said you loved me."

He moved to kiss her mouth and she turned her head. He pulled away, his expression becoming more predatory than pretend charming. "I have every intention of convincing you to come home with me tonight, babe."

In his eyes, her reflection was tiny and misshapen. The way she remembered that night was that she was perfectly fine walking, but he'd scooped her up even as she'd protested, and then they'd had an argument. Pru turned her head. "Oh, look, isn't that one of the board members of the LGSO talking to a couple of county commissioners? I bet it would be really embarrassing for them to see the principal violinist get slapped, wouldn't it?" she whispered back.

His face darkened as he stepped a few inches away. "We *are* going to discuss this."

She headed toward the door through which they'd entered

and he didn't pursue her. The walls tilted a few degrees to the right and her vision blurred as she began to hyperventilate.

She couldn't stay in the locker room. He'd find her and start to bother her again.

With one hand on the wall, Pru felt her way to the stairwell outside the kitchen that led to the basement. She could hardly breathe. The door clicked behind her. It took several seconds per step to make sure her foot would land on something solid. The farther she descended, though, the quieter everything became. She sat on the bottom step, in heavenly solitude as she waited for gravity to restore itself.

CHAPTER THIRTEEN

A few dying fluorescent lights buzzed and flickered, making the room dim and gray even in the best-lit areas and almost completely dark in others. Shawn eased his way along, winding through the basement's maze of heavy tables, stacked dining chairs, and shelves of assorted linens, toilet paper, and industrial-sized gel soap refills. He considered spooling out a roll of toilet paper like a modern Theseus. Still, relative darkness and silence was a welcome change from being either upstairs or outside in the bright heat. Shawn found some space on the rear wall and leaned his head against its solid coolness. He tried not to think about anything as the smells, tastes, and sounds from the ballroom dissipated from inside his head.

The effort didn't last long.

Cliff and Pru? Really?

That was difficult to picture, even if he closed his eyes and tried hard.

A loud series of heavy thuds and crashes—a miniature earthquake really—startled him. Just as he tensed and opened his eyes, someone soft thumped against him. He smelled a hint of wisteria.

"Oh, I'm—"

"Pru?"

"Shawn? What are you doing down here?"

Her hands were against his chest, and he grabbed her elbows to steady her.

"I wanted to get away from the crowd." He let out a

combination of exhalation and chuckle. "We must stop bumping into each other like this." She didn't react aside from shaking like a Chihuahua.

"Same." She backed away, swaying before she found the wall and leaned against it next to him. "I mean about getting away from everyone."

"You seem upset," Shawn said as her expression came into clearer focus.

"I'm fine." She gazed straight ahead.

"You don't sound fine."

She offered a flash of a smile that didn't quite make it to her eyes. "I'll be okay."

They stood side-by-side without saying anything. Each time they exhaled, and their shoulders released, the backs of their hands slid against each other.

Slowing his breath, Shawn focused on trying to keep his heart from racing. He wasn't even sure why it was, unless he somehow was feeding off of her energy. Best not to question it. Yogic teachings said to allow whatever feelings were present in any moment to travel through rather than cling to them or fight them off. They would go away eventually. Nothing lasted forever.

In the dim light, it was hard not to notice the sheen of her dark blue dress against her skin, highlighting her collarbones, throat, and jaw. "Won't your boyfriend be looking for you?"

"Boyfriend?" She furrowed her brow, touched her arm, and winced. Then her eyes widened. "Cliff is *not* my boyfriend. He hasn't been in a long time, and will not *ever* be in the future." Pru's jaw set and she straightened her posture. Her voice was firm, maybe even a little angry.

"Okay." A few seconds passed. "You don't know of another exit out of here, do you? That door from the kitchen automatically locks from the outside."

"I don't know. Maybe we can call security or something. I

don't have my phone. All my stuff's in a locker upstairs. Do you have yours?"

"Yeah." He grimaced. "I'm not always great about remembering to charge it, though. It's dead."

"I see." She smirked. "Do you often forget to put gas in your car too?"

Shawn hung his head. "I've gotten stranded on the road with an empty tank more than once." That earned him a chuckle.

They stared into the expanse of dining and cleaning supplies for a couple of minutes and then Pru went rigid. "Did he tell you we were a couple?"

He thought about whether to say no, that he'd just assumed, but decided to tell her the truth. "Yeah, while I was listening to you play." He looked down and pushed back a cuticle on his thumb. "I didn't mean to upset you. Do you, um, need some space? I can find somewhere else down here to hang out until a search party comes along."

"No." She extended a hand toward him then withdrew it. "You didn't upset me at all."

Shawn exhaled. He hadn't realized he'd been holding his breath after the question.

"Did you like the way we sounded?" she asked.

"I did." He leaned around to see what he could of her face. Her hair looked almost silver in the dim room. "I've never much liked classical music, but you sounded amazing."

She rewarded him with a big smile. "Thanks." He'd never met anyone so grateful for just plain, decent behavior or a genuine compliment. Pru was quiet for a moment. "You don't like any classical music at all?'

"No offense. It tends to put me to sleep. Even stuff like Wagner."

Her eyes widened, her mouth dropped open, and she touched her hand to her chest in obvious mock-horror.

"That's like saying you don't like movies. Are there any other huge categories of things you dislike?"

He tore his eyes from where her fingertips touched her clavicles. "I've never liked nut butters or most kinds of bread?"

She pulled away a few inches, squinted, and pressed her lips together. "I'm with you on the nut butter. I can't even stand the smell of it, especially peanut butter. But bread?" She squinted at him. "What else?"

"No way." He elbowed her. "Your turn."

"Fair enough. Let's see . . ." She bit her lip. When she released it, the image of sucking it between his teeth flashed. He silently admonished himself to quit it.

"Running. If you see me running, there's probably a bear chasing me."

Shawn chuckled. "We should try to find another way out before the Minotaur in an expensive suit finds us."

She was quiet, and he now remembered how embarrassed she had been in his car during the thunderstorm. He opened his mouth to explain the reference.

Pru perked up before he spoke. "Cliff's the monster. That's funny."

They pushed off the wall together and started to walk the perimeter of the cavernous, seemingly never-ending basement. The slower she walked, the more obvious her unsteadiness became. Shawn put his hand on her arm and she winced. "Are you okay?"

She pulled away and kept walking. "I'm sure I'll be fine." They rounded another corner. "It is kind of peaceful here, though." She turned to him. "What made you decide to get away?"

The fact that she wanted to change the subject wasn't lost on him. What had happened to her up there?

"Do you want the short or the long answer?" Everything

looked the same in the shadows. Shawn wasn't quite sure where in the room they were anymore.

She sucked her lips in and looked down as she thought it over. "It seems we have plenty of time to kill."

Staring straight ahead as they moved made it easier to get into some of his story. "My dad's a strategist who helps bring corporate funding to various political campaigns and organizations. I've been forced to go to these kinds of parties for as long as I can remember, and the self-congratulatory posturing was just too much tonight."

She stopped, so he did as well. "If that's all it was, you could've just gone home." Her voice was gentle rather than accusatory. Still, she'd caught him in a half-truth.

They passed a long row of top-to-bottom shelves of paper-wrapped, one-ply toilet paper. "I'm sort of at a crossroads in my life's trajectory," he continued. "My parents want to see me in a more stable, white-collar job rather than contractual gig work. I don't want to wear a suit and deal with the kinds of people who are upstairs for the rest of my life. I'm in Georgia trying to figure things out—how to make them happy without crushing my will to live. Working on their house was a good excuse to get some distance." He wasn't sure why he was telling her this, or why he'd neglected to mention that he wasn't single.

Actually, he knew exactly why for the latter, and tried to blink the notion away.

They were quiet for a while as they continued their search, or stroll . . . or whatever this had turned into. "That must be hard," Pru said.

He stole a glance at her, surprised again at the lack of judgment. "Your turn. Why did you come down to the basement? What prompted the escape attempt?"

Her eyes narrowed. "You haven't answered my question about that."

"Oh. You picked up on that." He winced.

"I'll give you a broad response as well." Taking a deep breath, all amusement left Pru's expression. "I'm the only one who survived a car accident that killed my family. Then my grandmother died, and she was everything to me. I went through most of high school living with my uncle—her brother. My friends are amazing, but they've got their own lives to live. I've spent all of mine terrified of my own company. I need to learn how to be okay without depending on other people. I can't be anyone's responsibility. I need to be ready for whenever they move on."

Shawn stopped walking, and she looked up at him. He was tempted to offer her empty reassurances. He also couldn't stop focusing on how soft the bow of her top lip looked, or the way shades of blue blended into the gray of her eyes, or her heart-shaped face.

Jesus.

They swallowed hard, almost in unison. "Seems like we both have things to sort out before our lives go on much further," he said.

"I'll tell you what my last straw was this evening if you promise to tell me yours." Her eyes were both dark and bright when they met his. She glanced down, then back up, continuing without waiting for him. "Cliff was being an overbearing jerk. I wanted to be somewhere he was unlikely to find me. If I'd gone straight to my car, he might've followed." She cleared her throat.

"Do you want to talk about it?"

Pru looked down. "Maybe some other time. We don't know each other that well yet."

Yet. That word should not have made him smile to the point where he thought his face might split. "Okay, fair is fair. What sent me looking for shelter was also that Cliff was being an overbearing jerk. I don't think he liked me helping you earlier. I figured it best to hide out before he came looking for me."

When he looked down, he found they were holding hands. Shawn couldn't remember when that had happened, but his was covering hers and she was gripping his back. She also seemed calmer. "All right, break's over. Let's find a way out."

Minutes passed. Every so often, that flower garden smell drifted past his nose. It wasn't perfume, he didn't think. The scent was almost visceral, like a mist. They still hadn't let their hands drop. Her thumb and index finger loosely held his thumb while she trailed the fingers of her other hand along the shelves. It had to be because she was having trouble in those heels. They were low, but she wobbled if they picked up their pace by too much. Every so often, the back of her nail slid against his palm and he suppressed a shiver. His involuntary reaction was nothing. He didn't want her to trip, though, so he didn't let go of her.

Yeah, keep telling yourself that's the reason.

Pru stopped short and tugged him backward. "Doorknob." She turned it, and the door opened not only to a stairwell, but to one with signage. Up one flight was an exit from the building in one direction and the passage back to the locker room with Pru's things in the other.

Neither of them moved. At some point their fingers had interlaced. "Hey, Pru, what do you think of sneaking out of here and grabbing a late dinner? You don't hate Chinese food, do you?"

Her eyes lit up. "That sounds like the best thing that could happen today — and I do like Chinese food." They clasped hands more tightly. "Let's get my stuff and go."

Outside, the sky was dimmer but the air was still muggy. Shawn was already sweating as he carried Pru's cello case to her car. He stopped to take off his jacket.

When he looked at her, she was focusing on him. "Can I

ask you a personal question?" she asked.

"Sure."

"Why did you stop at the BA? What did you want to do originally?" She frowned. "I mean, that's none of my business. Don't feel like you have to answer. I . . . Never mind." The last bit trailed off. She quickened her pace as they continued past an ocean of expensive cars toward the employees' section in the back.

Shawn shrugged. "It's fine. I wanted to go on to grad school. I like American Literature, I like writing essays and fiction, and I wanted to stay in academia and maybe teach to support the things I wanted to write and study."

They passed a particularly ugly BMW and Pru stared at it. "Who paints a car that costs more than what most people make in a year duckshit green?"

Maybe it was the combination of the words with her soft, Southern drawl and her vulnerable appearance, but Shawn started to laugh so hard that he staggered backward and had to lean against the vehicle in question. When he found his breath again, her arms were folded and she was smiling. "It wasn't *that* funny."

"Who taught you that kind of language, young lady?"

She rolled her eyes. "Just because I'm from the South doesn't mean I don't know swear words. I can curse a little bit in Yiddish too. Grandma taught me my first curse word when I was five."

Shawn grinned as they kept going.

"You have to admit that was a travesty of a car," she said with a shrug. "Anyway, why didn't you go to graduate school, then?" Before Shawn could answer, she added, "You wrote stories? Are any of them published?"

"A few, while I was still writing. I won a bunch of awards, got a reasonable handful of literary journal publications as far as undergraduates went, and my folks were pissed that I didn't major in something more profitable. When they found out about my declared major, they stopped paying tuition and I had to get part-time jobs and take out loans to finish college." He let his shoulders round. "Over the past few years, I've managed to pay off my loans. Now I'm trying to figure out how to support myself. Seems you need a graduate degree for most of the things I want to do."

Pru didn't say anything. They turned left, and her car was in the middle of the row. For the most part, people didn't say anything when he said that, they just gave him a pitying look. Shawn couldn't help thinking about all the fights he'd had with his parents about this. The guilt he tried so hard to compartmentalize every day poured through him like viscous black paint. What was he even doing down here, not to mention flirting with someone when he had no right to be?

When they reached her car and he lifted Pru's instrument into the hatchback, her expression wasn't what he had expected. He'd figured he'd see what little regard she had for him drain away.

Instead she touched his arm and steadied her focus on him. "I was really lucky. My grandmother put all her support and encouragement behind me when I wanted to pursue music. She told me that one day I'd write my first symphony and I could dedicate it to her. Even when I had my doubts, she never did." Their eyes met. "I'm sorry you never had that."

Their hands reached for the driver door at the same time. Another shiver ran through Shawn in spite of the thick, wet air around them. She let him open and close the door for her and then she lowered the window. "I'd love to see your stories. I don't think you're a loser at all. You just know your passion and haven't figured out a way to balance it with a job that doesn't make you feel like you're sacrificing it."

"You think so?"

"If you like writing, you should write." She made it sound

so simple. "I'm lucky to be paid to play music. But even if I had to do something else, I wouldn't be able to keep away, even if other responsibilities made it harder for me to be as disciplined. It's like it demands my attention, and then it takes over, you know what I mean? Keeping yourself away from what you love most hurts too much." She looked him straight in the eyes. "You seem like you're hurting."

Shawn's throat thickened. "Maybe," he managed. The thing was, underneath the nervousness, that was how she struck him as well.

"There's a good Chinese place not far from here. Just follow me. I'll wait for you at the parking lot exit."

"Sounds good." Shawn swallowed hard as she drove away. No one who mattered had ever told him anything like what she had.

Pru wasn't supposed to matter.

His parents called him immature. Helena said his head was in the clouds. By the time Shawn got into his car, their voices were clear in his mind.

Pru's fingers were calloused like his were, but her palm and the back of her hand were soft. This absolutely couldn't happen. Shawn followed her car down the road. Everything around him was cloaked in shadows until the combined glow of her taillights and his headlights illuminated his surroundings.

Chapter Fourteen

Pru followed the hostess and Shawn through the Dragon's Temple, where at least half the tables were occupied. She'd been here a couple of months ago and hadn't given much thought to her surroundings. Now, with the skirt of her dress bunched in her hand while treading carefully in her heels, she took in the plastic flowers hanging from the ceiling. Spotty yellow light from flimsy paper lanterns sifted through, adding an unnatural sheen to the leaves and petals.

They were led to one of the black lacquered standalone tables near a window. After their orders were taken, she watched Shawn take it all in. "I doubt that much on the menu is especially authentic. We can go someplace else if you want. My friend Edie and I used to meet here a lot when she worked at a smaller law practice a street over. That was a family law firm—a lot of child custody cases and divorces. It was hard, some of the stuff she saw people going through. I don't think I could ever do something like that. Barney, my great-uncle, was married before I was born. He never had any kids."

Shawn blinked a few times.

She was doing it again. She silently chastised herself to shut up, but her mouth wasn't getting the message.

"Anyway, my mom's whole side of the family's from New York City originally, and then they somehow all ended up in North Florida. I'm glad it wasn't central. I'm not a big Disney person. My parents took us to Disney World once when I was about five or six, and it was so crowded and overwhelming that when my dad tried to get a picture of me, my brother, and Pluto, I freaked out and kicked the character in the shin hard enough to make the person in the costume shout a very bad word, and I got in trouble. Anyway, I like this restaurant, but I bet it's not as good as what you can get in New York." Even having to take a quick breath couldn't quite stop her. "My uncle says as much about most foods in the South. I've heard just about every ethnic food up there is authentic and amazing."

Shawn sat back and raised his eyebrows.

"Uh-oh, you like Disney, don't you? I'm sorry. Tommy's boyfriend Andrew keeps telling me I'm the anti-Cinderella, and that I'm more likely to throw a shoe at someone than to lose it."

He smirked.

Pru widened her eyes. "Oh, not that I threw my shoes off in the park — that was a genuine accident." She peered at her lap and tried to think of a way out of this verbal mess.

"You look like you're thinking about saying something else," he said.

"I'm just trying to come up with a way to get my foot out of my mouth." She drummed her fingers on the table. "I hope the food doesn't taste like sweaty sneakers compared to what you're used to."

Shawn laughed loudly enough to make a couple of people turn toward them before returning to their meals. Recovering, he said, "You're thinking of the city. I'm from Upstate, so ethnic restaurants are hit-or-miss. I'm sure it's fine. I'm not that picky."

Lifting her hand, she rested her chin over the long edge of her thumb and set her teeth over the tip of her index finger. "I've always wanted to go up there, watch the New York Philharmonic play, and wander around the city."

"It's been a while since I've been out there." He crossed his legs and averted his eyes.

Their food arrived. Light from a small electric candle between them flickered over Shawn's face, randomly highlighting his cheekbones, nose, and mouth as the server's shadow moved across the table.

Shawn set his napkin on his lap, held a piece of tofu in his chopsticks and took a bite. He didn't do a very good job of hiding the puckered expression as he swallowed. "I've had worse."

Pru unrolled and arranged her napkin. "You're a terrible liar."

He drank some water. "I'm serious. This is perfectly fine."

As she picked up her fork, he cocked his head. "I've never gotten the hang of chopsticks," she said. "Tommy says I'm a lost cause."

Shawn came around, bringing his dish and taking the seat next to her, by the window. He angled the chair toward her and picked up his own chopsticks. "Hold them like this." He talked her through it as he arranged his fingers. The task seemed easy enough, but the chopsticks wouldn't balance in her hand. Shawn probably thought she was completely incompetent. "Here. Farther down." He adjusted her fingers with his, then picked up his own. "You pick up a piece of food like this." Grabbing a bamboo slice, he popped it in his mouth.

"Got it." As soon as Pru moved her hand, the utensils clattered onto the table. Her cheeks warmed.

"Let's try again." He held on to her wrist with one hand as he situated the chopsticks again. Dull pain spread along Pru's wrist. She couldn't stop a quick, startled inhalation. "Did I hurt you?"

She tried to force levity into her voice. "No." Before she could pull her hand away, though, he examined it more closely. "I hit my wrist on something earlier."

He narrowed his eyes. "Seems like you maybe hit it from the inside of someone's grip."

For a moment, she couldn't look him in the face. "I'll be fine." He didn't say anything in response, so she continued, "I'd like to try using the chopsticks one more time."

Shawn knitted his brows. "All right." He held Pru's wrist more loosely, positioning the chopsticks. She wasn't paying attention, though. She was staring at how gently he was circling her wrist and at the way the hair on his arms rose when he touched her. Their fingers fumbled around one another's, and their eyes locked as they looked up.

He darted his gaze back to their hands. "Very slowly now." Shawn guided her hand toward the plate, slid her fingers into position, and helped her pick up a carrot slice. "Now you've got it." As soon as Pru tried to take a bite though, everything landed back on the plate. Her teeth snapped down hard. Glancing sideways, she checked for his reaction.

"I'm kind of hopeless." She searched for signs of condescension in his face, but there was none as he watched her. Pru sucked in her breath. Their knees were touching, and his free arm was on the back of her chair.

Shawn backed up, sliding his knee away and letting go of the chair. "You're not hopeless. You just need practice."

"Can we try just once more?" she asked.

He reached out and helped arrange her fingers again. This time, Pru knocked the chopsticks against the edge of the plate, tried to catch them before they fell on the floor, and ended up grabbing the edge of the tablecloth. The plate tilted over the edge of the table.

"Look out." Shawn jumped up to pull her chair away. Pru started. Still clutching the tablecloth, she grabbed his waist and fell backward, bringing him down with her. She heard the clatter of the chair and dishes falling as the restaurant turned upside-down.

Shawn was gripping her so tightly that she couldn't breathe for a moment. He ended up splayed over her with his hand cradling the back of her head and his knee planted between her thighs, pinning down her dress. They stared wide-eyed at each other, panting. His face was as white as hers was probably red.

He sat her up with him. And now she was between his legs with her back to him. As they caught their breaths, four servers hurried over to clean up. "Are you okay?" His mouth was near the back of her neck. His breath was spicy. She could feel his heart beating against her back. Most of the diners and staff were now staring at them.

"Y-yes." They scrambled away from each other and stood up.

"I'm so sorry," Shawn said to Pru as she apologized to the servers. People were still murmuring to one another and watching the commotion. The servers waved her off, taking away the mess. "I didn't mean to manhandle you like that."

She scrunched her eyes shut. "This is why you can't take me anywhere nice." He didn't say anything, so she opened her eyes and put some bills on the table.

"Technically, I guess you just took me somewhere." He pressed his lips together and released them. "Can I at least leave the tip?"

"After I just embarrassed both of us? Please, let me." He wasn't going to want to be seen with her in public again. Then again, this wasn't a date. They were both just trying to get away from a stupid party — and from Cliff.

Shawn pushed the inside of his cheek with his tongue and seemed to assess her. Then he let his shoulders drop. "I'm not embarrassed, but okay. Thank you." He held the door for her as they left the restaurant.

"I hope teaching me yoga won't be as disastrous as teaching me how to eat." The sky was completely dark now. They walked toward the public parking lot.

"If it's any consolation, you looked and sounded great

tonight," Shawn said.

"Thanks." Pru looked at the ground and took tiny steps. "These shoes are the worst. Do you mind if we sit for a minute?"

"Sure." They stopped at a bench under a streetlamp.

A few cars drove past as Pru stared ahead. "The sky used to be so clear and bright at night, even downtown," she said, her voice quiet. A foggy haze spread across the sky, though a few stars looked as though they were struggling to fight their way through to shine.

"Just for the record, I don't get the whole Disney thing either," Shawn said. "I went there with some friends for spring break when I was in college. The place is like a gigantic acid trip." He winked. "Not that I'd know what that was like."

Pru laughed.

Shawn's brow was smooth, and his posture was relaxed. The stance could just be his own style of come-on, though—make her feel safe and then pounce. Still, he looked surprised each time they ended up in one another's arms courtesy of her own klutziness. If Shawn had wanted to make a move, he'd had better opportunities than this.

She wasn't even sure whether she'd object if he tried. Edie always said she trusted people too easily.

"You look lost in thought," Shawn said.

"What?" Pru blinked.

In the distance, the library's clock chimed ten. "We should probably call it a night." His voice was low and gentle.

They stood and continued toward the parking lot. "Watch your—"

Pru's body lurched into a forward freefall. Shawn jumped ahead and caught her beneath the armpits. Her face grew hot. "Oh, my God, this is beyond embarrassing. I'm—"

"Don't apologize." Shawn sounded sympathetic rather than annoyed. "I noticed that branch on the sidewalk at the last second myself." When she worked up the courage to look up at him, he smirked. "If I didn't know any better though, I'd worry you were trying to kill me." He let go of her.

Giving his arm a gentle shove, she relaxed. "You haven't made me angry enough for that."

He gave her a half smile. "You're not the Hulk, are you?"

Pru laughed.

"Are you hurt?"

She shook her head.

Shawn's shirt had come untucked and his tie was uneven. He pushed his hair from his forehead and they continued walking.

When they got back to Pru's car they faced each other, and he took up her hands in his. There were calluses at the base and tip of each finger. He slid a thumb along her palm. Pru shivered. For a few seconds, they hardly moved. "I enjoyed my evening more than I expected to," she blurted out.

His own breath stuttered a tiny bit. "Likewise." They leaned in closer, and Pru started to shake again. He pulled her into a hug. Her ear pressed against his shirt. She wrapped her arms around his waist as he rested his hand between her shoulder blades. Shawn smelled like Ivory soap and oily Chinese food, along with a hint of sweat. They clung to each other for what seemed like a long time.

"How's eleven the day after tomorrow for yoga?" His voice was soft.

"Okay." They separated and slid their hands along one another's forearms. Against the fog and streetlamps, his eyes were black and bright. He let go.

The loud banging on Pru's front door interrupted the last peaceful moments of sunrise the next morning. She tied her kimono, came inside, and looked through the peephole then opened the door for Joe.

His reddish, uncombed hair stuck out in all directions. He was wearing a Honey Nut Cheerios bee T-shirt along with a pair of cutoff shorts that had seen better days. He had a paper bag in one hand and a tray with three coffees in the other. "I heard from Cliff last night and figured you might need these."

He followed her into the kitchen. "What did he tell you?" Pru asked. She grabbed some napkins and three plates as he sat.

"He told me some guy in a bad suit was watching you all night, and that I should talk some sense into you. So, here goes my sense-talk. Cliff's an asshat. Keep ignoring him."

She covered her mouth to yawn but laughed halfway through it.

Joe smirked. "I told him to learn to take a hint." He pulled a cinnamon donut out of the bag and placed it on Pru's plate, taking a Boston cream for himself. "Something you want to tell me about the bad suit?"

She sat and blew on her coffee, making small, milky ripples as the vanilla roast smell washed through her. "Thanks for this. And his name is Shawn. He said you're a friend of his from college."

Joe finished chewing and leaned back, frowning. "Pru, look. Before you get too attached, you should ask him about—"

"I like him a lot."

His eyes widened as he sat straighter. "You need to know—"

"As friends." She took a big bite of her donut and grabbed her coffee to swallow it and the half-lie down.

A squeak and a thump came from next door. "In here," Pru called as Tommy came around into the kitchen to join them. He was still in his pajamas—musical-note bottoms and a black shirt. He ran his hand over his hair. "I thought I heard your car pull in, and I know you never come this early without bearing gifts. Do I smell coffee from Bella's Donuts?"

Joe looked up. "There's a frosted strawberry in the bag. Your two sugars, black is right there next to it."

Tommy gave him two thumbs-up. "You're my guardian angel." He sat and closed his eyes. "Just smelling this makes my morning better." Opening the bag, he looked at Joe. "Has Pru told you about her new man?"

Pru's head hung. "We're just friends," she said to her lap.

Tommy turned to Joe, whose elbows rested on the table as he held his coffee. "My left foot," he said. "You should've seen the way they were together a few days ago. You could've electrocuted yourself between them." Pru gave Tommy a light kick. "Is there a new development?" He bit into his donut and dabbed the corner of his mouth with a napkin as he chewed.

"I'm here because of Cliff," Joe replied. "He saw them near one another and started giving Pru a hard time." Without meaning to, she brought her hand to where her ex had dug his fingers into her arm.

Tommy caught her in the act and frowned. "Let me see."

"It's nothing." She stood with her coffee, filled a glass with ice, and poured the drink over it.

Joe and Tommy glanced at each other.

"I know you sometimes forget, but I'm a grownup. I can take care of myself." She returned to the table where she gripped her donut. Large crumbs landed on her plate.

"Let me look." Tommy gently lifted the hem of her sleeve. Five fingertip-sized welts circled her forearm. Both men stared at her. "If he gets anywhere near this house, "I swear I'll—"

"I'll be okay."

"Take pictures of the bruises and send them to Edie," Joe said. "Start gathering evidence if he hurts you again." He licked the cream off his fingers and stood to rinse his plate.

When he sat again, he took another sip of his coffee. "I've somehow managed to avoid that asshole for how many years? Until I gave a buddy some help with a job a few days ago. I will *not* let Cliff do that to you again." He pointed at her arm, which Tommy was still examining. "As for Shawn—"

Pulling at her sleeve, Pru said, "Tommy, please let go of me."

He released her. "Just remember, Joe and Edie and I all are here for you. You know that."

"I know." She picked up the other plates, scraped the crumbs into the trash, and put the dishes in the sink. Then she turned to lean on the counter and finish her iced coffee. "Joe, I know you feel bad about introducing me to Cliff, but he and I would've met anyway because we work together. I can handle him."

She couldn't hide from Cliff behind Shawn as a substitute for letting Joe, Tommy, or Edie protect her. No, she'd have to figure this out on her own.

Pru put her empty glass in the sink upside down so they'd think the clink of ice cubes was from that instead of her trembling hand.

CHAPTER FIFTEEN

Pouring rain meant working on the house wouldn't be worth the effort this morning since the plan had been to finish painting the porch swing and railings. Shawn was soaked just from carrying an umbrella from the apartment building to his car. His T-shirt and pants stuck to his skin, making him shiver when the air conditioner kicked in.

His backup plan of going to the hardware store was probably unwise as he thought about it. Visibility through the windshield was nonexistent, and the rain pounded the roof so hard the whole car shook. At least he thought it was shaking from the storm. But when he looked to the right, a bulky form was darkening the front passenger window. Opening the window a crack revealed Cliff's narrowed eyes and scowling mouth.

Great.

"Do you need something?"

Cliff folded his fingers over the glass and pushed down, forcing the window low enough to fit his head through. Water dripped from his dark blond stubble and his eyes were bloodshot. "Get out of the car." He was holding the glass too firmly for hitting the raise window button to do any good. "I *said* get out."

The lot was too full of parked vehicles to risk pulling out and weaving around the man without hydroplaning, even if he'd been able to see anything. With a glance at his useless, wet umbrella, he got out and shouted across the roof, "What do you want, Cliff?"

"I want a word with you." Cliff's feet made loud, hard splashes as he stomped and sloshed through the puddles overflowing from the small potholes in the pavement. All Shawn could think of when the man towered over him, face almost violet with anger, was *Creature from the Black Lagoon.* Shawn's heart pounded as if he were in his own personal horror movie. The veins in Cliff's biceps and forearms popped as he made fists. "Stay the fuck away from Pru."

The man loomed over him, his wet white T-shirt accentuating every line of his shoulder muscles and six-pack. Shawn made himself straighten as his stomach twisted. "Pru's a grown woman. Who she chooses to spend time with is her own business." He wasn't sure how well he was keeping his voice calm—his legs were shaking. "Did you really track me down just to—?"

Cliff jabbed his finger into Shawn's sternum. "I told you politely. She doesn't understand what she wants. She's mine." He shoved him against the car. The air left Shawn's lungs. "Do you understand?"

Shawn didn't break eye contact while he felt around for the door handle. "What I understand is that you're an overbearing bully with no self-control. I'm going to give you some advice. Get away from me and stay away."

Cliff stepped close enough for their sopping tennis shoes to touch. Without thinking, Shawn slipped sideways, farther away from the door and past his rearview mirror. Cliff closed the distance again. "What did you just say?" His breath smelled like alcohol and days-old coffee.

"I said step back and stay back." Rain bounced against the car like haphazard war drums as steam rose from the pavement. "You're lucky I'm as patient as I am. Get out of here." Shawn gave him a mostly ineffectual shove and moved even farther from the driver's side door.

The ground reverberated as Cliff stormed after him. As

Shawn got in front of the hood, and Cliff yanked him back by the collar. His anvil of a fist rammed between Shawn's shoulder blades. Shawn huffed just as his face hit the hood. Hot, wet pain burst through his head. Pink water slipped between his fingers as he braced to push up. Wiping the blood from his eyes, he turned around and wondered how bad the gash in his forehead might be.

The man's mouth twisted into a sneer. "You want to try and push me again? Try it. C'mon."

"This is stupid, Cliff. You've made your point. If you don't back off and go home, I'm calling the cops." The word "cops" came out as "copth" as his lips pulsed. As the world tilted, he thought about making a run for it back to the apartment, but his keys were hanging from his Star of David keychain in the ignition. When he turned to run, the rest of the parking lot revolved with him as he fumbled to get around the trunk and back to the driver's door.

Thunder boomed, shaking the earth. Unclear whether the sky had just darkened or whether he was on the verge of passing out, Shawn rounded the corner too soon. His hip clipped the edge of the trunk, and he was either falling toward the ground or the ground was rising to crash into him. Gravel scratched under his lids. His breakfast, along with the rest of his insides, raced to escape up his throat. He took some controlled breaths through his nose until the nauseous feeling passed. Somewhere over the pounding in and around Shawn's skull, he heard Cliff's retreating footsteps.

Anywhere between a few seconds and a few minutes went by before Shawn was steady enough to sit. It took longer before he managed to grab a door handle as leverage to stand. He leaned back on the car, shivering and soaked as he waited for the world to finish lifting and lowering beneath his feet. "Fucking hell."

On his way from the hot shower to his tiny bedroom, Shawn stopped at the fridge to grab a couple of bags of frozen vegetables from the freezer. Without turning on the lights, he curled into a ball on the mattress on the floor. He contemplated driving himself to the ER but getting behind the wheel seemed like a bad idea. Calling for an ambulance would make Cliff think he'd accomplished something if he were still hanging around somewhere. His heart raced. What if Cliff had stuck around to see which apartment he went to? Shawn waited, listening for footsteps outside. When none came, he rolled onto his back, shut his eyes, and put the bag over his face. If he didn't feel better by tomorrow, he'd ask Joe to take him to the hospital to be checked for a concussion. This wasn't his first rodeo when it came to being beaten up by bullies. He knew the drill.

He should have fought back harder.

Their encounter explained a lot. He'd offered to wait outside while Pru got her stuff from upstairs that night and she'd turned pale at the prospect of going back to that locker room alone.

In all likelihood, her friends knew what Cliff was like and served as some kind of buffer for her. That couldn't possibly be enough. Shawn's face numbed under the frozen carrots as his chest tightened. Calling the police and getting Cliff arrested for assault seemed like the best idea. But then Pru's name would get brought up when Cliff and he were asked what the fight had been about. As for himself, the less fuss made over this the better. Once Cliff was out on bail—and he was sure he would make bail—he'd make Shawn's life miserable. At least for as long as he was here, he'd have to protect Pru. He was as unsure about why he felt the need as how he was supposed to go about it.

CHAPTER SIXTEEN

The guard at the Sunrise Plantation community gate waved Pru through, and Miles, her Google navigator's tenor, British-accented voice, said to go straight. She turned off on several different streets, all named after some kind of flower or tree. The houses took up most of the small lots, which wasn't unusual, but there were tall white privacy fences instead of her neighborhood's chain link. Even with variations in style, the homes were one-story, with siding made to look like stone and wood. They all had concrete driveways and small front porches. She drove past all the manicured lawns and low boxwood bushes with flowering plants between them and turned onto Hibiscus Lane.

Shawn was on the front porch, standing on a stepladder and fastening the chain of a bench swing to the ceiling. He had on black gym shorts and a blue T-shirt.

"Hi, Shawn." He waved without turning his head. She couldn't see his face right away as she approached with her yoga mat, but she caught herself staring at the damp hair curling over the nape of his neck. She made herself look away. The front door was white with etched glass pineapples along each side.

"Hey, Pru. Give me just a minute. Hand me that big screwdriver to my right?" At the foot of the door were tools, a couple of paintbrushes, and a can of white paint spread over some newspapers.

She put the screwdriver in his hand and took a step back. It was hard not to watch him. The lower parts of his calves extended upward in a defined V, and a deep crevasse demarcated the upper muscles. His legs were tan. She could tell by the hint of a line of lighter skin under his shorts and shirt when he stretched to reach the ceiling. White paint stuck to the hair of his arms and legs. One long stripe ran between his triceps.

Pru pulled the drawstring at the hem of her tank top more tightly, then tied it off. Until now, she'd thought she was here because she had always wanted to try yoga. But there were classes she could have taken in lots of places if she was that committed. Her summer of independent solitude wasn't getting off to a great start.

He made a few more turns with the screwdriver and stepped off the ladder. "Want to try it out?"

Pru gasped. His bottom lip was swollen. Underneath his eye, an angry, bluish bruise expanded across his cheekbone. Furious red scrapes ran along his arms and shins.

"Oh, no." It was no use trying to keep the shock from her voice. "Let me see." Her shoulders trembled as she reached a finger up and, as if she were using a feather, traced it over and around his cheekbone. It felt as sharply defined as it looked, but thinner. Sweat rolled from his temple, between and around Pru's fingers, and disappeared into the bristle of his beard.

She brushed her fingers over a contusion on his cheek. She angled his face to see it more clearly. Sweat continued its descent around the blue veins of his jugular and past his frayed collar. The hair of his beard was lighter than Pru remembered — golden brown, with strands of darker brown mixed in. She pulled her hand away and stared. "Oh, my God."

"Is there paint on my face?"

"No," she replied. "What happened?"

Shawn waved off the question. "There was a minor misunderstanding with someone yesterday." He gave her a tight-lipped smile. "You should see the other guy."

She shuddered. "Did Cliff do this to you?"

He looked down at his pile of tools. "Yup."

Shuddering and hugging her shoulders, Pru said, "You need to call the police."

Shawn sighed. "Come sit." He sat on one end of the swing and patted the space next to him, so Pru sat as well, dangling her feet. "I don't want to make the drama even worse by pressing charges."

The back of her neck heated as she thought about what Cliff had done . . . and his probable reason. "My friend Edie's a lawyer. Maybe she can do something about him if you talk to her." She picked up her phone. "Here, I'm sending you her work number."

Shawn shook his head. "Thanks. If I change my mind, I'll call her."

Why were most men so stupid about this kind of thing? "At least take some pictures of your injuries and save them. Write down what happened too." Pru wished she'd done that when she'd tried to file a restraining order against Cliff. Without documentation, the judge had denied her, saying that if Cliff wasn't overtly threatening her and hadn't physically harmed her—he'd been cleared for what had caused her disfigurement—she had nothing to stand on.

He smirked. "Okay."

"You're not even gonna do that, are you?" He fidgeted his fingers in his lap, and she narrowed her eyes. "If you're not gonna do anything, then I'll make him leave you alone."

"I was going to tell you the same thing."

"I'm not scared of him." The words came out rushed. She averted her eyes. "I'm more worried about you." She glanced up in time to watch his gaze track to the bruises on her arm. His face clouded. "I can take care of myself." "Should you be doing anything physical if you're that injured? Does your head hurt?"

He shrugged. "Nah."

"Are you sure?" She frowned.

Shawn's features softened. "I am. I know what a concussion feels like, and I feel fine. If I start having symptoms, I promise you, I'll get help." He cocked his head. "Is all that bruising on your arm the real reason you were hiding in the basement the other night?"

Pru sat straighter and stared at him. "Cliff is my problem. I'll make sure he's not yours."

Shawn started. "Sorry," he said. "I shouldn't have said that." Their eyes locked, and they both looked away.

She scowled. "He's gone too far." Her voice rose, and she made fists in her lap. "Now he isn't just following me around like a stalker, he's going after people I care—my friends." When her hands began to hurt, she realized she'd made such tight fists that her knuckles were white. She released them and wiggled her fingers.

"He's following you?"

She didn't respond.

Shifting to face her, he frowned. "You're the one who should call the cops, Pru."

"I talked to Edie about that." She tugged at the hem of her shirt, folded it around her index finger, and let go. "It's very hard to prove stalking, especially when it isn't consistent. He wasn't doing much beyond bothering me at work until he saw us together." Her cheeks warmed and she pulled at her shirt again, stretching the weave until it was misshapen. "The burden of proof is on me."

He pushed off with his feet to make the swing move. For a while, they didn't say anything. Pru figured things would be peaceful here eventually, but the complex was still being built and mostly she heard construction sounds and cars. Her and Shawn's pinkies were almost touching. He linked his finger around hers. "I'm not gonna let him hurt you again — not if I can help it."

A spark of sensation tingled from the tip of her finger, through her hand, and up her arm. After a couple more swings, he said, "Let's go inside where it's cooler."

He stood to pick up her mat and held his other hand out to her. Pru stared at his injuries again. The man seemed strong enough to defend himself. Did yoga teachers ever hit people?

The door opened to a large, open floor plan. The kitchen began with a long granite countertop and dark wood barstools. Pru stepped in and looked around as Shawn shut the door behind them.

"Can I get you anything? There's bottled water in the fridge." He gestured toward the stainless-steel refrigerator opposite the counter.

Pru took another step into the empty room. Its walls were bare except for a row of large paint streaks in varying shades of cream. She scanned the floor. Most of it was still concrete, and off-white woodgrain planks were piled up by a window. She rolled her blue mat out opposite Shawn's red one on the finished side of the room. "I'd rather get started. I'm a little nervous."

"Don't be. I promise I'll be gentle." He winked, then cleared his throat.

Pru did her best to copy whatever he demonstrated, but while he looked strong and graceful in each posture, she stumbled and struggled.

"Okay, let's try a balance," Shawn said. He stood straight, pressed his foot into his thigh, and extended his arms over-head. "Try to look at something that isn't moving. It's easier to steady yourself that way." She nodded, stumbled, and righted herself. "So, this is tree pose, and with some practice, you can do this." He hooked a finger around his big toe and extended his leg out to the side.

She focused on one of the paint samples on the wall, but her gaze kept moving to Shawn's inner thigh and the way the hem of his shorts hiked up. She swayed as her foot slid down to her knee.

"You're doing great, Pru," he encouraged. "Try to avoid putting pressure on your knee." Their eyes met, and like a newly felled tree, she tipped over and toppled onto the mat, hard. Her arm throbbed where she'd landed on it.

Shawn squatted in front of her. "Did you hurt yourself?"

Sitting up, she rolled her ankles, then her wrists. "Just my pride." She shifted. Pain raced through her shoulders and the back of her neck, causing her to wince. "I need a minute to get my bearings."

"Here, can I help?"

"If you think you can, thank you."

He got behind her, gently pushing her long braid to one side, and she tried not to freeze up. His hands were on her back, and his heat sank through her top and beneath her skin as he moved his fingers along and between the backs of her shoulders. "Can I try to massage out that big knot?"

Pru couldn't find the voice to answer. All she could do was give him a quick nod, wincing again as sharpness shot across her shoulder blades.

"Try to relax your muscles." He began to knead her shoulders, working from the edges to her spine a few times, and then up to the back of her neck. She leaned against him, as if boneless. If he moved his hands farther up, they'd round over her throat. Pru imagined the tips of his fingers brushing along her jaw. Then she closed her eyes.

Without warning, a shiver of sensation released the tension. She yelped and jerked away from him. He took his hands off her, scooted away, and came around to sit next to her. "Was that painful?"

"No," she blurted out. "I don't know why I did that." Her

cheeks flushed and she averted her eyes. Why did everything she did around him turn out like a bad slapstick routine?

"Pru?" He leaned around to look at her so she sat up again. Shawn's brow was knitted and she could barely breathe. "What just happened? Did I do something wrong?"

If only she'd brought Matilda with her. He held his hands out and she took them. "I'm just naturally jumpy sometimes. I think the yoga can help though. I heard it's good for that over time."

"It usually is." Something about his open posture, the tilt of his head and his steady gaze, caused her to relax again by a fraction. "Maybe we can skip *savasana*, where you lie down on your back with your eyes closed. I'll show you how to meditate instead," he offered.

"Do I have to close my eyes for that?"

"Not if you don't want to." His voice was so soft and soothing she wished she could make it into a pillow.

"Will you stay next to me like this if I try?"

Squeezing her hand, he replied, "Of course."

Having his hand over hers, with his calm, quiet voice filling her head and his breath on her ear, was almost like having Matilda smooshing up next to her on the couch. The compression she needed wasn't there, but the reassuring stillness was. Pru closed her eyes, but light from the kitchen window filtered orange and pink through her lids. Even as her pulse slowed, the nearness of Shawn's body, the way it almost touched hers, made her jaw tense. She tried to sync her breath with his and listen to whatever guidance he was giving, but she was sure he was watching her.

She wasn't, in fact, entirely sure of what he was telling her. Mostly, she was just aware of his voice's cadence. The latter was so close to her ear that the rhythm of his words was more physical than aural. "When you're ready, open your eyes," he said.

Pru blinked a few times. "That didn't take long. I'm that bad at it?"

"That was almost eight minutes. You looked like you were doing great." She was sure it had been about thirty excruciating, self-conscious seconds. "How are you feeling?"

She scanned through her body. Her breath was more even, her pulse was steadier, and neither her brow nor her jaw were tense. "Better." She couldn't keep the surprise out of her voice. Their eyes met again. Shawn didn't move his hand from over hers, nor was he pressing down on it. She swallowed hard.

He tilted his head and blinked. For a few seconds, they didn't say anything. Then he patted her hand. "Good. That's what I like to hear." She could have sworn his voice caught a tiny bit before he stood and held out his hand. "Same time next week?" He helped her stand.

"Yes. Please." The reply came out breathier than she wanted it to. She hadn't made the conscious decision to get closer, but he closed the gap and she looked up at him. There was that lighter brown almost gold ring around the darkest rims of his irises.

Shawn put his arms around her back and hugged her. She wondered if he was looking down at her disheveled hair and what he must think of her. It turned out it really was impossible to teach her anything.

"You're a natural. I'm glad we did this," he said. His chin skimmed the top of her head as he stepped back. "See you soon."

Her muscles twitched as her heart beat faster, ready for fight, flight, or freeze again. "Okay." She rushed out, leaving her mat behind.

CHAPTER SEVENTEEN

Shawn waved as Pru pulled out of the driveway, watching her car disappear around the corner. Then he sat on the swing and took a few sips from his water bottle. He was supposed to be a professional. Still, what if he'd come behind her and pressed down on her hip bones—a standard assist for alignment in mountain pose?

She'd have frozen up. But what if he'd just held on to her from there? What if he'd been able to calm her again, and she'd leaned back in his arms? He'd have pushed her hair away and brought his mouth down to touch her ear. She'd have tilted her head to give him room, and he'd trail kisses to the nape of her neck. He'd smooth his hands down her arms and along that narrow waist. The faint wisteria smell that followed her everywhere would liquefy and pour through him. She'd turn around, and invisible vines would twist around them as they held one another. Tendrils would curl up and around their arms and the strong stems would pull their hips together, and they'd be bound.

This was a yoga lesson, not a booty call. He was a dolt.

He stood and drank some more water, then went in and out of the house a few times to bring the tools and paint inside. Once he'd set them down on some newspaper spread in the corner, he rolled up the yoga mats.

She's not thinking of confronting Cliff for real, is she?

Shawn looked at the wall where he'd painted streaks of possible colors for comparison. All of the rooms needed to be some variation of these samples of tan, cream, or eggshell.

There was still a lot of flooring to lay, not to mention bathroom and kitchen fixtures to install. He grabbed his phone, snapped a photo of the wall, and sent it to his mother.

Hi, Mom, he texted. *Here are your choices for all the rooms. Which one do you want for the main kitchen and living area, and which for the bathrooms and bedrooms?*

A few seconds went by.

Hi, sweetie. The middle one.

He looked up at the ceiling and exhaled. *There's no middle. If you start at the right, can you tell me which number? And for which parts of the house?*

Your right or mine? his mother responded.

Oh, my God.

Just pick your colors, Mom. Please.

Have you spoken to Helena? She, Candace, and I were looking at magazines, browsing different gowns yesterday. Not this again.

We're taking a break from each other Shawn typed. *Please stop pushing this.*

I liked a sleeveless one I found for myself, but we need to know what month you're planning. Helena said you hadn't discussed it yet.

Shawn dropped his head to his chest before he sent a reply. *Helena and I haven't spoken in a while. Don't buy anything. Gotta go. Love you.*

He headed for the garage to grab more paint supplies. Felt like stepping into a sauna. Georgia weather was insane. At least in New York they had seasons. Not to mention his family, Helena's family, and Helena. He pried open a can of paint and stared into the viscous beige liquid that would cover every scrape and smudge on the bare walls. He wasn't sure if he belonged anywhere.

Shawn wasn't sure how long he'd been at it, but when his phone buzzed, two walls had been painted and it was getting dark out. He wiped his hands on his shorts and answered his phone.

"Hey, Joe. What's up?"

"I'm bored. Feel like a pint?"

Shawn's stomach growled. "Actually, yeah. Make it somewhere with real food and you're on. I can meet you in about forty minutes. I need to head home and clean myself up."

The Fisherman's Public House was dimly lit, decorated with anchors, fish nets, reels, and boat wheels. A large black-and-white photo of a trawler hung on the wall by his booth. Shawn nursed his beer and thought about earlier. Helena was supposed to be his perfect match, according to everyone who knew them, and they'd been on and off for about three years now. He wasn't even sure what love was supposed to feel like—if this was it, the rom-coms she liked watching exaggerated things by a lot. Probably their relationship was based more on habit and horniness.

"Hello? Anyone in there?" Shawn blinked. Joe sat across from him, waving his hand in front of his face. Fish netting draped over the incandescent fixtures above the tables made strips of Joe's dark red hair look brown and his pale blue eyes darker. Mostly, Shawn saw soft bulk.

"What happened to you?" Joe gestured at a giant bruise on Shawn's forearm.

"Got into a tussle, that's all." Shawn folded his hands in his lap, hiding his arms.

Joe sat back. "Judging by your face, it looks like more than that. Have you seen a doctor? How's your vision?"

Shawn sighed. "I don't need a doctor, my vision is fine, I doubt I'm concussed, and before you ask, I'm not calling the cops."

"All right, now that that's settled, where were you, who

were you with, and how did you piss them off?" Joe turned his head as a waitress brought him a glass of beer and took their orders.

"Sorry. Lost in space." Shawn sat back. "How've you been?"

Joe frowned. "I'm great. You're deflecting. Plus I know that dreamy, if black-and-blue, look on your face. Whose boyfriend beat you up?"

Shawn hoped he gave Joe a withering look. "You've been sitting on your ass too much. When's the last time you worked out?"

Joe laughed and patted his belly. "You answer my question, I'll answer yours." His phone dinged. He looked at it and muttered, "What in hell does he want? One obligatory invitation and suddenly we're chums."

"What does he want?" Shawn asked.

"To be one of the performers for my event," Joe replied, holding up his phone for Shawn to read. He pulled it away when Shawn rolled his eyes. "Back to your life. You were just about to tell me about the eventful night you had."

"Nice try. No one. I'm not thinking about anyone—it's been a long day."

Joe grinned. "Yes, you are thinking of someone. Who is she, and are you going to take her back to New York to show her your bedroom? Did you take down your Pamela Anderson and skateboarding posters when you moved back in after college?"

"Now I'm never going to give you a name, pal." He grinned back. "And they were of Halle Berry. Pam Anderson had too much plastic in her."

Joe lowered his chin and smirked. Shawn almost wondered if he already knew.

"Okay, fine," Shawn admitted. "There were also a couple of her too." He took a long drink of beer and stared at his friend. Joe threw his head back and laughed.

The waitress came by and set down their food. The evening came and went. By the time he got home, Shawn was sure he and Joe had had some kind of conversation, but he remembered neither what they talked about nor what his burger tasted like. What was he going to do about all this?

For Helena, end things once and for all. As far as Pru, wanking off would have to suffice.

Shawn glanced around his dingy month-to-month apartment as he walked toward the bedroom. If he went back to New York, but was single again, he wouldn't even be able to afford to live in a place this good. He was almost thirty years old. Here he was, thinking about pretending to be some knight in shining armor for Pru, and he was barely taking care of himself. If she knew what he was really like, she'd be repulsed.

Fuck my life.

What he was feeling was just lust and fantasy. He was sick of Helena, sick of his parents and hers carving out a life he didn't want. Pru was a convenient, imaginary escape hatch. That was it. And Helena was hot — Joe wasn't wrong about that. Most of it was even real, except for her breasts, and the nose job from when she was a teenager. As he thought about it, she might have had a tummy tuck and ass augmentation at some point as well.

Shawn didn't bother washing up. He stripped down, got into bed, and stared at the ceiling as he reached between his legs, not thinking of anyone in particular.

CHAPTER EIGHTEEN

Pru sat on a park bench by the playground and watched as a couple of mothers helped their young children across the rainbow-striped monkey bars. Only nine in the morning, but the strong sun already made her skin sting and her head ache. Still, the risk of potential skin cancer was a better option than the risk of being somewhere more private.

More sets of kids and parents arrived. Four children made beelines across the artificial turf toward the swings as three women set out bags of snacks and sunscreen. Pru relaxed a little. The more people here, the better. She closed her eyes.

"That'll be us someday, sweetheart." Cliff sidled in next to her and planted a dry, minty kiss on her cheek. She hadn't even noticed him coming.

Pru opened her eyes and scooted away until she was close to the edge of the bench. Even though it must already have been around ninety degrees, Cliff looked cool and comfortable in his gingham short-sleeved shirt and khaki shorts. He was wearing a pair of Ray-Bans, and his smile was even and warm. He was watching a couple with a toddler walk toward the playground.

She imagined slitted snake irises behind the dark lenses. "No, it won't."

"Do you remember our first date?" He didn't wait for an answer. "I brought you roses. They were red, and I asked if they were your favorite. You smiled at me and blushed — it was so cute — and thanked me. You said you liked pink better."

"I also remember that Matilda hated you instantly. Dogs' instincts are always right."

Cliff laughed and reached for Pru's hand. She whisked it away before he could grab it. Instead, he slid closer to her. "She must be old by now, isn't she?"

Pru stared at him.

"I'm glad we're doing this, babe. I've missed you."

A few more people passed the bench—three kids and another adult couple holding hands and smiling at their children. "Pru, please look at me."

It was the "please," and his soft, pleading tone that made her turn her head. His forehead was smooth, and his mouth was neither in a thin frown nor a condescending sneer. For a few seconds, she saw the handsome, talented gentleman who'd chosen her above all the other women in the orchestra who coveted him. He put his hand over hers on the bench.

"I know what an asshole I can be sometimes. I understand why you left. Things escalated out of my control. I'm going to try to do better." She tried to slip her hand away, but he closed his fingers around it.

She yanked hard and he let go of her. "Cliff, you hurt me. You disfigured me just because I told you I didn't think you interpreted a Mozart solo correctly." Her head and chest tightened. "In the hospital, you told me you had half a mind to let me die." She'd gone to the police that time and pressed charges. Even with that kind of assault and Edie's help, Cliff had still gotten away with it. His family had money and influence and they were friends with several Superior Court justices. Everything was swept under the rug.

Cliff's shoulders dropped and he pulled off his sunglasses. "But I felt so bad about that. I went out of my way to offer to drive you to and from rehearsals and brought you flowers." He pouted and widened his eyes, like one of those plastic dog banks put out on store counters by the Humane Society.

Pru straightened and slid herself out of arm's reach. She narrowed her eyes. "You made jokes about it. You said I got what I deserved." She wasn't sure what to make of his expression. Were the rims of his eyes turning red? Was he going to cry? He looked down and sucked in his lower lip. When he met her gaze again, there was a tear on his cheek.

"It was a defense mechanism. I didn't know how to handle what happened." He sniffled. "You didn't even thank me for wanting to help you."

She raised her voice. "You don't get to be the victim here. Don't turn this around on me."

"Mind if I tell you a story? I don't think you've heard this one."

Pru rolled her eyes. "Sure, why not?"

"When I was a boy, my parents and grandparents made sure I had anything I could possibly want. They're very well off. You know that." He took a breath and let it out slowly. "What I didn't have was their affection. They were always busy, always sending me off to one place or another, whether it was to camp or off to entertain myself. When I was in school, no one was all that interested in me unless I could either give them something or make them look good."

In spite of herself, Pru envisioned a beautiful, lonely little boy, so stifled and sheltered that he never learned how to receive love, never mind reciprocate it. He was right—he'd never told her this before.

Cliff moved closer and put his arm around her shoulders. She stiffened. "You always give me what I need—your devotion and love. I know you want that for me—I can see it all over your face. I'm glad you decided to go out with me today."

Shivers spiked from beneath Pru's skin and cold sweat beaded on her brow. She took a deep breath and forced herself to look at him. "This isn't a date, Cliff." Speaking made her stomach seem to dislodge and work its way toward her throat. "I asked you to meet me here, in public so you could look me in the face and see how serious I am. I don't like you, and I certainly don't belong to you. I don't ever want you near me or my friends again."

"You don't really mean that." He brushed his fingers along the side of her neck.

Her skin chilled. "Stop."

"Don't play hard to get. It doesn't suit you." He brushed back some of her hair.

"Don't touch me, Cliff." Pru jerked her torso back. Cliff took his hand away.

Before she had a chance to recover, he leaned in and kissed her cheek. "Enough." His tone was made sharper by his saccharine breath. She almost gagged on the overwhelming bergamot in his aftershave.

Pru pulled her face away and grimaced. "I'm leaving in ten, nine, eight . . ."

Cliff leaned in and put his face close to her ear. "Have you shown that janitor of yours what you look like under that dress? I'm the only one willing to have you as is." His breath in her ear was like a thin, hairy root darting from his mouth, trying to lodge itself in her and feed off her. She wanted to get up, but her feet wouldn't comply. She sat paralyzed as tears welled and began to run down her face.

"Babe, don't cry." He wiped some tears away with his finger.

Pru imagined the scene in *Alien* where the *Internecivus raptus* was breathing down Sigourney Weaver's face. Tears fell faster. Her heart beat into her stomach, and her breath sharpened as she broke away from him and stood. He stood as well and took up her hand.

Her muscles clenched as she yanked it away. He held on more tightly and tugged back. "Let me go." There was a monotone fury to her voice that even she didn't recognize. She lifted a leg, stomped into his instep, and then kneed him between the legs. Cliff's mouth hung open. His eyes bulged as he staggered a couple of paces and fell onto the bench. He glared at her as he jumped to his feet. He looked like he wanted to scream bloody murder.

"I'll say it again, Cliff. Stay away." Pru turned to leave. Her insides were hot, and she was sweating all over as her limbs shook. She was sure her knees were about to buckle. Instead of running, she walked as calmly and briskly as she could manage without looking back. No one followed her.

Blood pounded between Pru's ears. She turned the radio up over the air conditioner and engine but still couldn't hear whatever was playing. She drove to the farthest front corner spot in the parking lot, which was blessedly under a large tree, and let the car idle while she leaned back and held her hands over her face.

How had she just managed that? Less than a year ago, she'd have let Cliff drag her away. Her diaphragm was a trampoline for her heart and stomach. She flung open the door, ran to the tree in front of the car, and dug her fingernails into its bark as her head dropped and gravity forced her to her knees.

She dry-heaved a few times, then leaned against the trunk. Her bones were done supporting her right now. A slight breeze broke the still, stifling heat. Her breath lengthened. She focused on that rather than the racing thoughts that warned her to drive away at top speed. After a few moments, the nauseating panic abated.

Pru stood and looked around. Still no Cliff. As far as she could see from across the lot, his car was gone. What would she have done right now if she'd opened her eyes and he was in front of her again, like at Geoff Reid's cocktail party? She shuddered at the thought and breathed through the next wave of nausea.

That wouldn't matter — you're here. Nothing bad is happening to you.

The thought was in Shawn's voice. She opened her eyes and blinked. The sky was cloudless, clear, Crayola blue. "Oh, my God." She pulled out her phone.

Are you around? she typed.

A few seconds went by before Shawn texted back. *I'm working on the house. What's up?*

Can I come over?

There was no lag this time. *Sure. The door's unlocked.*

Pru took one more big breath and looked through the pine needles above her. Giddy, she got into her car.

CHAPTER NINETEEN

Shawn dropped his paintbrush into a bucket of water, swirled it around, and left it to dry on the newspapers he'd spread in front of the wall he'd been working on. He didn't dare check the bathroom mirror. He knew he'd see a sweaty, filthy, disaster of a face that desperately needed a shave. A few days had passed since his incident with Cliff and shaving still smarted. Besides, the beard partially disguised the yellowing bruises on his face.

He washed his hands in the kitchen sink, then rubbed cold water over his face and through his hair. He was wiping his hands off on his paint-streaked shirt when Pru knocked on the door and let herself in.

She was wearing that same green dress he'd seen her in when they'd met by accident the first time. Had it really only been just over two weeks ago? Her hair was pulled up into what might have been a bun at one point, but long blonde strands drooped from the top of her head. She smiled as one piece fell in front of her mouth. She tucked it behind her ear. "It worked." She sounded exuberant.

He hesitated then smiled back. "What worked?" She took another step into the room and the memory of the way that dress stuck to her like a second skin materialized. Thankful for the kitchen counter separating them, he leaned in on his elbows.

She came to the other side of the counter, pressed her hands on its edge, and bounced on the balls of her feet a few times like a little kid. "The yoga. It worked today." Her cheeks were pink, and her eyes were on the grayer end of blue in the lighting. Before he could ask her what she meant, she took a few steps over to him, threw her arms around his neck, and hugged him.

Shawn hugged her back, and the question momentarily retreated from his mind. It was all he could do not to cup her face in one hand and press his lips against her forehead. Her graceful, surprisingly strong arms rested over the tops of his shoulders. Her long, warm fingers interlaced behind his neck tickled where his hair brushed against it. He suppressed a moan. Her head was against his heart, her soft breasts pressed against his chest. He spread his fingers against her mid-back and resisted the urge to let them roam. A velvety scent washed through him, one that he more tasted than smelled. He could only describe the sensation as "purple."

What had he taught her that warranted this? He should let go. They should both let go . . . anytime now.

Instead, she sighed, and they pulled closer together. *Brahmacharya.* He silently repeated the Sanskrit word for "restraint" a few times, resting his head over hers. A few seconds passed.

He had to end this. He needed to tell her "You're welcome" for whatever he'd done and let go of her. He let his hand wander down to the slope of her waist.

Brahmacharya. Brahmacharya.

She sighed so quietly he felt it more than heard it. His breath caught, but he forced his hips to stay still. Pru looked up at him. She was smiling, sort of, but her gray eyes were limpid and watchful.

Patting her back, Shawn took a step away. That felt like one of the worst decisions of his life. "So, what exactly did yoga help you do?" He took another step back and grabbed a bottle of water from the fridge for her.

She accepted it and took a few sips. "I saw Cliff. I told him to leave me and my friends alone. I was really nervous, and then I was too rattled to drive right away. I thought I was going to be sick a couple of minutes later but still, I did it." It all came out in a flurry of words, and then she turned pink and wrinkled her brow for a moment before her eyes brightened again. "I let the feelings pass, just like you said to, and they went away. I breathed, I paid attention to what parts of my body were tense, and I was okay after that." She sounded as if she'd experienced some kind of miracle and she was attributing it to him. "Thank you so much. I can't wait to learn more."

Shawn narrowed his eyes and frowned. "He was bothering you again?" He'd always thought that being so mad you saw red was only an expression, but for a few seconds his head was a furnace and the room tinted with his burgeoning anger.

He walked around her and she followed him into the living room. "Come sit." She sat cross-legged on the floor, and he took a seat across from her. "What did he do to you? Was he stalking you?" His gaze set on Pru's forearm, where faint gray marks were still imprinted.

Her eyes shone and her cheeks were pink as she smiled. "No. I asked him to see me in public, so we met at the park, by the playground."

"Why would you have done that? He could've hurt you."

"Probably not, at least not intentionally. When he grabbed my hand and wouldn't let go, I kicked him between the legs and walked away."

Shawn's eyes widened as he tried not to sputter the water he'd just sipped. "He grabbed you."

Averting her gaze, she opened her palms in her lap. "Yeah."

"And you—" He couldn't finish the sentence. "No way." He wasn't proud of himself, but he relished the mental picture of Pru kicking Cliff in the balls. "You are a tangle of contradictions, Pru. Has anyone ever told you that?"

She shrugged. "Anyway, he was too busy keeling over to chase me down."

"Wait, would he have?" His muscles stiffened. He looked her up and down and imagined Cliff shoving her around — or worse. In the shadows cast by the flooring he hadn't yet laid, he made out new bruises on her arm. His jaw tensed. It wasn't enough that Pru's thoughts raced all over her brain. She set his emotions swinging like a high-speed Foucault pendulum. He'd oscillated from perplexed to horny, to angry, to amused, to angry again, all in under twenty minutes.

He should ask her to go.

Pru folded her hands in her lap. "He might have." She frowned. "Now that I'm thinking about it, you said non-harming was part of doing yoga. I meant the yoga helped with the calming down part, but I hurt him on purpose." She winced. "Did I mess up?"

Shawn reached over to touch her hand, but she shifted at the last minute and his hand landed on her thigh. He froze. He stopped breathing. Imagined pulling her into his lap. He blinked hard and took his hand away as shame kicked him from behind a couple of times. "No." Letting out a breath, he felt relieved to once more be back on neutral and familiar turf. "Have you heard the story of Arjuna?"

Leaning her elbows on her thighs, she rested her head in her hands. "Tell me." Pru looked up at him, lips parted. He focused on the way they moved, the whiteness of her teeth and the tip of her tongue as she spoke. Her eyes were like the sky parting clouds after a storm. To wrench his gaze away from her and cast them toward the floor between their feet was almost physically painful.

"Oh, come forth into the storm and be my love in the rain."

"That was nice, Shawn. Is that by Arjuna? I don't think I understand what it has to do with non-harming." She winced as if embarrassed, the way she did when they'd talked about

"The Legend of Sleepy Hollow."

He thought he'd just recited that in his head.

Shit.

"No, sorry, I just got sidetracked. That was from a Robert Frost poem. It popped into my head for no reason."

"It's nice to know I'm not the only one who jumps around from one unrelated idea to another." Pru smirked and looked down.

"Okay, back to non-harming." He stretched his arms up, interlaced his fingers, and lowered them again. It was time to return to planet Earth. "In the *Bhagavad Gita*, Arjuna was the most revered member of the warrior caste. He rode out on his chariot one day to lead the ultimate battle between good and evil. His charioteer was a man named Krishna."

Pru leaned in, eyes focused on him. He cleared his throat.

"The problem was that half the people on the demons' side of the fight were beloved family members and friends who'd been corrupted over time. When he saw people he loved on each side of the field, ready for the generals to lead the charge, Arjuna cowered in his chariot and told Krishna to take him away because he couldn't bring himself to kill his wayward kindred. But the rules of the ancient caste system were rigid. He was born to lead battles. Shirking your gods-given duties was an unforgivable sin. Krishna tried every argument he could think of to convince Arjuna to carry on, but nothing got through to him."

Pru looked down. "I don't know that I'd be able to hurt the people I love. I don't blame him."

She pushed herself closer. Shawn focused on what felt like miles instead of inches of floor in between them. Borrowing from another tradition, this had to be how Tantalus felt. His mouth went dry, and he was tempted to sit on his hands.

"So, what happened? Did he get in trouble for not fighting?"

"Almost," Shawn said. "But here's the thing. Krishna

wasn't Krishna the charioteer. Krishna was the *god* Krishna. And he revealed himself to show Arjuna the universe without any of the filters that shield human beings from its vastness and light. Arjuna saw with complete clarity the way everything was interconnected. He could only handle it for a short time—the reality was too intense for people who aren't deities. But after experiencing, just for a moment, his place in the universe, he understood his responsibility to the whole of creation. At that point, he led the charge into battle."

Pru bit her lip. "All right."

"The real lesson here was that when God shows you your place in the cosmos, you do what they tell you to do without question. My point is there's a difference between harming out of malice or insensitivity and harming because it's a means of self-defense or the most responsible thing to do at the time."

He reached out and held on to her fingers. "If you were genuinely sure that Cliff was going to hurt you, you did what you had to do to protect yourself." Letting go, he leaned around and caught her eyes. "It's not like you ran him over in the parking lot or something."

"I, um . . ." She reddened. They were quiet for a few seconds. "I actually almost did run him over recently. And it wasn't because I wasn't paying attention."

"Okay." He rubbed the back of his neck. "Do I want to know the rest of this story?"

Pru bit her lip. "It was on the last day of orchestra rehearsal. He tried to grab me. Then he followed me around and tried to cage me in, so I got into the car and pulled out fast." She dug her fingernails into her palm. "I knew he'd get out of the way, but I did almost crash into someone's car. The guy behind the wheel gave me the finger." She twisted her fingers together.

"That was you?" He stared at her and guffawed. "I was so

pissed at whoever it was that nearly T-boned me. Now that I know the whole story, I'm taking back the rude gesture. I met Cliff for the first time that day. He had it coming."

Pru's eyes widened, but the rest of her face was blank. "I—"

"I'm not upset, Pru."

"I probably need to do more yoga." She looked at him wide-eyed. "I didn't realize I was so angry."

He chuckled. "We'll work on your rage issues.'" He made air quotes. "You didn't hurt anyone or anything." He looked past her, gathering his thoughts. "I think you should get angry more often about being bullied, but in the meantime, I don't want to get you mad at me now that I know the possible consequences of crossing you." He grinned.

She didn't return his grin. "I don't think I could ever be mad at you."

Taking up her hands, he leaned in closer to her. She could have almost fallen into his lap at this point. Shawn shivered as heat rose between them. "Pru, I—"

"Thank you." She stood, and he stood with her.

He reminded himself that A) she came here about yoga, B) he might be on the verge of being engaged, and C) he should not be a douche.

"My goal this summer was to stop having to lean on everyone to prop up my self-esteem. You're helping me a lot. I'm so glad we met." She put her arms around his waist and hugged him.

Shawn touched his hands to her upper back. "Me too." His voice cracked. Then he kissed the top of her head and took a step away from her. "I'd better get back to work." He smiled.

Pru smiled back. Hers looked more genuine than his felt.

After she'd left, he couldn't keep the brush steady as he tried to finish painting the wall.

CHAPTER TWENTY

The two string bags of groceries dug into Pru's elbow as she let Matilda guide her down the Main Street sidewalk. Downtown was busier than usual for a Monday. The sky was bright, but not brutally so yet, and the humidity had lifted a little bit. They wound through and around throngs of young-looking people as they came in and out of the shops and restaurants. Even the green, which was usually a quiet place for Matilda to do her business without getting distracted, was full of teenagers. They were sitting cross-legged on blankets, eating pizza slices, throwing Frisbees around, or sitting on swings meant for younger kids.

People "awwed" and reached out to pet the dog in spite of her orange service dog vest as Pru tried to drag her toward the trees in the back. Matilda was in her element, though. She didn't stop to play, but she did slow down, clearly enjoying the attention. As she got closer to where they were going, a teenager with light hair and a *Gorge View Graduate* T-shirt hurried over, intercepted them, and leaned in to grab Matilda's head and scratch behind her ears. Matilda didn't respond. She knew she was on duty when the vest was on.

"Sorry, but this is a service dog."

The teenager didn't stop petting her. He did look up at Pru, though. "You don't look blind to me."

Pru's neck warmed and her heart sped. "She's not that kind of service dog—she's working now, so please move aside." Matilda must have sensed the change in energy because she backed away from him, pivoted, and began to lead Pru away.

He yelled, "Bitch" as they left him.

It was going to take forever for the dog to concentrate on what they came here to do until Pru calmed herself. She was trying to remember the breathing exercises Shawn had taught her again when the phone buzzed.

"Uncle Barney, hi. I was going to call you later."

"Great minds, honey." His voice was strained and gravelly. "What's new in your life?"

Balancing her phone on her shoulder, Pru dug around her purse for a poop bag as Matilda sniffed the base of a tree. "Not much. Orchestra season is over, so I have a break. I want to come down and see you."

Her uncle was quiet for a few seconds. "Listen, sweetie, save your money. I'm in the hospital again."

Pru halted. Her service dog backed toward Pru and held still, ready for Pru to lean on her for support. "Why?"

"Nothing major. Just a little pain. It's nothing too serious, but they had to biopsy a few things. I'm going home tomorrow. Nancy . . . remember her from next door?"

"Of course I do." Pru snapped her fingers and pointed to the tree again. Matilda returned to her sniffing.

"She's gonna check in a few times a day. And I've got a nurse coming in to help me in and out of the shower. I'll be fine. You stay where you are so you can visit when I'm healthy. Better yet, stop sending me money I don't need and go on a nice vacation. Were you accepted into that program again?"

Pru winced. She'd been paying his considerable hospital bills for the past year—everything that was too experimental for Medicare to cover. With Matilda's hip surgery and follow-up treatments only just paid off, there was hardly any money left to spare. He didn't know that, of course—he would've been furious with her.

"Yes. I was invited up to Maplewood for later this summer.

I haven't accepted yet, though." The offer came with room and board in Dobbs Ferry in Upstate New York. That was a prestigious opportunity — a series of workshops and lectures paid for in part by donors and grants, and in part in exchange for a series of concerts with various combinations of musicians. She'd worked hard on the audition recording, but she planned on turning it down. Barney's health was too fragile, and she had to stay nearby.

"Sweetheart, this will be the third time. They're not going to keep offering. This is your career. You should go," he scolded.

Pru bit her lip and watched as her dog finally squatted. "I'll think about it." She stepped forward to bag the poop.

"Prudence. My angel. I'm an old man. I don't have anything left in my life that's undone. You're young, and you still need to live. Go on your trip. Play for me."

She tried to keep her voice from breaking. "You're not done living. I'm coming down tomorrow."

"I will make the nurse turn you back out again." Even though thin and scratchy, his voice was firm, like when she was a kid. She could almost see his finger jabbing at the dining room table for emphasis. Then his tone softened. "Pru. It's okay. *I'm* okay. It will make me happy if you go up there and send me pictures. I'll be here when you get back. Then I'd love to see you."

"I . . . I'll think about it. I promise." She took a few steps toward the tree, knelt with Matilda's help, and scooped the poop into a bag.

"That's my girl. I gotta go. A pretty nurse just came in. Goodbye, darling." Barney hung up.

Pru took a shaky breath, tossed the bag in the garbage, and let Matilda lead her back to the sidewalk. She'd meant to stop by the music store for more rosin, but her chest was beginning to constrict and her eyes were tearing up. "Let's go home,

Matilda." Pru's head burned. She didn't take her eyes from the blurry sidewalk as they walked at a fast enough pace for the world not to compress around her.

CHAPTER TWENTY-ONE

Shawn dug around for his keys as he headed for his metered spot along the sidewalk on Main Street. Just as he found his car, his phone lit up for probably the tenth time that morning. Most of the texts had been from Helena. He considered temporarily blocking her. Instead, he turned off his sound.

Opening the trunk, he dropped his pile of resumes into it. Next to those was a stack of yoga class fliers, but he had nowhere to hold a real class, and he didn't like taking people's money for that, anyway. From a gym or an organization willing to pay him, sure. Actual people who came to him in need of whatever yoga could offer? Not so much.

His father and Helena each had called him an idiot for that in the past. Meanwhile, he'd left seven resumes around town today for handyman work. Between the orchestra building's cleanup and Geoff's party, he had more than enough money for now, even some to put aside after rent, utilities, and filling his car. That wasn't going to last long, though.

He reached up and closed the trunk. As he turned around, a yellow lab in an orange service vest came into view from the opposite direction. Shawn recognized the gait of the woman behind it, then her calves as her light blue skirt swished around her knees, then the long braid that had fallen over her shoulder. There was a sudden lightness in his chest as his adrenaline kicked in. He smiled more widely than he should have. "Oh, hi Pru."

She stopped and Matilda sat, mouth open and tongue lolling out one side in a goofy grin. "Hi," Pru said without looking up. "It's okay. You can pet her. Say hello, Mattie." Pru's voice was expressionless. The lab began to wag her tail and pant. A long line of drool hung from her mouth to just above the ground.

Shawn scratched Matilda's head, but he continued to look at Pru. Her shoulders were shaking. "Are you all right? Do you need help?" When she looked up, Shawn's first instinct, which he tamped down, was to draw her into a hug and swear to fix whatever was wrong. Pru's eyes were red and puffy, and tears streaked her face. "Do you want to grab a cup of coffee and talk about it?"

Pru bit her lip and nodded. If only he had tissues on him.

Every few steps, Matilda stopped and held still. Then Pru would put her hand on the dog's back and lean into her, as if Matilda were in charge. It also seemed as though it was the animal, not the human, who determined when it was okay to keep going again and at what pace.

Slowing, Pru pointed and said, "Here." They stopped in front of a glass door full of handprints. Why did no one bother with handles? "They'll let Mattie into the diner. Not every place does, even though they're supposed to."

They sat in one of the black vinyl booths at the back of Lila's Diner. It was a well-lit little place with white floors, a clean chrome-and-white counter with round black swivel stools, and large hooded red lights overhead. A server came over right away and took their orders for tea and coffee.

"Do you want anything else?" Shawn asked. "Maybe you should eat."

The corners of Pru's mouth twitched up as she shook her head. "It's the same no matter where we're from. If we were raised by a Jewish maternal figure, food's the panacea for all that hurts."

Shawn grinned. "Are you implying it isn't?"

Laughing a little, she grabbed a napkin to dab her eyes.

Their server arrived and set down her tea and his coffee, as well as a bowl of water and a couple of dog biscuits on a placemat for Matilda, who grunted as she gobbled them up.

They watched passersby out the window without saying anything. Past girlfriends used to be impressed that he wouldn't hound them with question after question, guess after guess about what was on their minds. They misinterpreted nearly three decades of being kowtowed into silence for patience.

Pru took a few sips of her tea. "My uncle's had cancer for the past two years. I've been covering a lot of his expenses, even though he doesn't want me to. Medicare won't allow the more experimental treatments. He took a turn for the worse three months ago, then he got better, and now he's in the hospital again. He won't let me come and visit." Her voice began to break. "He says I worry too much."

Leaning forward, Shawn rested his elbow on the table and propped his head on his hand. Pru took another sip and mirrored him. "He and Matilda are the only family I have left. He helped raise me. Mattie's seven. She's already had one hip replaced six months ago. I've just caught up from that, and I'm not sure what else I can sell or put aside for Uncle Barney." She swallowed a sob. "I'm not even all that worried about that—I'll go into debt if I have to. He can't die. I won't let him. He can't leave me."

Now Shawn's eyes were getting wet. He thought about his network of family—parents, aunts, uncles, two living grandparents, and a slew of cousins. For a moment, he tried to imagine being the only one left. Suddenly, his parents' constant haranguing wasn't so annoying anymore.

He extended his arm across the table and held his palm open, unsure, yet again, of what to say to her. "I guess being in an orchestra is only slightly more lucrative than being a yoga teacher. I'm sorry—for all of it."

Pru closed her hand around his and he did the same. "The LGSO comes with a pretty decent salary for one person if you don't have a lot of expenses. It's just that I've plundered a lot of my savings between the two of them. I mean, I can still pay the bills — I don't have many since Tommy won't let me pay rent — and I can cover groceries and little stuff like that, but I'm getting worried."

"Not to pry, but if he's covering your rent, why not just divert some of your usual charity donations for a while?"

Pru was silent for a moment.

That was the definition of prying, and he was a *schmuck*.

She took a breath. "Because things are tight, but I have an income. I'm caught up on everything and I still have some savings left. It's just dwindling fast. The food pantry and the shelter for people in flight need more than I do. I'll at least have a roof over my head. And Tommy jokes that I don't eat much anyway."

Shawn added "generous to a fault" to the list of things about Pru that he liked.

"I know the feeling — about the money trouble part." He wriggled his fingers in between hers and swallowed some coffee with his free hand. It was already cold. "I'd offer you a platitude about things working out, but I don't like them."

"Me neither." She picked up her tea, took a small slurp, and put it down, making a face. "I let it get too cold. Do you want to go?"

Shawn reached into his pocket for his wallet while Pru opened her purse, and they both put some cash on the table. "I've got it," he said.

Pru frowned. "I can still afford a couple cups of coffee or tea."

"Please let me get it, Pru. You got dinner last time."

Her shoulders dropped. "Okay. Thank you."

He slid out from his seat. "My pleasure. Can I give you a

lift home?"

They didn't say much in the car, but it was only about a ten-minute drive. Pru leaned her head against the window and closed her eyes. Her breathing slowed right away, and her body was limp by the time he pulled up in the driveway.

Shawn twisted around to look at Matilda. "So, what do you think, Mattie?" he said, keeping his voice down. "Can you help me figure her out? What do you do for her? How can I make up for the rest?" Matilda hopped onto the floor from the back seat and leaned her head over the console. She licked his hand.

Pru remained asleep as Shawn let his car idle. Tommy's car was gone. It was hard to reconcile the confident, elegant person he saw playing the cello with the trembling, rain-soaked stranger, the nervous, awkward yoga student, and the emotionally spent woman before him.

What would he be like if he got his wish and his family didn't bother him anymore? It seemed like every conversation he had with his father for the last ten years had devolved into a disagreement. He tried to imagine the man being gone from his life forever—especially with so much unresolved. Shawn remembered vacations—just him and his parents or with extended family. He'd grown up with holiday celebrations and Saturday afternoons kicking a soccer ball in their large backyard with cousins and uncles. He remembered countless tearful conversations with his mother about math homework and girlfriends. His throat tightened.

Pru opened her eyes. "Anxiety," she mumbled, pushing her hair back and sitting up. "Mattie is a service dog for almost constant, life-disrupting anxiety. It doesn't even have to be triggered sometimes. The symptoms just kick in. That's why I shake so much."

Shawn felt the blood rush from his face. "I shouldn't have said—"

"I was mostly asleep, so it's okay. Not many people ask my dog before they do me." She smiled at him, and he saw the woman from the party again—the one who looked content and happy while playing her cello. "I'd better go inside and lie down. Thank you, Shawn. Thank you for this afternoon."

He got out without turning off the car. She and Matilda followed him to the trunk. "Do you need help bringing these in?" He held up her grocery bags.

"No, but I appreciate the offer." Pru's shirt had become untucked from her skirt, and both were rumpled. Like last time, that strong wisteria smell hung in the air. Everywhere he saw or smelled it now, he automatically conjured the image of her, drenched in front of her house. Shawn wasn't sure if Pru was shaking, but he certainly was.

He took a step forward, and she met him halfway for a hug. Her hair was starting to stick out from the braid, nearly poking up his nose, and he picked up the faint scent of salt from her sweat with the flowers. They each moved to peck each other on the cheek and their mouths landed closer than intended, like falling feathers. They stood stock-still until she lifted her chin by the smallest fraction, a natural, involuntary movement rather than something deliberate.

Please, don't let this stop.

Pru took the tiniest breath, and he registered her earlier tears layered in Earl Grey tea. He let the bags drop to the ground.

Shawn, you're a moron.

Her lips were warm on his skin, just a fraction of an inch from the corner of his mouth.

Shut up. I don't care right now. This has to happen.

He swallowed. Her jaw contained none of the tension he'd noticed earlier today. They swayed as their heads made tiny movements, gliding their closed mouths back and forth like skaters floating across the ice. Her breath pirouetted down to the bottoms of his lungs.

Don't stop. Don't think.

Cupping his hand behind her head, they added more pressure against each other's lips and their mouths parted slightly. The tips of their tongues touched.

After a few seconds, she pulled back. Her brow knitted for a second, but the blue rays in her gray eyes glinted when she bit her lip and smiled at him. She picked up her bags.

"Anytime you need someone, I'm a phone call away," Shawn half whispered, touching her arm. "I mean it."

She reached for his hand, and he gave it a quick squeeze. "Okay." She hurried up the porch steps and waved from her door's threshold.

After waiting to make sure she was safely inside, Shawn pulled back onto the road. As he began to drive away, he thought he saw her watching him from her window.

He shouldn't have let that happen. Yet he put his fingers to his lips, as if he could hold the kiss there longer.

CHAPTER TWENTY-TWO

Shawn pushed his sunglasses up the bridge of his nose and paced across the stucco patio of a half-renovated antique of a house. The sun had just begun to rise behind Joe and him, turning the sky dull pink. He could have sworn he saw the grass displace in a distinctly slithery pattern in the weed-filled yard. He frowned. "We're not anywhere near a pond or lake or something, are we?"

"Not that I'm aware of," Joe replied. "Cottonmouths aren't likely able to bite through calf-high leather boots, though. We're good regardless."

They looked around Sylvia Meyers's back yard. She was a professor at the College of Greater Atlanta who had just bought the sprawling old house. Joe had been trying to get into her good graces — and her pants — for months. He'd told her she'd get twice the work for half the price by letting him and Shawn clean up here.

The two men tucked their pants into their work boots, then took turns dousing themselves with Insect Shield. "Hopefully this will ward off the Chihuahua-sized mosquitoes," Shawn said.

"You're exaggerating." Joe grinned. He made a face as some of the bug spray mist got in his mouth. "They're more like rat-sized."

Shawn laughed.

They had their work cut out for them. The house might have been part of a small plantation at one point, but now "plant" was the operative word. Like most residences he'd seen around the area, the house took up most of the land.

Sylvia had hired professional landscapers to take care of the front and side yards. Shawn pushed his sleeves farther into his gloves. The two men gathered their gear and headed toward the back right corner.

There was nothing to mow—everything was too dense for a mower to get through. Joe held his hand to his forehead like a visor. "Shit on a stick."

Shawn grinned and grabbed a long-handled weed puller. "Very poetic. I can see why you became a Shakespeare scholar. Let's start with the perimeter back here and work our way to the center."

"Sounds like a plan." Joe started whacking away at the dense, thorny vegetation. "Shakespeare was rarely anything but crass, and I've earned the right to be crude. You can too if you finally apply to a graduate program and make something of yourself."

Shawn walked parallel to him, widening the path with his own tool. "Maybe." He jumped back as a garden snake glided past his foot.

"Or you can just up and marry your girlfriend."

Shawn thwacked his weed puller so hard that the blade got stuck in the hard Georgia clay. "Or not." He steadied his stance and yanked it out as hard as he could, causing him to stumble and fall into a thick patch of thistles. Standing, he tried to wipe the thorns out of his clothes.

Joe looked him up and down. "You all right?"

Shawn turned back, felled the thistle plants, and resumed his path. "No, in so many ways." He'd managed to go the whole week without seeing Pru. He'd been relieved when she had to cancel yoga for a rehearsal for a private function. It was early June. He hadn't spoken to Helena much, either. Every time he thought about his girlfriend, he wished she were Pru. He wasn't sure how to make either the want or the guilt stop.

They continued in silence as they rounded the corner. The

day was starting to get hot, and they had to finish this before the daily downpour.

By the time they finished and had raked the detritus into the woods and returned to the patio, they were dripping with sweat. Balancing one hand on a dilapidated plastic chair, Shawn pulled off his boots, wriggled out of his thorny coveralls, and did his best not to cut himself while removing his gloves. Joe leaned on the wall once he'd taken off his own protective gear.

"I don't suppose you've got a comb," Shawn said.

"Why, got a date?"

He narrowed his eyes at him. "No. So I can try to get more of the thistles out of my hair."

"I don't. Sorry." Joe pursed his lips. "Who is she? Tell me for real this time."

Shawn went cold and sat. "Who's who?"

Joe frowned. "Levinson, I was your roommate for four years up at Buffalo. I know what you look like when you're pretending to be stupid."

Shawn studied him and narrowed his eyes. "I don't think I can tell you. And at any rate, we're just friends. We've only known one another for a handful of weeks."

All he needed was for his family to think that not only had he abandoned Helena but was cheating on her too.

Joe waggled his eyebrows. "A description then?" He made a Dr. Evil gesture with his hand and adopted the accent. "Throw me a freakin' bone."

Shawn laughed. "Fine. Let's see . . ." She was so clear in his mind—every version of her that he'd met so far. "She's relatively short but has what look to be perfect boobs, a tiny waist, and an ass you just wanna sink your fingers into." He smirked. "Will that suffice for your pornographic fantasies?"

Joe laughed. "You always were the silver-tongued poet between the two of us. I need a little more."

Shawn closed his eyes for a moment. "Long blonde hair and gray eyes that sometimes look blue, so they're fascinating to stare at, even though I try not to. That would unnerve just about anyone."

His friend drummed his fingers and, no longer smiling, folded his arms. "More."

"Okay, let me think." Shawn took a deep breath. "She's talented and generous to a fault. She's living almost as much at poverty level as me because she gives all her money to other people . . ." He thought some more. "And she's one of the nicest people I've met down here." He looked at Joe again. "How's that?"

Joe frowned and stared at him.

"You already knew," Shawn said, realization dawning.

He leaned in and clasped his hands. "I wanted to hear it from you. I wanted to hear how you talked about her." Joe let out a breath. "Pru *is* special. She's all of those other things you said. She's got a stubborn streak and a hell of a backbone, but she also has a lot on her plate, and in the eight years I've known her, she's always been emotional. If you start something with her and she trusts you enough to let you in, it will destroy her when you go back home."

Shawn looked at his lap.

"Look at me," Joe said. Shawn lifted his head. "She dated a complete shithead, and everyone who cares about her watched her confidence crumble piece by piece while they were together. She hadn't had much experience before him as far as I know, and she hasn't trusted any man romantically since then." He dropped his arms by his sides. "What I'm trying to say is tread lightly with her. She will pour everything she can give into your hands if she falls for you—and she's gonna be either all in or all out when it comes to stuff like this. If you dump Helena and start dating Pru, please, just don't break her heart."

CHAPTER TWENTY-THREE

Soft music piped from hidden speakers around the dining room of Chez Véro. Pru used the edge of her spoon to lift back the cheese that sealed her onion soup, and some of the brown liquid spilled over the edge of the brown porcelain crock. She inhaled the earthy, sweet fragrance and peeled back more of the cheese with her spoon.

The dinner rush hadn't quite started yet—only five other tables had filled. Even with about twenty or so tables in total, the restaurant had an open, airy quality with its light polished wood floor, blond furniture, and mauve upholstery and table linens. An unlit red-brick hearth filled the back wall.

Shawn held the menu open like a book and stared at it.

"Do you need help translating the entrees?" Pru asked.

They'd been texting for a week since that one kiss that had sent her reeling. But this was the first weekend of a brand-new month, and a brand-new start. Tommy had objected, but she was sure she knew what had to happen from here if she was to keep to her summer goal though. At least, she was pretty sure.

"My French is pretty rusty." He flicked the yellow tassel attached to the leatherette binding of the menu. "It wasn't that great even at my best."

"Mine's not perfect, but I learned to get by in French, Italian, and German in graduate school." She read off the items on the menu, translating as she went, and he made a selection.

"You know so much about culture and languages. Why don't you display your degree, or talk about it much?" Shawn sat back. His arms made small jerky movements, as though he was wringing his hands under the table. His jaw was tight, and lines creased his forehead.

"I don't feel the need." She shrugged. "I'm proud of it and I don't actively hide it, but I already know I have a doctorate. I don't need a reminder on my wall. And there's zero reason for me to make it the topic of conversation."

His eyes twitched.

"My level of education and what I do for a living don't define who I am," she said.

"That is probably one of the most yogic things I've heard you say."

"I have an excellent teacher." She dipped her spoon into the soup and sipped a small amount to test the temperature. "This is so good. Try yours."

Shawn took a spoonful, shutting his eyes as if to savor the sweet, dark flavor. "Wow." They smiled at each other. He straightened and cleared his throat. "But that's an important lesson—not to define yourself by outside standards. It's hard to remember sometimes." He took a sip of his Vouvray.

"Thank you." Her stomach fluttered as the silence between them lengthened. His posture was stiff, and every time he spoke, something unsaid lingered between them. He was probably about to tell her lessons were off. She shouldn't have kissed him when he was just trying to be nice to her. For the past few days with hardly any contact, she wondered what had possessed her to do so.

Her train of thought was distracted by Timéo, the owner's cousin. He stood at the table in his black button-down shirt and matching slacks, pen and pad readied to jot down their order. She rattled off in French what she and Shawn wanted.

"Is this handsome man your boyfriend?" he asked, still in French, raising his salt-and-pepper eyebrows.

"I'm not sure, but when I find out, you and Claudette will

be among the first to know," Pru replied in the same.

"*Oui, bien.*" He winked before he walked away.

Shawn smirked. "You just said you were barely passable in French."

"Here, I'm usually fine. I'd be pretty lost in France though, I bet."

"Have you ever been?" He twirled some cheese onto his spoon.

Pru nodded. "With my grandmother and uncle when I was eleven, for Uncle Barney's business trip. Somewhere around the house is my little Eiffel Tower souvenir." She smiled. "What about you? Have you been to Europe?"

"Nope. I've never even gotten a passport. Everyone keeps saying I should before I get back with . . ."

He shivered and trailed off, took a big spoonful of soup and looked like he nearly choked on it. Grabbing his wine glass, he took a few swallows.

An hour later, as they waited for their boxed leftovers, Pru had had enough of their evening-long, stiff, halting conversation. They'd gone stumbling gracelessly from topic to topic, with Shawn constantly looking down and frowning. She was shaking badly enough to have trouble holding her water glass in the end, but he hadn't seemed to notice.

It was still light outside as they made their way down the cracked, weedy sidewalk toward their cars. They'd met here instead of coming together. They passed the older, less well-maintained brick stores, a 7-Eleven gas station, and a florist that had been in business since the thirties as they walked in tense silence. The humidity was mercifully light this evening, but something heavy hung in a thick cloud between and around them just the same. He hadn't even held her hand or hugged her all evening.

When they reached the public parking lot, Pru stopped and looked at him. "You're upset about something. Was it what happened when you drove me home a few days ago? I'm really sorry about that. I promise I'll—"

"Me too." Shawn shut his eyes and exhaled. "We shouldn't have done that. I think we need to take a couple of steps backward." He reached into his pocket and put on his mirrored sunglasses.

Pru gripped her upper arms and shivered. This was why they'd gone out in the first place, to somewhere neutral. In retrospect, this place had been a bad choice. What had she been thinking, suggesting a romantic atmosphere to ask for a platonic relationship? "Okay. I mean, yeah, you're right." She dug her fingers in hard enough to know she'd probably be bruised later.

He leaned back on his car, his hands hanging at his sides, shoulders slumped. "You told me you needed to try to be independent, and the thing is, I like you a lot, but my life's pretty complicated right now." He sounded tentative and resigned, and he wouldn't look at her. "I wouldn't be able to live with myself if you got hurt because I was careless." The declaration came out as a half-whispered mumble.

"Shawn." He lifted his head. She had no idea what she wanted to say next, even though she'd rehearsed the conversation in her head. All she could think about was the time he'd recited Robert Frost to her impromptu as a rainstorm began. His mouth was a tight, straight line. He inhaled with a small shudder, and she saw her distorted reflection. It seemed a perfect image of how she was feeling. "It's all right. I was thinking the same thing for a similar reason, you just brought it up first. I like you a lot too, and I wasn't sure how to say any of it without hurting you."

He pulled the corners of his mouth back. "We're on the same page, then. Are we good?"

Focusing on looking resolute as her legs and chest shook, she opened and closed her mouth a couple of times before she was able to get any sound out. "We're absolutely fine," she managed. "Except for that one thing, nothing's really changed, has it? Two friends kissed for a minute. Not a big deal, right?"

"Of course not." He smiled for real this time and hugged her. His chest was warm, and his heart was racing.

Pru shuddered and put all her energy into holding off tears. She stepped back, and they dropped their arms. "Okay," she said. She walked around to her own driver's side door and opened it.

Shawn got into his car. "I'll see you around, Pru."

This was for the best. This was what they both wanted. Nothing had changed.

She pretended to do something on her phone while she watched him drop his head back on his seat, shut his eyes, and then straighten, take a big breath, and drive away.

CHAPTER TWENTY-FOUR

When Pru opened her eyes, the birds imprinted on her kantha quilt were a misshapen tangle wrapped over her legs and around her middle. She squirmed and kicked to free herself, then sat up. The sun was so bright through the window that she had to squint and use her hand as a visor. She'd overslept several times since that conversation with Shawn after dinner.

Now Matilda was sitting at the foot of the bed, waiting for breakfast. Pru had missed sunrise again.

Swinging her legs over the bed and stumbling over BOB, who'd fallen from the nightstand, she knelt to grab the vibrator. She carried it into the bathroom to wash it as well as herself and get dressed. When she returned and went to let Matilda outside, she said, "Just the two of us again, huh?"

She stepped outside onto the porch. The air wasn't quite hot and soupy yet. In fact, she felt a tiny breeze that would have been pleasant anywhere else. She pinched her nose with one hand as she held a plastic Kroger bag in the other and headed to pick up Matilda's poop. The dog trotted around the yard, sniffing along the fences. Pru dumped the bag in the outdoor bin and they went inside.

The front storm door creaked just moments after Pru finished her dry toast. That was about all she could stomach most mornings lately. Tommy tapped on the door before opening it a crack. "Are you decent?"

Pru laughed. "As a human being or as a clothed person?"

He came in and peered at her through the kitchen pass-through, wearing a white T-shirt with astronaut cats on it. Pru was pretty sure that was Andrew's shirt. "You'll have to decide the first question for yourself. I thought we could go for a walk since you're dressed."

Pru stood. "Let's go, Matilda." The dog, who was lying by Pru's feet and waiting for crumbs to fall, moved to stand. She stumbled for a moment as she found her balance. Tommy and Pru frowned at each other. Matilda wagged her tail when she saw Pru get the leash from its hook.

"She's okay," Tommy reassured. "C'mon."

The neighborhood had originally been meant for young families with white-collar jobs back in the forties and fifties, but as the population aged, so had the area. Pru and Tommy walked past the brick-front houses, all of which had concrete porches and white carports. Everything was in good enough repair, and most of the small front yards were neatly mowed, with zinnia and marigold beds beneath the front windows. Large, established trees lined the sidewalks. Toppled tricycles and half-deflated soccer balls decorated a few yards, but the area mostly consisted of single-family homes occupied by retirees and duplex rentals inhabited by college students.

Pru inhaled the magnolia scent that the breeze blew across them, and Tommy smiled. It had been too long since they'd taken a walk together. They strolled in the comfortable quiet that came with years of friendship. As they rounded the corner at the four-way intersection between Malcolm and Ashley Streets, he finally said, "I haven't seen Shawn in a while. What's up?"

Pru picked up her pace without meaning to, and her friend hurried to catch up. "I think we kissed," she said.

Tommy squinted. "You only think so?"

"It was more like our mouths touched by accident, kind of, and then we kept them there."

He laughed. "I think that counts." Then he was quiet as

they walked by a manicured, colorfully flowered yard and the one next door, which was overgrown with tall, spiky grass. "But you haven't heard from him since?"

Pru watched their feet as they walked. "Well, we went out for dinner last week, and decided we should just be friends. We haven't spoken since then—not even texts." She did her best not to sound disappointed.

"I'm sorry."

"Yeah. It's for the best." An airplane flew overhead, drowning out any possible conversation. By the time it had passed, Matilda was starting to pant. Pru pointed toward the next street, which led to their own.

"You don't sound convinced," Tommy said. "Maybe you should talk to him about it some more." They paused at a streetlamp in front of a whitewashed brick house with red shutters.

Pru scuffed the toe of her sneaker along the sidewalk, making a faint half-circle in a light layer of dirt and pebbles. "I don't think I want a relationship. I need to quit looking to cling to people."

They kept walking until they came to an intersection. Tommy pursed his lips and drummed his fingers on the corner stop sign. "There's a difference between clinging to people and allowing people to care for you, Pru." He touched her arm. "He's not Cliff. You used to date all the time in college, and then he knocked you down so hard that you never got up again. I think you and Shawn really like each other. Why won't you let him help you find your feet?"

"I don't know." Her voice creaked, and she let Tommy pull her in to lean her head on his chest. "I'll ruin it. I'm too messed up. It's not the right time."

He rubbed her back. "That's a load of garbage. You're overcomplicating things. He might make you happy."

"That's the problem." Pru pulled away. "I can't make

myself happy right now. I don't remember a lot about what that feels like. It's not fair to put the burden on anyone else. And besides, he doesn't want to date me."

They started to walk again in silence. As they turned the next corner back onto their street, Tommy said, "I bet you're wrong." He took a slow breath and continued. "Look, I know you've been occupying yourself. I know you know how to take care of yourself. And I definitely know you're good at taking care of the people you love."

They mounted the three steps to their front porch. Tommy opened his door and waited for her to go inside, and then they headed for the kitchen, which was opposite and identical to Pru's except for its pale yellow and blue décor. Tommy filled a bowl with water and set it on the floor for Matilda, grabbed a large pan hanging on a rack overhead, and took out eggs, milk, and bread.

"What are you doing?" Pru reached around to rip some paper towels from their stand and knelt to clean the water Matilda had slobbered all over the floor.

"We're having French toast. Get the cinnamon from the cabinet right above you when you stand." She did as asked, poured two mugs of coffee, and set them on the table. She sat and watched him soak the bread in the egg mixture he'd made. He turned around. "I'm trying not to push you too hard into a new guy's waiting arms, but I wish you'd give yourself a chance to be happy—and you're not happy when you're all alone." He dropped the eggy bread onto the heated pan.

Pru sighed. "I know. But this is important to me. Whatever was happening between us, it needed to slow down. I can't do this." A silence took over the conversation as Tommy flipped the bread in the pan and listened to their breakfast sizzle.

When their breakfast was ready, he brought over their

plates. "I'm going to give you some tough love, Pru. You *can* do it, you just *won't*. It's time for you to crawl out from the rock Cliff buried you under. The sun is up, the sky is blue — meet a brand-new day."

"I know," she said. "Do you think you'll ever get tired of quoting the Beatles' song to me?"

He chuckled. "Change your name to Martha, Julia, or Michelle, and I'll switch songs."

She rolled her eyes, took a bite of her second breakfast, and hummed. "This is so delicious." Putting her fork down, she added, "I'm making my way out, but I have to get strong enough not to be hurt again."

Raising his eyebrows, Tommy took a sip of coffee and closed his eyes. "That's not how it works."

"But it will for me. I'll make it work."

With a sigh, he opened them. "You do understand this is your twice-orphaned child-voice talking, don't you? This is fear and anxiety, Pru. You're standing in your own way."

"I'm going to make myself emotionally self-sufficient. I don't need someone to love me — not like that — to be happy." Tommy drank more of his coffee, watching her while she put another forkful of food in her mouth. It had started sweet, but the aftertaste had become bitter.

CHAPTER TWENTY-FIVE

Pru opened the door, and Edie walked in with a large pizza from Ralph's Brooklyn Deli, which she set on the coffee table. "Starve no more. Sustenance has arrived."

"You are my savior." Pru grinned.

Andrew, who had on a red polo shirt with a Coca-Cola logo, jumped up from the couch. "I'll grab the beer." His shiny black hair flopped into his eyes and he pushed it back.

"Get a haircut while you're up," Tommy teased.

Andrew smirked at his boyfriend, eyes glinting. "Get one yourself unless you're going for the Bob Marley look. Besides, in Chinese culture, long hair is a sign of nobility."

Edie looked from one to the other. "The long dreads help thin out those baby cheeks."

"You'd look good with a long ponytail," Pru said to Andrew. She cued up Netflix while Matilda drooled at the smell of garlic, basil, oregano, and whatever other things Ralph used to make this magical thing of beauty. "Go to your bed, Mattie." Matilda sulked to the corner of the room and plopped onto her cushion.

The four friends squashed together on the couch and clinked their bottles. "To your first big case. May it be a success," Tommy said.

"It will be a success. Edie's going to win, and then she'll conquer the world," Pru said. "Regardless of her wishes, we will follow her orders blindly and gladly."

Edie laughed. "I'll drink to that."

Ninety minutes' worth of '50s sci-fi B movies and a

devoured pizza later, all four of them slumped, too full to move. Andrew, hands resting on his slightly rounded belly, turned to Tommy. "You'd best digest all that food fast so I can do wicked things to you later on."

"I will run laps up and down the street until I puke if I have to." He grinned and winked at Pru.

She pretended to gag. "Eww, Tommy."

"That is way too much information," Edie piped in. "I don't care about the sex talk, but the other image is harshing my food mellow." She hoisted herself from the couch and started to pick up plates and bottles.

"Don't do that, this is your party," Pru said. "I think Tommy should clean up as penance for what he said."

He groaned and rolled his eyes. "Fine. But later on, I'm gonna tell you the story about streaking across campus when I was a sophomore. Pru's probably still got pictures."

She laughed. "I'll have to look for them later."

Andrew shut his eyes and shook his head, then stood. "Sit back down, Edie." They changed places and he looked at Tommy. "Go do as you've been bidden. I'll break down the box to put in the trash outside before we go back to my place."

"Why are you going there when you're already here?" Edie asked.

Tommy grinned. "We might get noisy. Matilda started barking at the wall last time."

"Talk about harshing the mood." Andrew laughed and looked at Tommy. "Have you told them?"

With an even wider smile, Tommy held up his left hand. He was wearing a silvery band with small green stones circling it. "We're engaged."

Pru jumped to her feet and threw her arms around him. "Oh my God, I'm so happy for you." She moved to Andrew and hugged him hard. "This is so amazing."

Edie, who also had risen, wrapped an arm around Tommy

and examined his ring before kissing him on the cheek. "So, tell us everything." She dragged him back to the couch.

Andrew sat between Pru and Tommy and leaned forward on his forearms. "I said I wanted to take him somewhere nice to celebrate my promotion. I got on my knee just before dessert."

Pru maintained her smile and tried to keep track of the conversation beyond that. Some of it was static. She rose to take a few things into the kitchen but in reality, she needed to lean against the counter and remind herself to breathe.

"I meant to tell you on our walk, but I was worried about you." Tommy's voice was soft—she hadn't even heard him come in.

Pru opened her eyes. Her friend was leaning on the refrigerator with his hands folded in front of him. "Tommy, I don't think I could be happier for you if I tried." She looked down. "I know you're almost always at one or the other place, but when are you—"

"We're not moving in together yet. But Pru, sometime in the fall I'm going to put the house on the market. I wasn't sure how to bring up that conversation." He came over and stood alongside her. "I'm not gonna let you be homeless, though. Just stop donating your imagined rent and start saving it."

She leaned on his shoulder. "Tommy, I'm twenty-six, and I have a job. I'll figure something out. This isn't your problem." Her eyes burned, but she wasn't going to cry. She was not going to make him feel guilty for living his life.

Reaching around, he wove his fingers between hers. "I know you better than that. We're going to sit and have a conversation and find you a place to live where you'll be happy and safe. But I'm worried about you not having me around in case . . . you know."

Pru moved to sit at the table. "That's why Matilda's here. And you're not . . ." The thought hadn't occurred to her until now. "You're not moving far away, are you? Does Andrew's promotion mean moving to Marietta?" She knew he worked at a satellite office for Coca-Cola.

Walking around, Tommy stood behind her. "I don't think so since my job's still local. But we might have to find somewhere halfway at some point." He rubbed her shoulders. They were so tight that even a little bit of firm pressure hurt, but she ignored the discomfort. "You will not be without me, though. You know that, right? I'm a fixture in your life. You'll never be rid of me."

Pru stood and hugged him, burying her head against his shirt. Now she couldn't stop herself from crying. "I suck as a friend. I'm supposed to be supportive, and I'm so glad for you, and I'm so scared. I'm thinking of myself instead of my best friend."

He rocked her and kissed the top of her head. "You're being human, baby girl. And Andrew adores you. He's a hundred percent behind working together to make sure we're all gonna be okay."

She clutched him more tightly, then pulled away to smile at him. Letting go, he used his thumbs to wipe away her tears. "This is what I meant on our walk, though. It's okay to depend on and let people love you. No one's cutting you loose."

"Shawn said he wanted to cool things off before I even said anything."

Tommy stared off for a few seconds. "I bet he's just as scared as you are. Slowing down is one thing. Cutting ties is a whole other matter."

Everyone left around midnight. Pru changed into a tank top and a pair of sleeping shorts, had some tea, brushed her teeth, and shook out her hair. As she drifted off, the dream hit—the hard crunch of metal and shattering of glass, the smell of burning gasoline. Sammy next to her, his little hand reaching for hers, screaming as fire consumed him. The image morphed into Cliff. But instead of burning up, he was pushing her into the fire. Shawn was there too. He was about to pull her out but at the last second turned and walked away.

Pru jerked awake, startled, but she couldn't move because Matilda had laid herself across the length of Pru's body. Dreams were so annoyingly literal sometimes. "Let me up, Mattie."

The room was pitch dark. Her whole body trembled so hard she had trouble finding the floor right away as she tried to stand. She couldn't slow her breath and could barely keep up with it. So she headed for the bathroom to look for her rescue pills. She took four tries to open the prescription bottle and dump the last one into her hand, which shook so much that she missed her mouth altogether. The clonazepam tablet fell into the sink and slid down the drain.

Pru's ribs seemed to link shut around her organs.

She started for the living room, where she'd left her phone. Matilda followed, grabbed the phone from its charger, and set it on the pass-through. She jumped up and put her paw on the edge of the phone, steadying it. Pru wasn't sure who in her contacts list she hit—she couldn't focus, and her coordination was nonexistent.

Shawn yawned as he answered. "Hello? Who is this?"

"Shawn, is that you? Please, please come over." Her voice was thready. A gigantic sob was making its way through her stomach and up to her throat.

"Pru? What's the matter?" He sounded wide awake now.

"Please come. *Please.*" The last word was drowned as she began to cry. She gulped for air, but she was crying so hard she could hardly breathe.

"Okay. I'm throwing on some clothes right now. I'll be there in a few minutes." He hung up.

Without any warning, the room blurred and tilted hard to the right. Pru stumbled into the wall and sank to the floor. Hugging her knees to her chest, she closed her eyes. The room rocked, and she thought she might be sick. She tried to crawl to the bathroom, but as soon as she got on hands and knees, the room slanted again, sending her careening against the wall. Her stomach roiled as she struggled to sit.

There was a heavy knock on the door. "Mattie, get the door," Pru gasped. The dog jumped onto her hind legs and nosed the chain latch until she could catch it in her teeth and undo it. Then she pawed at the doorknob until it turned. She backed up as Shawn rushed in.

"Oh, my God, Pru." He was at her side on the floor before she knew it and put his arms around her. "Can you move?" She couldn't answer. "I want you to sit up and lean back on me, and I'll hang onto you."

"I can't tell where up is." Her heart pounded faster.

"All right. I'm gonna help you then." Shawn maneuvered himself behind her. With one hand over her shoulder and the other on the side of her rib cage, he guided her to sit against his chest. He scooted them both back until he was leaning on the wall, then wrapped his arms and legs around her. "I want you to breathe. Can you do that for me? I'll do it with you." He took a slow, deep inhalation, then let it out. "You do it now. You can do it."

Pru took a big, nauseating, gasp. But when she let it go, she hiccupped, gulped, and felt gravity shove down on her shoulders as she started sobbing again. Matilda wrapped herself next to Pru. "Don't let go. Don't go." Her voice was high and panicked as she tried not to pant.

"I'm right here." Shawn's breath was on her ear. She shut her eyes as he kissed the top of her head. "I won't leave until you tell me to. I'm here, Pru."

Somehow the sound of her name combined with his mouth

by her ear made her chest begin to pry itself open.

"I'm here with you. Just breathe, however you can do it."

Her pulse began to slow, and after what felt like hours but probably was only a few minutes, she could take deep enough breaths to stop crying. When she opened her eyes, the room was once again steady and still.

CHAPTER TWENTY-SIX

Rocking Pru in his arms seemed unwise if she was this dizzy, so Shawn put his cheek against hers and held her as tightly as he could. After a few minutes, she seemed calmer and wasn't shaking as much. Eventually she pulled away and he loosened his hold. She pivoted to face him, wrapped her arms around his back and nuzzled her head under his chin. "Thank you," she whispered into his chest.

"Of course." He hugged her again. "Anytime you need me, I'll do whatever I can to be there for you. You don't have to be alone." He almost said something else—something that probably wasn't true, but Joe's warning kept coming back to him. Then again, so did the sad look on her face, as well as his sense of loss, maybe even grief, as he'd driven away that night.

She rested her head on his chest, and he looked down as she looked at him. She bit her lip and released it.

Shawn kissed her forehead and Pru kissed his chin. Then their lips were touching, first gently, and then with more and more pressure, until their mouths parted. He held her jaw in his hand and traced over it with his thumb.

Don't you dare do this, Shawn.

His inner voice faded to white noise. He registered her palm against his face and her fingers gently settling over his cheekbones. As he inhaled the combination of toothpaste and tears on her breath, he found that her lips were fuller than he'd remembered. Now he was definitely the one shaking. He'd had a reason not to kiss her, hadn't he? Shawn tried to

Dear Prudence

---

arrange a thought—any thought—but the neurons firing through the thickening static between his ears short-circuited. There was just warmth and softness between them, her short breaths and his, and the sound of their small gasps as they pressed together.

He cupped her cheek and opened his mouth more. She slid her tongue past his lips and all he could manage was to acquiesce. He pushed his tongue back and her quiet moan reverberated through him. She was holding him. She was breathing for him. He was hers.

Maybe she was Zeus and he was Metis. Maybe she would swallow him whole. He wrapped an arm around her more tightly and plunged farther into the kiss. Pru gasped and swung a leg around his waist as he scrunched her hair in his fist. Its texture was thicker than it appeared. He picked up that faint wisteria scent that wound past his nostrils and settled on the back of his tongue.

Shawn let go of Pru's hair and slid his hand over her lower back and around her waist. She pulled away. He glided his mouth behind her ear and along the side of her neck. She sighed, relaxed, and leaned in.

"I changed my mind. I don't want to go backward," he murmured against her.

Angling upward, she planted kisses along his jaw. "I'm sorry I pushed you away."

"I'm the one who's sorry. You didn't do anything wrong." He found her mouth again and slanted his over hers.

She slid her hands to his shoulders and broke off the kiss. Her lips had darkened and her cheeks flushed. As she clenched his shirt in her hands, he thought he noticed her hips rock. He fought down the urge to settle her more purposefully between his legs. "Shawn, I—"

Matilda chose that moment to shove her paw between them and against his crotch. Her heavy foot knocked and

147

pushed against his erection. He covered his painful reaction with a laugh.

"This is turning out to be a weird night," Pru said with a chuckle. The dog had a point, though. This wasn't why Pru had called him here. He kissed her forehead and helped her up as he stood. They sat on the couch, where he put his arm around her shoulders. She grabbed his fingers and leaned on him.

"Do you feel like talking? Did something trigger you?"

Wrapping her free arm around his waist, she sighed. "It's so stupid. It was such a long time ago."

"Pain is pain, Pru. It doesn't matter how long ago it happened. Your brain and your body can work hard to bury and ignore a lot of things, but that doesn't make them go away."

Says the pot to the kettle.

Taking a deep but shaky breath, she pulled herself closer. "I dream about that afternoon of the accident sometimes, but it doesn't feel like a dream. I see it from my own perspective as a little girl. Sammy and I had been playing tic-tac-toe on the back of a fast-food napkin. I looked out the window, and the sky was so blue it looked like a cartoon. There was a huge jolt. My head hit the back of the front passenger seat, and his hit the window. Metal crunched, and glass was everywhere. I remember screaming for my mom, but her head was slumped forward, and so was my dad's. Blood was all over the dashboard. I heard sirens. Then I smelled gasoline, and something in front of us exploded so loudly I couldn't hear anything else. Smoke filled our car, and the last thing I remember was coughing and trying to warn Sammy his clothes and hair were on fire."

Shawn picked up her hand and kissed her palm. "Oh, Pru."

"But that's not what the trigger is for me," she continued. "In the next part of the dream, I'm reaching out and holding onto my brother's blackened arm. It's completely ash and starts to crumble at the shoulder. Then his eyes pop open.

They're milky blue, and we're both burning from the inside. Black smoke puffs out of my mouth." She ignored a tear rolling over the bridge of her nose. "After that, everything is white, and there's nothing under my feet, and I just scream and scream."

He hugged her and she threaded her arm around his torso. "I don't trust that story to many people."

Dipping his head down, he kissed her again. This time, their kisses were more tender as they trailed them along one another's jaws and throats, then found each other's lips again.

"Don't let go of me," she said.

He kissed the salty, wet corners of her eyes. "I won't." In return, she kissed his chin, and he pulled her onto his lap. "I . . ."

He stopped himself. They didn't know each other well enough to say what popped into his head. Or, maybe they did now — at least, he knew her. If he was really going to do this, he had to tell her everything.

Finding her mouth again, Shawn kissed her harder. He'd tell her later. That was a shitty thing to do, but he was fairly certain his heart would stop if he wasn't touching her. Tentatively, he slid his hand farther down, pausing at the side of her breast. Her skin was so soft. She made that same half-sigh, half moan. When he got to her waist, he lifted the hem of her top. Before he could touch her, she pulled away, drew his hand back, and stared at him. Her jaw started to tremble, and her eyes were wide and afraid.

CHAPTER TWENTY-SEVEN

Without Shawn's weight and breath on her, the tremors began again. Tears threatened to roll down Pru's cheeks. She hugged her knees to her chest.

Shawn shifted to face her. "I'm sorry. I shouldn't have just assumed—"

"It's okay. I'm—I'm just . . ." She wasn't sure what she was. She was needy—she felt scared and safe at the same time. Just looking at Shawn's messy hair and hungry, confused expression made her insides ache.

Hopeless. She was hopeless and she was going to mess things up again.

He was hard. She wanted to palm the outside of his shorts and work her hand underneath and through one of the leg holes. Fluid stuck her sleep shorts to her inner thigh, threatening an embarrassing mess.

He would take one look underneath her shirt and leave.

"I want to." She took a deep breath, cleared her throat, and tried to steady herself. Then she moved over to him and rested her hand over his heart.

Shawn took that hand, kissed each of her fingers, and replaced it on his chest. There were dark circles under his eyes and his shoulders dropped. "Pru, you just exposed everything about yourself to me. You just relived some major trauma. This isn't the right time, and I was wrong to have pushed you."

"Please don't go." Wet drops slid down her cheeks. She was pathetic.

He hugged her. "I'll stay all night if you want me to. I'll sleep right here."

She wished they could kiss some more. She wished she was brave enough to show him her thick, raised scars and disgusting, hard flesh.

"In the little wheeled cart between the sink and the tub are extra toothbrushes if you want one, and extra sheets, blankets, and a pillow are in the closet just outside the bedroom." Gripping onto him for support, she stood and led him to the bedroom, Matilda in tow.

Pru sat cross-legged on the bed and waited until Shawn returned from washing up. "Lie down," he said when he returned. He tucked the thin quilt around her, then knelt at the side of the bed.

Reaching out, she touched his cheek. "Thank you."

"You're welcome." Shawn leaned in to kiss her, this time with his mouth closed. After lingering for a few seconds, he straightened. "I'll be right outside the door. Goodnight, Pru."

Curled on her side with Matilda against her, Pru reached over and turned off the lamp. She waited for the light in the living room to go out. As the air conditioner's initial rattle and low hum kicked in, her muscles softened—even the ones in her face. She closed her eyes and sank into a deep sleep.

CHAPTER TWENTY-EIGHT

Shawn opened his eyes halfway. The room was dark, the vague outlines of things were blurry, and the whole space was faintly perfumed with wisteria and mint. He closed his eyes again as he stretched. His back was kinked from having slept in the same twisted fetal position all night, and he was almost painfully hard.

Sitting up, he rubbed his eyes and looked around. From around the corner, he saw Pru outside the sliding door, facing away from him. Her sleep-mussed hair hung down to her lower back and her arms were at her sides. He remembered her hair bunched in his hand last night, how perfect she had felt when she'd settled against him, and the way she'd held on to him.

Standing, he opened the back door. "Good morning."

She turned around and lowered her gaze toward the floor with a small smile. "Hi." From the quietness of her voice, he thought she might be blushing, but it was still dark out. "I always go outside and watch the sun come up unless it's raining. Join me?"

"Let me just splash some water on my face. Be right there." When he looked out the glass door again, her outline and shadows made him think of how soft she'd been before she'd pushed his hand away from under her top. She'd just told him a few nights ago that she needed space. They both had said so. Last night, she was emotionally fragile—he wasn't.

He walked into the bathroom and stared at his reflection before brushing his teeth.

Congratulations, Shawn. You're the world champion of selfishness and mixed messages.

Walking back outside, he found her on tiptoes, burying her nose in a pink magnolia blossom. Shawn wrapped his arm around her from behind, reached up and pulled the citrusy-smelling flower and part of the branch off the tree. "Here you go." He pushed her hair away and tucked it behind her ear.

Turning, she smiled up at him. "Thank you."

He smiled back. "You make it look better than the tree does."

"I meant for last night." She squirmed a little. "I'm not very good at receiving compliments, but thank you for that too." Looking down, she added, "And I'm sorry for what happened."

Shawn took a step back. "I was way out of line." She stared at him and he closed his eyes and grimaced. "You were upset — you were huddled on the floor — you couldn't even stand up without help." Opening his eyes again, he found that hers were wide, and her lips parted. "What I did was practically assault. I —"

"I meant about me." She held his gaze. "I meant about calling you in the middle of the night and making you come out here, and then . . ." She swallowed and he watched the muscles around her throat expand and contract. "You came here to help and I caught you off guard when I did something inappropriate — something you specifically said you didn't want to happen. I hadn't planned to — I had no plan at all. I'm embarrassed about being so needy and helpless. I ended up manipulating you into —"

"What?" He put his hands on her shoulders. "Pru, I will come to you for any reason, whenever you want me to." Her lips parted. "But when you pushed me off so fast — did I scare you or hurt you?"

"There are things about me you don't know. Even worse than what I've already said. I'm not sure I can tell you. I'm not sure if I'm ready for that." She wrapped her arms around his waist and rested her unflowered ear against his chest.

He rubbed her back. "We're missing the sunrise."

With their arms wrapped around one another's waists, they watched as the sky moved from dark to dusty blue, then pink, then yellow, until the whole morning was illuminated and bright.

CHAPTER TWENTY-NINE

Standing on the front porch, Pru held on to Shawn tightly one more time and pressed her mouth against his. He kissed her back, lips parted, and Pru inhaled the hazelnut roast she kept for when her friends visited.

Stepping away, he smiled. "I'd better go. I'll text you when I get to my parents' house, okay?"

"Okay." They touched fingers as he turned to leave. She did a quick body scan only to realize her heart was racing. That made her grip the top railing on the porch. "Shawn?" He stopped halfway across the yard and turned around. "Please don't change your mind back."

He took a few big steps back to the house and looked up at her as she leaned against the railing. "With love's light wings did I o'er-perch these walls, but parting is such sweet sorrow."

He came back up, wrapped one arm around her waist and the other around her shoulders, and sealed his mouth against hers. She might have forgotten how to breathe, but it didn't matter. He broke off the kiss and they touched foreheads. "I won't change my mind and I have no intention of ending up like those two characters." He grinned. "I'll talk to you soon. Promise."

As his car pulled away, shivers went through her, the way they might through a little kid when they see their birthday cake. Years had passed since she'd felt like that. From the corner of her eye, she saw Tommy's car in the carport. She took a couple of steps over and knocked on his door.

He answered in a pair of bike shorts and no shirt. "That was a sexy goodbye. I didn't know you could open your mouth that wide."

"Yeah you did. Remember that time Andrew made baklava cheesecake?"

Chuckling, Tommy stepped aside and gestured for her to come in. "I'm making breakfast. Did you finally get laid? I haven't seen you smile like that in ages."

She followed him into his kitchen and grabbed some juice glasses from his cabinet. Then she set out the pitcher and silverware and sat, watching him. When he moved, the almost life-sized violin and bow tattooed on his back moved with him as if music were playing. The black of its pegs and chin rest and the reddish-brown of the body rose and dipped along the faint lines of his muscles. His physique was always a startling contrast to his smooth, round cheeks.

He set two plates of eggs and toast on the table, grabbed some farmer's market marmalade from the fridge, and pulled on a T-shirt that he'd draped over a chair. He sat across from her. "Tell me everything."

An hour later, once dishes had been done and things put away, they headed to the living room which, like his kitchen was a mirror image of Pru's. However, she'd fixed hers up as cozily as she could with as few resources as possible. Tommy's place, meanwhile, was all Ikea stainless-steel and light-colored furniture, with a few framed photographs on hung shelves and some landscape prints on the wall behind his couch. His was a real one, rather than the secondhand futon she'd bought for herself.

Pushing back in the recliner, she asked, "Well, what do you think?"

Tommy grinned. "I think that you have a boyfriend, my dear. He's even quoting Shakespeare to you. *Mazel tov*." He stretched his legs along the length of the couch.

Pursing her lips, she took a few seconds to think about that. The space behind her brow and temples pulsed. "I'm not sure you're right."

"It was from *Romeo and Juliet*. Definitely Shakespeare." He winked.

Pru tossed a throw pillow in his direction but she couldn't help a small smile. "I mean about him being a boyfriend. I'm not sure what's going on."

"Decide what you want to be going on and then ask. I mean, he knows your stuff, right?"

"Not all of it." She bit her lip.

Tommy swung his legs over, stood, and looked down at her.

"I don't think I'm good enough for—"

Tommy held up his hand and she closed her mouth as he walked around and sat on the edge of the coffee table in front of her. Pru pulled the recliner upright. "You are *not* damaged goods," he said.

She frowned. "We didn't say anything about being a couple."

"You're overthinking it." Her friend folded his arms. "I know what I saw while I spied on you through the window, Pru. I doubt he'd see what you see when you look at yourself."

Her hand automatically rose and settled on her waist.

Tommy stood and held out his own hand.

She let him haul her up to stand and he rested his hand where hers had been. "Those are battle scars, not defects." They hugged for a few seconds and Tommy patted her back. "I've got summer administrative bullshit meetings today. We can discuss this more later. Talk to him."

Sitting in her straight-backed chair that afternoon, Pru shut her eyes as she went through her scales. The sky was already beginning to darken. It was going to storm all day. She allowed the notes to carry her elsewhere as the wind picked up and the first heavy drops splattered against her window.

When she finished the last of the minor scales, she stood to dig through her sheet music. There was the matter of some difficult pieces to practice for when LGSO reconvened, and she couldn't avoid them forever. She found the Prokofiev, set it on her stand, and glanced at her phone. She had five messages.

One from Tommy read, *I'll take any excuse to get the hell out of this meeting about filling in the new lesson plan paperwork. I've got my ringer on. Call with an emergency, I'm begging you.*

I'll rescue him when I'm finished practicing. She figured she'd give herself three passes through the hardest part. That would be enough to accomplish at least something before she got too frustrated. She willed away the memory of the disastrous attempt in front of the whole cello section last time.

Then she looked at Edie's message. *Tommy said you had a panic attack. Call me.*

Pru replied *I did have one, but I'm okay now. There's news, though. We'll talk later.*

She had to bounce what had happened last night off Edie. She hovered her finger over the phone icon then lowered it. Edie was going to be stressing over her big case. They could dissect her new relationship, if it was that, in a couple of days.

Uncle Barney had texted. *Just checking in. Love you, darling.*

She'd call him back in five minutes. How happy would it make him to know she'd met someone? A better question was how she'd gone from not knowing her relationship status to having a full-blown, committed love affair so quickly.

Then there was one from Cliff.

Come have dinner with me tonight. Let's work through what happened." That wasn't going to happen even if hell froze over. She highlighted his number and blocked it. Uncle Barney, from 300 miles away, had known that relationship was no good before she did. Everyone knew. She might be wise to

Cliff now, but that didn't mean she didn't suck when it came to seeing what she wanted to see.

Oh, my God. I've convinced myself that I'm in love with someone I know next to nothing about. I'm an idiot.

That was Cliff talking, though. What she needed was to stand on her own two feet for a while longer. She had to show Uncle Barney that she could take care of herself. She reached behind to scratch Mattie's chin. When Matilda got older, it would be Pru taking care of the dog rather than the other way around, like it was now. What was it like to love someone without needing them?

She scrolled down to her last message, from Shawn.

Just came back from the hardware store. Caught in the storm while driving. Can't stop thinking about you.

That one made her smile.

CHAPTER THIRTY

Shawn sat on his parents' porch swing and watched as the sky opened up. He wondered again why someone would choose to live somewhere like this. It wasn't as if the rain cut through the humidity by much. Mostly, it just made everything even wetter than it already was.

He went inside and, from the large front window, watched as trees, still held upright by wood supports, swayed in the wind, leaves tearing from their baby branches. The impatiens' and rhododendrons' stems bent, dropping petals. Shaking his head, he walked toward the flooring planks piled in a corner.

He was about to lay one down when his phone buzzed. The only reason he checked was because someone was supposed to be delivering cabinet doors for the master bath at some point today—or it could be Pru. When he saw who the text was actually from, he groaned.

Hiya it read.

Hey Helena.

He waited a few seconds as three dots on the screen wavered.

You haven't been returning my calls or replying to messages. Is everything okay?

He closed his eyes. Everything was so far from okay right now.

Busy morning, noon, and night he texted back.

Look, can we call instead of text? she wrote.

Sure.

Shawn waited for more than a minute, and then his phone

buzzed again, a call this time. He picked up.

"Hi, how's it going?" He kept his voice neutral.

"Fine. I finally got the official promotion. You're talking to the youngest supervisory manager of human resources that Jupitelligence Software has ever had." Helena sounded triumphant.

"That's great. That's what you wanted."

"It's what I deserve."

He began to sort through different lengths of planks. "Well, at any rate, good job. Thanks for telling me. I've got to—"

"That isn't the reason I called." Helena's tone was softer now. "I've thought about things a lot while we've been apart, and I've decided we should stay together."

His shoulders stiffened, and he tried not to sound irritated. "Helena, I was the one who wanted to get away. You wanted me to stay. Your choice was already clear. I'm the one who needs space."

"I've made my decision."

"It isn't yours alone to make. I'm not an employee." He heard her take a breath to speak so he hurried along, raising his voice. "I don't want you pushing me, I don't want you contacting me, and I don't want to do this anymore. When I said I needed to get away, I meant it." For a moment, Shawn wondered whether he'd have had the balls to say this to her face. As it was, he knew that shuddery breath before her tears fell. He wondered if she had to work them up just so he'd hear them.

"Shawn, you belong to me."

His head began to heat. "Well, *gosh*, if you put it *that* way." He didn't bother hiding the disdain in his tone. "Do you even hear yourself? Have I made a fucking decision at all in this relationship yet?" He began to pace.

"Shawn, how can you say that?" She sounded like she was crying for real. Somehow, it wasn't as potent to him over the phone as it was in person. "I've been everything to you, and now you're hurting me. It's not fair. I want you to come back up here."

Shawn put the phone on speaker to start laying the floorboards in place. "What about what I want?"

She took a breath. "You're just confused."

"I am not confused."

"I'll have my secretary work out some dates with your folks and send you plane tickets. We'll talk." Without another word, she hung up.

She was probably right about one thing. They were going to have to have this out in person. He'd have to face her at some point.

He started hammering so hard that he didn't hear the UPS truck come and go.

An hour later, as the rain began to stop, he checked outside. The large cardboard box sitting there was soaking wet and falling apart. After ripping it open, he brought pieces of cabinet in one by one.

He needed to call Pru. He also needed to step away from both women in reality, one because she was pissing him off and the other because he was having too hard of a time staying away. What the hell had he done last night, and what had he been thinking this morning?

CHAPTER THIRTY-ONE

Pru parked her car in the employee lot around the back of the hotel and popped her trunk open. The closest spot was still far from the service doors, and the wet blacktop shimmered against a sky so vividly blue it almost hurt her eyes.

After waiting for the last vestiges of cold air in the car to dissipate she got out, tugging her black dress back down. The skirt was just wide enough to accommodate her cello, but it was fitted through the bodice and kept hitching up every time she sat for too long. Pru sighed. Had this party been for someone other than Joe, she might not have accepted the gig.

She steadied herself on her low black heels and took a deep breath. If she didn't know any better, she could have sworn the pavement was melting and sticking to her soles.

Her hard, bright silver, humidity-proof cello case was a lot bulkier than her regular one. She'd splurged on it after her instrument had warped in the summer heat a few years ago, nearly ruining it. The expensive Eastman Master instrument had been a gift from her grandmother when Pru had made it into the National Youth Symphony at fifteen. Esther had died that very year. When it warped, it had cost a small fortune to repair. The cello would have been less expensive to replace with an identical one, but she just couldn't bear the thought.

She leaned in until she was on tiptoes to grab the case, then pulled it toward the edge of the hatchback with a series of short, hard tugs. When it wouldn't budge far enough, she hoisted herself halfway into the car, letting her feet dangle, and inched herself forward to get a better hold. With a grunt, she wrapped her arms around the middle and jerked her weight back. It moved about two inches. She felt the front of her skirt bunch up, her body now wedged beneath the car's ceiling, her nose pressed against the hard polycarbonate. Her hair, which Andrew had helped arrange into an intricate, elegantly braided bun before she left, brushed the fabric lining.

Well, this is typical, isn't it?

She heard footsteps hurrying from behind her and scrunched her eyes shut. With luck, whoever it was wouldn't notice the spectacle.

"Want some help with that?" Shawn's voice, right behind her.

She managed a muffled, "Yef, pleef."

"Coming behind you." His hands were on her calves. He wrapped his fingers around them and gave a firm tug. She slid a few more inches and felt the back of her dress hike up more. Sweat pooled in the backs of her knees, trapped beneath her stockings.

"The case still won't budge," she gasped.

"But you are a little. Let's take care of you first." He tugged again. She slid farther, but her feet still hung a few inches from the ground. A shoe dangled from her toes and fell. She thought she heard fabric rip as it caught on the case's latch.

Pru stared out the window and watched the faint steam from her breath disappear along with her dignity.

Chapter Thirty-Two

Shawn was having a hard time not staring at the lines of Pru's calves and mid-thighs. Her black stockings had seams running down the center, accentuating them.

Stepping forward again, he assured himself he could help her without being creepy. "Do you think you can widen your legs? I'm gonna try pulling you out by the waist if that's okay."

She tensed, then jerked her legs apart, and the back of her dress hitched to right below her hips. He exhaled slowly. "All right, here I come." Stepping between her thighs, he was soon touching the bumper. He shouldn't have looked down. Now he saw the scalloped edges of her stockings, which had gold and teal embellishments woven through them.

Christ.

"This is going to get a little familiar." He leaned in until he was practically lying over her. Then he dug his fingers around and under Pru's waist. She started and her leg jerked up.

He hopped backward to avoid getting kicked in the nuts. "Did I startle you anyway?"

"I didn't mean to do that." She sounded embarrassed. "It's okay. Go ahead and try again."

Shawn situated himself between her thighs once more and wrapped his hands around her waist. This time he tried willing his half hard-on to disappear before pulling. He could see from here that her panties were plain white cotton, and damn if that wasn't a hundred times sexier than that expensive stuff Helena wore. With the front of her dress bunched beneath her, the back of her dress hugged her body almost as closely as that wet dress had when they got caught in the rain. He was going to have to pull her closer to his groin to help her out of the car.

Fuck.

"Gimme a sec." He tried to take a few cooling breaths, but instead of going from half-mast to lowered, he got completely hard. As he pulled her out, he backed away.

On the ground, she stumbled in her one shoe and turned, while he held on to keep her from falling. Her dress was torn almost all the way up the front of her leg. Mascara smeared beneath her eyes, making them appear deeper and darker. Small trails of makeup streaked past her temples and onto her cheeks, and half her hair had escaped from where it had been pinned. He took a half step toward her, ready to smooth it back somehow, but stopped when she began to tug her dress into place. The neckline wasn't especially revealing, but he watched as a trail of sweat rolled down her chest and past her cleavage. He turned to the side, untucked his shirt, and faced her again.

Pru put on the other shoe and glanced at him. "What?" She put her hand to her face, looked at her palm, and grimaced. "Oh."

"Don't think I'm stupid, but you look beautiful—more so than usual." Shawn drew closer. More makeup-laced perspiration threatened to drip into her eyes and down her nose.

Pru laughed. "I don't think you're stupid, but you probably need to get your eyes examined." She put her clean hand on his face, and her fingers swept his cheekbone. "You shaved."

Tingling heat spread beneath her hand, past his skin and into his chest. Her wet, melty complexion had turned pink. Shawn lifted her hand away and kissed the inside of her wrist. "Let's get inside. How'd you even get that into your car? It's almost as big as you." He stepped around and lifted the case out of the car.

"It usually isn't a problem. It just got wedged in this time." She reached up and closed the hatchback. "Thank you," she said with a smile. "You saved the day yet again."

Shawn shrugged. "I aim to please."

"I'm probably the biggest disaster of a human being you've ever met." Pru turned even pinker.

"You've never seen me drunk." After looking around for a second, he leaned in and kissed her. His touch was meant as a light peck, but she softened against him and put her arms around his waist.

And back up to half-mast I go.

He smiled as she pulled back and wiped the lipstick off his mouth with her fingers.

When they reached the building, he held the door open and the air conditioning blasted over them. He was suddenly aware that his shirt was soaked. The employee entrance was empty. They leaned on the white, blank wall next to the glass double doors. A few yards ahead, the small foyer split into a four-way intersection. Voices and the sounds of movement came from straight ahead. He glanced at the goosebumps on her arms, which were hanging limply. Her chin quivered, and her mouth twitched.

"Are you all right?"

She barely got the word "yes" out as she burst out laughing. He stared at her. Her belly shook, and she wrapped her arms around her waist as she folded forward. Tears mixed with the streams of sweat, foundation, and mascara down her cheeks. Eventually her breath slowed. Still flushed and smiling, she leaned back on the wall and turned her head to him. "Sorry. It was either that or crying."

Shawn grinned back at her. Her bare shoulders were especially smooth and pale against the black fabric. He kissed her temple. "Are you usually this much fun?"

Her smile faded. "Why?"

"Just so I can be prepared for next time." The words came out drier than he'd intended.

Pru wiped either residual tears or sweat from her eyes with the heel of her hand, then said something he couldn't quite make out. He leaned in closer. "Say again?" The back of his hand brushed hers.

Up close, he could see where some of her lipstick had bled and smeared above her upper lip and into the corners of her mouth. For a second, he thought about using his fingers to wipe it away. Then a vision of licking it away flashed. He was in so much trouble.

"I said, I'm usually pretty boring, but I'm glad there will be a next time." She shifted, and they loosely held hands. "I only look unusually terrible when you're around."

"You look perfect from where I'm standing. And I can't imagine you ever being boring." Deep in his brain, a miniature of himself waved his arms in the air, gesturing for him to back away. A kaleidoscope of butterflies flitted in his stomach. On his shoulder, a twin miniature scolded that he was behaving like a teenager.

He put a hand on her shoulder and started to lower his face to hers.

"What on earth happened to you?" A female voice registered shock and exasperation. Shawn jerked away. A tall, slender, brown-skinned woman in a dark pink cocktail dress stood a few feet away with her arms folded, frowning.

Pru turned to the woman. "Long story short, I had a lot of trouble with my cello case. Edie, this is Shawn. Shawn, this is my friend Edie."

He walked around and shook her hand. Edie looked from him to Pru a couple of times and tsk'd. "Follow me. Do you know where the men's locker room is?"

"Yeah." He rubbed the back of his neck. "I need a shower before I change into my suit."

Edie turned to Pru. "I'll take care of the hot mess that is yourself." She poked her finger beneath a rip in the side seam of the dress's bodice. "You're gonna need stitches."

"You're not a doctor." Pru grinned.

Her friend laughed. "But I can play one with the right person." She looked from Shawn to Pru again. Shawn looked away.

When they dropped him off in front of the men's changing room, Shawn listened to the clicks of the women's high heels. He thought he heard Edie say, "You've been keeping this from me. Tell me about your knight in sweaty armor."

CHAPTER THIRTY-THREE

Pru stood as still as she could in front of a three-way, full-length mirror in the ladies' lounge. Behind her, Edie perched at the edge of the lavender-colored round couch in the middle of the plush, beige carpet. "Hold your breath," she told Pru.

She sucked in her stomach and suspended her breath for Edie to finish stitching the side seam of her bodice.

"All right." Edie allowed Pru to exhale.

Edie had stitched the tear too tightly, though. The waist conformed even more firmly to Pru's body, and her breasts threatened to pop out. Now the garment looked more like the top of a corset than a dress. She stood straighter.

"All right. You look and smell better from the neck down. Now, keep your head still so I can do something about your makeup and hair." Edie draped a couple of hand towels around Pru's neck and shoulders then began to undo her braid. "He's hot," she said as she handed Pru wipe after wipe to clean herself off. "I forbid you to screw this one up." She began to twist Pru's hair into an updo.

"I'm not dating him. We just sort of bumped into each other a couple of times." It wasn't hard to talk, but it was a bit of an effort to take a deep enough breath to form more than a few words at a time.

"You are terrible at lying. Look up."

Pru tilted her chin for Edie to apply fresh makeup. "That must have been some couple of bumps, the way you were staring at his biceps and the way he was staring at your mouth. Don't tell me BOB has competition for your affections."

Pru wheezed over a laugh and rolled her eyes. "Okay, fine. I don't know if we're dating, but we're sort of circling around it."

"I've got a good feeling about this one. Make the circle smaller." Edie smiled. "Look at you." She put her hands on her hips. "I did a damn good job given what I had to work with." They'd used what they could scrounge from a few women's makeup cases and decided to simplify her hair into a twist. "You're lucky you've got my fairy godmother services on retainer."

Forty minutes later, she sat in the semicircle of musicians and the last vestiges of tension released. She and the others looked at one another, the violinist nodded, and they launched into the Dvořák. The cello solo was technically complex, but this was one of her favorites, and not nearly as difficult as the Prokofiev. Her limbs were more fluid, and the hum of the crowded ballroom faded as the music flowed through her. There were only notes and harmony. The swirl of suits and dresses in the room was a soft, peripheral blur for the next hour.

After applause and bows, Pru straightened and waved, smiling as Edie came over. In the chandeliers' lighting, her friend's skin practically glowed against the low-cut pink satin. Pru took a few tottering steps, the best she could do given the high heels and tight dress.

Edie took her by the elbow and led her to the open bar as recorded music piped through the speakers. "Let's go say hi to Joe."

The man in question was holding court with a couple of people whose backs were to them. A brunette woman in four-inch stilettos had slid her hand underneath one man's dark blue jacket and looked like she was trying to figure out a way to squirm the rest of herself in there too. The man took a step away, but she followed. Pru squinted. He looked familiar from behind, but Joe waved and distracted her. "Hey, birthday boy," Pru said.

"My two favorite ladies." Joe's brown eyes were already glassy. He put down his drink and pulled Pru in with one arm and Edie with the other. "You sounded incredible. You were the best one," he told Pru and gave her a wet kiss on the cheek.

She laughed and wiped it away. "I heard you were promoted to full professor. Congratulations." She wriggled out of his grip and turned to look at the people in front of her. She almost didn't recognize the man in the midnight-blue suit and neatly combed, medium brown hair. Shawn's posture was straight and relaxed, and his eyes softened when he smiled at her.

Pru thought about the lines of his biceps and thighs when he did yoga with her, and the wall of solid muscle from his chest and abdomen to his shoulders and back. She'd felt but never seen his torso up close and personal—at least not completely—but knowing they lay beneath the polished exterior of his crisp white shirt and perfectly fitted jacket and slacks made her want to grab him by that matching blue tie and drag him somewhere private.

"Edie, this is my old buddy, Shawn Levinson." Joe handed each woman a glass of champagne from the bar. "Pru, this is Shawn in nicer clothes and without that scraggly animal clinging to his face." He winked at her.

Extending his hand, Shawn took a step toward Edie. "Nice to meet you."

Edie shook it. "Hello again." Pru watched as Edie examined him.

As Shawn took another step toward Pru, the brunette woman grabbed his arm and stepped with him. He tugged his arm away from her.

Shawn's apparent companion approached him yet again. Edie stepped around Pru and tugged at the woman's sleeve hard enough for the stranger to stumble back a few steps. The brunette frowned at Edie.

In what Pru considered a fine display of acting, Edie said, "I can't get over those shoes. Who makes those?"

Shawn stood closer to Joe and Pru. "Please make her go away," he muttered under his breath to Joe. "She's like a human barnacle." He put his hand on Pru's shoulder.

Joe laughed. "Go dance with Pru." Shawn raised his eyebrows at her and offered his hand.

"I think we're even. You just came to my rescue this time," Shawn said as they approached the dance floor. "I met that lady about twenty minutes ago." Pru smiled. "And you guys sounded great." They faced each other, and he put his hand on her back, holding hers near his shoulder. "Even to my ignorant and untrained ears."

They didn't say much as they began to move together, but when she looked up at him, he was completely focused on her, as if they were the only two people in the room. She also hadn't noticed the graceful ease in his movements until now. "You told me you were a terrible dancer, but it's the opposite."

He squeezed her hand. "Thanks. I've suffered through events like this for my dad's work since I was in my teens, but I think you're defining *dance* generously. And you're pretty good, yourself," he added with a smile.

She laughed. "I just can't move very much because of the way Edie fixed my dress. There's less room to be a spaz." As they moved, he became quiet. "What are you thinking about?"

His ears turned pink. "Please don't slap me if I tell you the truth."

She stood still. "Okay."

He sucked his lips behind his teeth and released them. "I'm trying not to stare at the tops of your breasts."

Her own face and neck warmed, but she chuckled. He looked like he was leaning in to say something but took too big of a step. The tight fabric of her dress resisted, and she gasped and tripped over his foot. Shawn stepped in to catch her, but another pair of hands yanked her back.

"There you are." Cliff stood behind her and clamped his hand over her shoulder. "Joey didn't invite me to play. I was disappointed not to be part of the performance."

Pru's throat tightened. She tried to hold her breath to avoid the heavy smell of whatever musky cologne he'd doused himself with.

"Dance with me, Pru. C'mon." He grabbed her hand and started to walk away.

Shawn followed them and frowned as Pru wriggled her hand from Cliff's grip.

"I don't believe you were invited," Cliff warned Shawn.

"I don't believe you were, Cliff," Pru muttered.

"One dance, Pru. Stop making me the mustache-twirling villain when I'm the one who's rescuing you." He got hold of her hand again and held it more tightly.

"I don't need rescuing at all," Pru said. "And we talked about not coming near me or my friends." She pulled away from him, but he stepped closer to her.

Shawn frowned. "You heard her."

Heart pounding and face heating, Pru frowned back. "You stay out of this." Her hands began to sweat enough for her to wrest her hand from Cliff's grip. "And you go away."

She looked from one man to the other and imagined the squabbles between preteen boys over any attractive cheerleader in middle school. No one ever won the damned fights—nor the girl, usually. Pru sucked in her cheeks and willed herself not to lose her temper and storm off. If she left

Shawn and Cliff to their own devices, things were likely to get uglier fast. Besides, she couldn't walk that fast in these shoes, anyway.

Chapter Thirty-Four

Shawn took in Pru's red-faced scowl and Cliff's condescending, punchable smile. He straightened. "Pru, do you want to dance with Cliff?"

"No." Her voice was strained.

Cliff leaned his head next to Pru's and kissed her ear. She grimaced. "You're adorable when you're frustrated," he cooed.

Shawn curled his hands into loose fists and forced his arms to remain at his sides.

"Haven't you missed dancing together? You'll like it once you remember," Cliff continued. Shawn even wanted to beat up Cliff's voice right now.

"Cliff." Joe came up alongside him and clapped him on the back. Shawn could tell he was exaggerating the friendly, tipsy demeanor. "Been looking everywhere for you. Come meet someone."

Cliff let Joe lead him off toward where Edie was watching with her arms folded. Joe looked over his shoulder and mouthed, *You owe me."

Shawn put his hand on Pru's shoulder. "You're shaking. Do you want to get out of here?" He glanced over at where she and the other musicians had been. Someone had already taken away the setup, which meant her cello was waiting in the back room, all packed up.

The angry color faded from her face and neck until she went pale. "If you don't mind."

As they made their way down the corridor, Edie caught up

with them. "He is the biggest tool in the shed, and I work with lawyers all day long. Pru, I don't want you going home alone in case he follows you back." She looked at Shawn. "Can you stay with her for a while? I caught a ride in with another friend. I can take Pru's car back."

Tugging at his sleeves, Shawn said, "I uh, hadn't thought that far ahead. Joe brought me here." He warmed. "Sorry. I didn't realize—"

"I'll drive," Pru interrupted. Her voice squeaked.

"Okay," Edie said. "I'll go get your stuff." Before either of them could reply, Edie hurried down the hallway and disappeared around the corner. Shawn wasn't sure what to say or ask as they waited for her. Pru's breathing was fast and shallow.

"Can you take a big, slow breath for me? Pretend you're filling up your belly like a balloon." She stared at him. "Like this. Put one hand over your chest and the other on your belly." Her torso and legs shook as she tried. "Breathe in and fill up your chest. You see how it lifts up when it's full?" She nodded, but it looked like the seams of her dress were straining against the effort. "Only do as much as you comfortably can. Don't force anything." He waited. "Now exhale in the opposite direction. Let the air go from your chest and draw in your belly. Good. Do it again." Some of her color had returned after the fourth or fifth round, but she was still trembling as Edie came in again with Pru's purse and cello.

"Here you go," she told Pru, but she rolled the cello case toward Shawn, casting him a glance. "Maybe you should drive." Pru nodded, and Edie handed Shawn the keys.

Shawn rolled the cello case and Pru trailed behind him. Dark now, the air was still thick, if a tiny bit cooler. "I'm thinking maybe we can go to my place," he said when they got in the car. He adjusted the seat and mirrors. "And when you're more settled, you can either go home yourself or we can figure out what to do. Or we can go for a drink first, if you want."

Pru took a sip from the warm water bottle she'd left in the console. "Your place if that's all right. I don't think I can handle a crowded bar." She stared out the window as he drove. In his periphery, she seemed to be shaking again — or still.

He stole glances of her profile at every traffic stop. There was a kind of silvery light to her — like the moon. She'd leaned her head back on the seat and shut her eyes. Her hands were clasped so tightly in her lap that her skin was white. The tiny bones that extended to the base of her fingers were clearly delineated, and a couple of small, blue veins pulsed against her skin. Pru's face was also tense. Tiny lines extended from her eyes and her small mouth. From this angle, it was hard to tell if there were tears as well.

Shawn sighed as he pulled into a parking space in front of his apartment building. It was a square, squat, ugly thing with a mildewy pool in the back, whose concrete porch featured rickety plastic lounge chairs and weeds that poked through the cracks in the cement. The brown paint on all of the apartment doors was peeling.

She got out of the car. "I'm on the third floor," he said. "Do you mind walking? The elevator usually smells like bleach and death."

Shawn offered his arm and noticed a hint of a smile in return. "Lead the way," she said as she accepted it.

CHAPTER THIRTY-FIVE

"It's not much." Shawn sounded embarrassed as Pru looked around the living room. The industrial low-pile carpet looked as though it might once have been brown but had faded to uneven gray patches. A scratchy-looking plaid couch that looked like a reject from a Brady Bunch set sat near a matching chair. A small flat-screen TV hung against the dull white wall. "The furniture came with the place, except for the TV and the bed." He glanced toward a door ahead of them. "The bed's really an air mattress. I had them haul the original bed away because it was every manner of gross." He gestured to the couch. "Have a seat. Can I get you that drink? All I've got is beer."

Pru sat on the couch and leaned back. "Please." When he returned with an open bottle, she pushed the label on the glass with her thumbnail. "I probably should explain what happened tonight." Tears burned at the corners of her eyes. She tried to blink them back.

"You don't have to if you don't want to." Shawn sat a few inches away from her. "I am curious though."

"Thanks." She squirmed to find a comfortable angle.

Shawn watched her. "I can probably find you something to change into if you want to hang out for a while." Pru raised her eyebrows. "It's the least I can do after the complimentary wardrobe change at your place. I was thinking about ducking into the bathroom and changing too."

She briefly imagined hugging one of his shirts around herself, inhaling his scent. "It's getting late. I don't want to keep you from sleep."

"As long as you feel like staying here, I'm happy to have you. *Mi casa es tu casa.*"

Chin shaking, she bowed her head. "I'd like to stay," she whispered to her lap.

"Follow me." He cleared his throat. "For the record, sleep keeps me from you." Pru was glad she was behind him so he wouldn't see her trip in response.

Shawn's bedroom was a tiny space, cramped with a full-sized mattress on the floor, pillows askew over a rumpled blue blanket. An ugly warped brown dresser and a pile of laundry in the corner completed the space. He dug around in the middle drawer and produced a white *I Love New York* T-shirt and a pair of black drawstring gym shorts. He held them out to her.

"Thank you." Pru's mouth was dry.

Their fingertips brushed as she took them. They both froze for a second. He stepped closer and stared at her. After a few seconds, Shawn lifted her hand and kissed it. "I'll see you in a few minutes," he said in a soft voice.

Pru's heart beat all the way down to her stomach as she tossed the clothes on the mattress and closed the rest of the space between them. He pulled her in by the waist. His breath shook and his heartbeat was fast. She reached up and combed her fingers through his hair. He shivered. His cock was hard against her. She couldn't resist pressing even closer.

He put his hand behind her head and kissed her. She melted into him. She and Edie sometimes liked to make fun of all those romance novel clichés, but literally, she almost felt as though her insides had turned to mush and she was on the verge of going boneless. He pushed his tongue past her teeth, feeling around the insides of her cheeks. She pushed her hips more firmly against his. He pushed back, groaned, and slid his tongue in and out of her mouth slowly as they rocked against each other. She thought about reaching her fingers beneath his waistband.

He would see how damaged she was. "Shawn."

His fingers splayed across her lower back and traveled down until he was cupping her ass. She mashed her mouth against his and set her teeth on his lower lip.

She should at least warn him.

He groaned again, then pulled away. He was breathless, and his dark eyes shone. "I'd better, uh . . . I'll be in the living room." Grabbing a shirt and shorts for himself, he hurried out.

When he left, Pru reached around to unzip her dress. The teeth fought her fumbling fingers, gnashing the thread as she tugged hard until the fabric ripped down her back. She slid out of her ruined clothes and flinched as her fingers brushed along her waist. Her stomach knotted.

She pulled on her borrowed outfit and stared at the shut door. She could stay here and pretend she'd fallen asleep. On this side of the door was safety and a lost opportunity. On the other side was what might have looked like a run-down living room, but it could just as well have been outer space. Putting her fingers on the handle, she took a deep breath in case the air was sucked out of her.

CHAPTER THIRTY-SIX

*S*hit.

Shawn tilted his head back to get the last swallow of his beer then walked into the kitchen to grab another one. This had to stop. For two days, his whole life had revolved around Pru and the seemingly endless, aching hard-on since that night at her house. The whole idea of being in Georgia was for this *not* to happen. Why did he keep having to remind himself of this?

He opened the bottle, set it on the counter, and rubbed the back of his neck. When he heard the door open, he looked up. Pru had let her hair down, and it fell past her lower back. He could see a hint of dark lace from her bra through his white T-shirt. The shirt came down past her hips. His shorts were baggy, hitting just below her knees.

He did his best to take a cooling breath. Pru was here in his home, his clothes were hanging off her, and both his heart and his cock were dying to relieve her of them. "Feel like a movie or something?"

Pru grinned. "Are we doing Netflix and chill now?"

He lowered his gaze to his hands. "I just figured it was a way to pass the time."

"Oh." She blinked. "Okay." Her voice got quiet. "If you would rather I go . . . I just thought . . . ." That last word was almost a whisper.

Shawn patted the couch. "Please." Her disappointed expression was like a left hook. He wasn't sure whether it was selfish of him to want to keep her here. A movie and a beer were all he could think to offer. They gave him something else to look at and something to occupy his hands. "I want you to stay."

She lifted her eyebrows and smiled. "Do you like *Doctor Who*?"

Shawn dug between the couch cushions to find the remote and then took a seat in the corner. "What's that?"

Pru's jaw dropped but her face lit up. "Oh Grasshopper, you have much to learn." She sat cross-legged next to him and took the remote from him, scrolling until she found BBC America. "We can't go any further in this relationship until you understand and enjoy riding along in the TARDIS." She scrolled through the programs. "Please tell me you at least like Terry Pratchett."

Shawn watched her profile and smiled. Her shoulders and temples were relaxed. "Yes. Terry Pratchett is awesome." His throat had gone dry and his voice broke. Hitting the start button, she leaned against him. Without thinking about it, he put his arm around her shoulders and pulled her closer.

About two hours later, when he switched off the end credits, neither of them moved. "Well?" she asked.

"I'm kind of nonplussed. That was great, but I'm not sure about the production values—y'know, the rubber masks and fake settings." He kissed the top of her head. "I did like the scarf and hat."

Pru reached forward and took a few swallows of her beer.

Shawn couldn't tear his gaze from her neck as she swallowed. He slid his hand around her waist. Her hand rested on his thigh, just at the hem of his shorts. He half hoped she'd move it higher up. She shivered.

"You okay?"

"I am." She nuzzled his arm. "I like this—just sitting with you, doing normal stuff. It's such a change for me from when . . . ." Staring at some indeterminate point in the room, she closed her mouth and took her hand off him. "There are things I should probably tell you."

Doing his best to keep his gaze steady, Shawn ignored the way his throat clenched around his own secret.

"Cliff and I were together for about two years. Even though it's been a year since we broke up, he thinks he owns me. You saw that much."

Shawn shifted so that they could face each other better. That also gave him a better view of her inner thighs. When he was a kid, he'd sometimes helped his father replicate a family recipe for buttercream. Pru's skin, especially right there, made him remember the smoothness of the cream and the hint of salt that lingered on his tongue after he scooped some from the edge of the bowl with his finger. He licked his lips and refocused just as Pru met his gaze, her gray eyes darkening.

"We didn't go out much. He used to like to hang out with his friends at sports bars or at their houses. Then I found out his friends all brought their significant others to their get-to-gethers. Once, when he was fixing to leave, I asked if I could go with him." She shut her eyes and made and released fists. "He said . . ." She shuddered. "He said I wasn't exactly arm candy. Later on in the relationship, he used to joke that I was still in training to be presentable."

Shawn couldn't keep his mouth from hanging open. "I beg your pardon?"

She bit and released her bottom lip. "He can be mean as all get-out, but he was right—I'm not exactly sexy. I'm not look-ing for a compliment or anything like that, it's just true. I'm short and spazzy. I'm too pale, and my hair just sort of hangs there like spaghetti." She took another few sips of her drink.

"He was wrong." Shawn tried to keep his voice even, when really he wanted to shout at Cliff. "He was absolutely wrong. I haven't been able to stop thinking about you since we met, and we both looked like drowned rats that day." He held his hand out to her. She rested hers on top of it. With his heart pounding into his head, they traced one another's palms with their index fingers.

Pru's hand stopped moving, and she wrapped two fingers over his index finger. "You haven't seen how grotesque I am."

He shook his head. "You and that word don't belong together."

"They do," she protested, shutting her eyes. "Only Tommy and Edie know about what happened. Cliff and I were sitting by a fire pit. He never gets a *little* angry. He's either sweet as pie or madder than a wet hen."

Those phrases, combined with her Southern accent, made his chest warm even as he braced himself for what couldn't be a good memory for Pru to relate.

"We had an argument," she said. "I got up to leave, and he shoved me so hard I fell sideways and landed on the grating. I think he might've waited a few seconds before he pulled me out and called nine-one-one, but I can't be sure. When he finally took me home, he told me that now I was branded as his. He called my burn scars our disgusting little secret."

Shawn was going to have to force himself not to beat the crap out of that man next time they met. He'd never considered himself a violent or angry person before. "Is that what you think?"

"I'm not a commodity, but it doesn't feel great to be told over and over that I'm a freak. There are some parts of me that are ugly and broken. I'm pretty good at messing things up within moments of meeting people."

Shawn lightly ran his palm over her waist and around her back. "Not with me. Not on day one, and not now." Pru's lips parted. "Even the parts you think are damaged, even the parts of you that still hurt—are perfect and beautiful. I've never thought of you as defective. There can't be anything about you that I don't love." He suppressed a gasp.

Did I really just say what I heard myself say?

185

Her lashes were wet. "I'm terrified, Shawn."

You and me both.

"Can I kiss you again?"

Pru shook some more, but her expression softened. She grabbed his forearms and he leaned in. They crushed their mouths together.

What have I just done?

He moved his mouth to her jaw, her shoulder, her neck, and she dropped her head back. When she hooked her legs around his waist, his resolve crumbled. Like watching a movie of himself—he couldn't stop, his brain just along for the ride.

Shawn lowered her to the rough cushions. She pressed her fingers into his back as he kissed her again. Their mouths opened wider and wider until he imagined them as Charybdis twins, spiraling downward into each other, each of them drowning. She pressed against him and widened her thighs against his groin then reached between his legs.

He settled on top of her, and she hooked a leg around him. He pushed his hips against hers. She slid her tongue into his mouth and dipped her fingers past his lower back and under his waistband.

Shawn brushed his fingers along the side of her breast, then slid his hand beneath her shirt. That was when he felt it—the bumpy, hard texture of her skin. She shoved him back and scrambled to sit, looking pale.

Shawn sat back, his erection pushing up and against his clothes. "Can I see? Please?"

She held her breath as he raised the hem of her shirt and lifted it over her head. The tops of her breasts were gorgeous against her navy bra. He almost forgot what he was doing, but her posture was rigid. He ran his fingers along a network of scarring just above her waist and around to her mid-back, almost to her armpit. He pulled her close again. "You're beautiful."

With that word, she relaxed in his arms. "I trust you."

Reaching around, he kissed the nape of her neck. She shivered, so he did it again. This time she whimpered. "I've been dying to do that." He kept his voice to a low whisper. She dropped her head forward. He made a mental note—she really liked that spot. He did it again, a little harder.

Her breath stuttered.

The next time he tried it with the tip of his tongue. She made a small moaning sound as she arched her back, squeezed her eyes shut and grabbed at the couch cushion. He slid a hand up her shorts leg and worked his fingers past her panties. She wasn't just wet, she was soaked and completely smooth.

Her hips moved faster and faster as he moved his finger in and around her. Not that he had a ton of experience, but he was sure he'd never turned anyone on like this. It had never occurred to him that there was a powerful sensory feedback loop to sex. He wasn't even undressed, but he couldn't imagine being more turned on.

Pulling his finger out, he pressed his clothed cock between her thighs and looked down at her. "Are you sure you're okay with this?"

"Yes." That was the most beautiful sound he'd ever heard. Her breath was jagged as she pushed her fingernails into his ass and ground against him. "I love you, Shawn."

This was so different than with Helena, who used a lot of lube and had a choreography that they never veered from by much. They even spoke nearly scripted words of endearment, using that same word. He'd never be able to say that to Helena again.

Oh, no.

"Pru, wait." Everything hurt as Shawn pulled away and sat on his heels—not just the obvious impending blue balls, but also his heart and head constricted. She sat as well. "I'm so sorry. You have no idea. The more time I spend with you, the more I need. It isn't just because I can hardly look at you without wanting to touch you. It's just being with you."

The corners of Pru's eyes crinkled as she sucked in her bottom lip and smiled. He wanted to cry. "I feel the same, Shawn. I didn't even know I could." She caught his eyes. Hers were clear, and he dreaded the coming storm. "Why are you sorry?"

"Pru, we can't do this, as much as I want to. My home is in New York. I'm not staying down here."

She inched back.

"I wish things were different—"

"They can be." Her hands began to tremble. "You can work here, can't you? You can go back to graduate school. You can even stay with me and you won't have to pay rent—at least not for a while." Her cadence sped. "Or I can audition for another orchestra, or just teach music, and be with you. I won't mind teaching. I think I can get used to it. I might have to go down to Florida a lot to visit my uncle, but if we love each other, as long as we can be together—"

He pushed his tongue into his cheek and she quieted. She was mapping out an entire future based on what, a handful of weeks? He couldn't have meant what he'd said before.

Pru reached for him but Shawn shivered and scooted back. He fought the urge to retreat to the other room by himself, the way he often did when Helena started talking about future careers, plans, and his place by her side. His hand was dead weight when he lifted it to block her. "I also technically have a girlfriend up there, and we—"

As the color drained from her face, Pru seemed to stop breathing for a few seconds. She nearly fell against the coffee table as she stood. "You just *now* remembered her?" Her voice sounded as though it was scraping against broken glass. Grabbing the T-shirt, she wrestled herself into it inside-out and backward. Even though she was trembling, she scowled and balled her fists. She gaped at him for a few seconds, grabbed her keys from the coffee table, and without bothering with shoes, went to the door. "Why would you say all those things to me?" She put her hand on the knob.

Shawn willed himself to get up, but his body remained cemented in place. Everything he wanted to say wouldn't budge between his brain and his mouth. A fat tear plopped onto his thigh and his chest heaved. "Don't go. Please, Pru. I'm so sorry."

"I gutted myself right in front of you twice, and you let me do it each time." Her voice broke. She turned her back, walked through the door, and pulled it shut behind her.

Shawn buried his face in his hands.

Fucking Helena.

Gorgeous, wealthy Helena, who his family was sure was the answer to their good-for-nothing son's problems. That meant she was the answer to their problems. His future was a narrow, empty tunnel toward that woman. He couldn't imagine himself walking through it. Pru hadn't been showing him a carefully constructed outline of a life together where he had a role to fulfill. No, she wasn't asking him to get a better job or put a ring on her finger. She'd just suggested he follow his original dream. All she wanted was for them to be together—and he wanted that as well. The amount of time they'd known each other didn't matter.

I'm in love with Prudence Blum, and my head's been too far up my ass to admit it.

He stood and rushed out the door. Looking over the railing, he saw Pru in her car. The interior lights were on and she was wiping her eyes.

Barefoot and half-naked, he called out to her as he rushed down the three flights of filthy concrete stairs. By the time he got to ground level, her taillights were disappearing out of the parking lot.

CHAPTER THIRTY-SEVEN

Pru pulled a pastel-blue throw blanket around her shoulders and huddled on Edie's oversized, light-yellow living room chair. It and the matching loveseat were like soft sunlight against the sky-blue walls. The light birch floor's wide planks made the room seem bigger than it was, though. Pru closed the blanket around herself more tightly, cocooning herself from the agoraphobia setting in.

"Honey, you should eat something."

"I can't. I don't think I remember how."

Edie stood behind the chair and rubbed Pru's shoulders.

After leaving Shawn's, she'd sped to her friend's apartment and alternated between ranting and pacing and sobbing in Edie's arms.

That was the first night. Three days had passed now, and she still hadn't left, letting Tommy take care of Matilda in the meantime. Today she was in a borrowed T-shirt and wrap skirt. Edie had washed Pru's hair and piled it on top of her head in a damp, messy bun.

Pru stood, and invisible hands pressed on her shoulders. Her back and leg muscles were leaden as she shuffled across the room, dragging the blanket with her to the table where her phone was charging. "I've got like six messages from him just from this morning."

"Keep ignoring them," Edie said. "I'll be your hypothetical attorney here. Direct interaction with the opposition never leads to a good outcome. You came here for me to protect you."

Pru squinted. "I came here because I needed my friend."

Edie hung her head. She'd just straightened her own hair, and it slanted past her face, briefly obscuring it. "You're right. I apologize."

"Maybe he just wants to give my dress back."

"Do you even want it back? It's all ripped up anyway." Her friend walked around to face Pru. "Here, give me the phone." Pru handed it to her and Edie started typing.

"Don't text him. Don't be my lawyer."

"I'm not even dignifying his texts by reading them." She handed it back and Shawn's messages were gone. "Onward and upward. What's on your agenda today?"

"I need to go home. I want to hang out with Mattie and try to lose myself in practicing." Pru looked down.

"You can hole up here as long as you want. I know Tommy is loving spoiling Matilda, but we can ask him to bring her over for you. As long as she's got her vest, the neighbors can't make an official complaint to the management."

"Thanks. I want to try to be normal again — or at least whatever semblance of normal I can find." Pru took a deep breath. "I need to take on private students again. That'll keep my schedule full, at least, and I can send more money to my uncle." She folded the blanket as she headed for the chair and draped it over the back. "I also need to save more for Matilda's vet bills. She'll probably need her other hip replaced at some point. Those things are what are important."

"Taking care of yourself is what's important." Edie looked at the clock on her cable box. "I've gotta go meet a couple of new clients in two hours. You gonna be all right?"

Pru forced a smile. "I will."

"Don't try to drive until after you eat. I've got some hard-boiled eggs and pineapple juice in the fridge." Her friend hugged her and held her head against her shoulder, rocking gently. "I will not have you falling down a rabbit hole over this. I'm your safety net, okay?"

"Thank you."

"I'll check on you later. Make sure you have your phone on. Don't reply to Shawn when he tries again."

That wouldn't be a problem. Every time Pru thought about replying, she couldn't think of anything to say. "I promise."

Edie slid on her blazer and shoes and headed for the door. "Love you to pieces, Pru."

Pru stared at the door for a few seconds after her friend closed it. The thought of the acidic sugar that was pineapple juice made her stomach cramp. Instead, she had half of an egg and a glass of water. Relatively certain she was strong and clearheaded enough to drive, she cleaned up and headed home.

Pru glanced around the diner and picked at a piece of dry toast. Another three days had passed since she'd come home from Edie's. Everything looked the same as it had when she sat in this very same seat, pouring her heart out to Shawn — the clean, bright flooring, the shiny red, white, and black retro décor with chrome accents along the bar, even the same two servers as that day, in their red-and-black-striped polos. Still, it was as if she were on a plane of existence askew to the real one.

Staring out the window, she watched the Main Street traffic pick up as the clock on the square rang eight. The air had already begun to shimmer with exhaust fumes as the sun rose and the temperature began to climb.

Her barely eaten toast was mostly a pile of crumbs. Picking up a crust, she took a small bite. That little bit of bread tasted like dry sand, and it scratched her throat. She was out of tears for now, so at least there was that. She was just pulling some cash from her wallet when Cliff slid into the seat across from her. "You look terrible," he said.

Pru leveled her gaze at him. His face was still shiny with shaving oil. He waved to get the waitress's attention, and she brought over a cup of coffee. "Let's have breakfast and take a walk before the weather turns. You look like you need me." He emptied a packet of sugar into his mug, stirred, and took a sip.

"No."

He leaned in. "I want to be here for you. I warned that jerk to stay away from you. Look how miserable you are. You should have listened to me." He extended his hand palm-up on the table. "I'll take you back, you know. I forgive you."

She slid out from the booth and grabbed the edge of the table for support. "Don't follow me."

That only got a chuckle from him. "You know I can't stay away from you, babe, especially when you're this confused and upset." He closed his hand over hers.

"Let go, Cliff." He didn't move.

She stared at his generically handsome face, and the hints of his shoulder and chest muscles beneath his pink polo shirt. He'd arranged his mouth into a sympathetic pout, and his clear, cornflower blue eyes had that wide, sad cartoon-puppy expression he'd used to manipulate her so many times. "Then I'll help you stay away." She picked up his cup and tipped it over his lap. He turned red and barely suppressed a shout. The three other diners in the restaurant turned to stare. A bus-boy with a large tub of dirty dishes froze in his tracks. Pru turned and, as if walking against high tide, found her way to the front of the diner.

"Prudence, get over here." Cliff deepened his voice.

The bells above the entrance jingled as she let the door shut behind her. Through the diner's window, she saw him pulling napkins out of the dispenser. She picked up her pace. There was still some sunlight filtering through the dark gray clouds when Pru reached her car. She didn't remember driving home, but when she got inside, the sky was dark, and the rain had washed away everything outside until the world was unrecognizable.

Tommy extended his legs along the couch, Matilda sprawled over him and snoring. Pru sat across from him on the floor, her laptop on the coffee table.

"I am absolutely certain Barney wouldn't want you draining your savings for him."

It was the first of the month, which meant Pru's last paycheck until September when the orchestra reconvened. Pru hit *yes*, and the transfer went from her checking account to her uncle's medical account.

"He's my grandma's brother," she said. "And he gave me a home after she died." She took a deep breath, remembering the police coming to the house to tell her that a drunk driver in a large truck had plowed into Grandma Esther's little white Neon. She'd just gotten dressed to meet her friends and drive to a party. "I adore you to the moon, but he's the only relative I've got left."

"You can't shoot yourself in the foot like this. Barney's got plenty of money. He told you as much."

"He lives in a bungalow on an undeveloped beach and hardly spends any money, probably because he hasn't got any. He's exaggerating so I won't worry."

Tommy folded his arms. "He was the CFO for three different Fortune 500 companies over the course of his career. We're talking about six- and seven-figure earnings for one guy living below his income modestly for the past couple of decades."

Pru locked eyes with him. "You don't have to keep vigil over me. I know how to budget, and I want him to have whatever I'm not using. Besides, I'm going to have to get used to not having you around." Even though she knew she wasn't fooling him about her mood, she forced a smile. "Have you guys set a date? Are you having an engagement party? I want to play at it for you."

"You're changing the subject, and the answers are no, yes at some point, and we'd love you to." Tommy sat back. "I'm worried about you."

"I'm actually feeling a little better, and I'm making some extra money lately."

He looked her over. "At least you're less of a hermit."

It had been a week since Pru's encounter with Cliff. She still needed a calendar to remind her each day that time was passing, since they all still blended together. She'd been leaving the house every couple of days though, marking time by seeing one new middle school cello player and a couple of viola students at their respective homes. Now it was only evenings and nights that set her crying, and occasionally mornings until she got into her routine. It was worse when Tommy was over at Andrew's house instead of next door. She didn't dare tell either of them that.

Pru stood, put her phone in its charger on the kitchen pass-through, and squashed herself into the other corner of the couch. Tommy lifted his feet to make room for her and she settled them on her lap.

He sighed. "You might be able to fool other people, but I still see it all over your face. I'm seriously thinking about asking Joe to have a word with his *friend.*" He made air quotes around the word.

Pru leaned back. "Don't. This isn't high school. I was stupid enough to let my guard down and I got hurt for it."

"Letting yourself feel things isn't stupid. I mean, sure, if you trusted Cliff again, I'd be first in line to shout some sense into you, probably with a megaphone to your ear. But it's okay to take emotional risks." He shifted and Matilda rolled onto her back. "Remember when I first met Andrew, and all I wanted to do was numb out over Jason a year after breaking up?"

Pru nodded.

"What did you tell me?"

"That's different." She forced herself not to look away.

"Uh-uh. I want to hear exactly what you said to me." He raised an eyebrow.

Pru dropped her head forward. "I said going through life afraid to let someone love you was no way to live. But that's not the same as this. I knew better. I got carried away and—"

"And that was brave. *You* are brave. You're certainly not stupid. You've got your doctoral certificate shoved in a drawer somewhere in case you need reminding." He drummed his palms on Matilda's belly until she rolled off him and shook herself out. "Plus your besties have your back. We got this." He reached back and grabbed his phone.

Pru heard more than one pair of footsteps come up to the front porch less than an hour after Tommy spoke with Edie and Joe. She was getting up to answer the door when she heard Edie's raised voice. "You've got an oversized pair, for sure," she was saying to whoever was with her. "See this? This is what she needs right now, not you. She needs her friends, she needs a *Doctor Who* mini-marathon, and she needs a whole pint of Ben and Jerry's Brownie Batter."

A man said something back.

"Go home. Go anywhere else. We're picking up all the crap you dropped at this poor woman's feet."

Pru took a step closer to the door. Tommy came around and pulled back on her elbow, shaking his head. She recognized Shawn's voice now, but she still couldn't make out what he was saying. She started to shake. "Let Edie handle this, Pru," Tommy said.

She planted her feet, neither pulling from Tommy's grasp nor sitting back down.

"No, she doesn't need to hear your apology." Edie's voice was a low burn. "You've said more than enough. Leave. Take that shit with you. Donate it to a funeral home or something." Shawn's voice was louder now, but still unclear, with Edie interrupting every word or two.

"Bye, Felicia. Go on. Otherwise the ice cream's gonna melt, and that'll be one more way you'll have messed up her life."

A few moments later an engine started and Edie let herself in. She held up a plastic bag from Kroger. She hadn't changed from work, and she slid her heels off as soon as she shut the door behind her then shrugged off her blazer as Tommy disappeared into the kitchen to get spoons. "Don't suppose we can watch David Tennant instead of Matt Smith? He's cuter."

"Thanks, Edie." Pru plopped onto the couch. "I should probably talk to Shawn."

"No, you shouldn't," Edie said. "You don't need his lies and half-truths."

Tommy returned. "I'm with Pru. Smith is funnier."

Edie and Tommy sat on either side of her and Pru cued up the first episode with the eleventh Doctor.

"We should wait for Joe." Pru paused the television. She wondered where she'd go if she had a time machine. Everyone she loved might not be in her life if others hadn't left it. How radical would the difference be between who she was and who she could have been? Still, she couldn't stop looking at the door, wondering if Shawn might come back. Could this have had any other outcome?

Edie gently kicked Pru's ankle and gestured toward the TV. "I know what you're thinking."

Pru picked up her spoon. The Doctor, for all his

protestations about being a loner in nearly every version of himself, rarely traveled alone. Even time lords needed companions on their journeys.

CHAPTER THIRTY-EIGHT

Shawn let his car idle at the end of the block. He wondered whether he should go bang on the door now that Pru's self-appointed security guard wasn't there to block him. He started when Joe pounded on his passenger side door. Joe waved and Shawn lowered the window.

"Are you going to or from?" Joe's brow was smooth, his mouth a tight line. "I know which one I'd recommend after the text I just got from Edie."

Shawn dropped his chin to his chest. "I'm surprised my balls are still attached to my body."

Joe opened the door and slid in next to him. "Once Pru's done kicking herself for trusting you, Edie will be the least of your troubles. Pru might cut them off herself with a newly strung bow when she moves from heartbroken to royally pissed." He scowled. "I fucking told you what would hap-pen."

Shawn straightened. "Now wait a minute. I would never hurt her on purpose. Ever."

Joe lowered his chin and narrowed his eyes. "And yet."

He tried to come up with a rejoinder, but he couldn't. "I know this is my fault." He shut his eyes and thudded his head back on the headrest. "I've made up my mind though. I just need to apolo—"

"Well, that's interesting," Joe interrupted. Shawn turned his head. Joe had stiffened and was watching a shiny, pow-der-blue Lexus drive by.

"Meaning?"

"Meaning," Joe said as he shifted to face Shawn, "that was Cliff's car heading toward Pru and Tommy's place."

"Fuck. Get out." Shawn put his foot on the brake and shifted into *Drive*.

Joe opened the door but didn't leave. "Stay out of it for now. Don't be a self-appointed hero. Decide what you want to say to her once you can wash all that guilt off your face. Figure out whatever screwed-up thing you've got going on with Helena. We'll all deal with Cliff, trust me."

"You'd better."

Joe got out of the car and leaned in. "Do you think she's dumb enough—or wounded enough—to fall back into his bed? If you think that little of Pru, do her a favor and stay away for good."

Shawn gripped the steering wheel. "Of course I don't think that. I—"

"Then I am telling you, as your friend and your only advocate here, get lost."

Shawn reached into the back seat and handed him the grocery store bouquet he'd picked up on the way in. "Give her these?"

Joe rolled his eyes and took them. "Go to a liquor store, go home and get drunk until you pass out before you can do any more damage. I'll intercept Cliff and send him packing." He shut the door, went back to his car and pulled away.

Stomach twisting and heart slamming against his throat, Shawn watched through his rear mirror and waited for Cliff's car to come back down the road. When it did, Shawn pulled out in front of it as it approached. He hit his hazard lights, got out of his own car, and stepped around to lean on his trunk, arms folded.

Cliff's brakes squealed to a stop. He slammed his door shut

and got out. "What are you doing in the middle of the road, asshole?"

Shawn shrugged. "Takes one to know one. Leave Pru alone."

The man took a couple of steps forward, fists clenched by his sides. "I'm going to tell you this once more, because you clearly weren't smart enough to understand me the first two times. Maybe that's why you literally work cleaning up other people's shit instead of having a real job."

Shawn almost wanted to laugh. The moron thought his and Joe's farfetched, impromptu story was true. "I'm pretty sure us shit-cleaners are more useful to the world than you are."

"Pru is my girlfriend. Don't even breathe on her." Cliff's voice was low and menacing.

Shawn pushed away from the trunk and stepped up until they were nearly chest-to-chest. "Apparently you're the one who doesn't seem to understand the word no. At least I'm not so full of myself that I think I deserve her. Back off and stay away, prick." He shoved his hands into Cliff's chest, making him sway backward. "If you want me out of the way, move me yourself."

A shadow loomed. The next thing Shawn felt was a heavy, fleshy weight against his chest and the air huff from his body. He opened his eyes in time to see Cliff's fist speed toward his face. Shawn raised his arms and stepped aside. There was a loud thwack as Cliff punched the trunk.

Shawn straightened and threw all his weight into a punch to Cliff's gut. Dull pain throbbed through his knuckles and into his wrist. The man's muscles might as well have been made of Teflon.

His opponent stumbled back and his face darkened. He rolled his shoulders, squared his jaw, and reared his arm back. Shawn ducked but not in time. Cliff's fist clipped his shoulder, knocking him sideways against the car.

There was a blur of skin before Shawn regained his bearings. Hot wetness spread over Shawn's lips before he registered the painful stinging and throbbing. He wiped blood away from his face "Gonna break your damn fingers, Cliff," he lisped. He balanced against the car and lifted his fists.

Cliff laughed and shoved him away. "In your dreams. That's the only place Pru's ever gonna be too." He walked back to his car, pulled around, and drove off.

Shawn hunched forward and rested his hands over his thighs. Maybe he wasn't that bright, letting himself get beaten up exactly the same way twice—except voluntarily this time. Shawn got back behind the wheel and started to pull away. If standing in front of Cliff's fists was what it took to keep that loser from bothering Pru, so be it.

CHAPTER THIRTY-NINE

Pru looked up as Joe let himself into the house. He had two bouquets tucked beneath one arm and a twelve-pack of Sam Adams in his other hand. Edie got up to close the door behind him.

Joe handed her both bouquets. She frowned and opened her mouth, but Joe said quickly, "The pink roses are from Shawn. The cheap-ass grocery store chrysanthemums are from He Who Shall Not Be Named, who was just pulling up when I got here. I sent both packing."

Pru watched as Edie looked over her shoulder and frowned at Joe before heading into the kitchen with them. Pru recognized the "I call bullshit" expression on her friend's face but wasn't sure what that was for.

"Cliff came?" she asked. She'd been about to peel the lid off her ice cream, but now she set it down. "He's like a vulture who thinks I'm carrion."

Joe sat next to her and found his pint of Chunky Monkey in the plastic bag on the coffee table. "You're being too complimentary." He grabbed two water bottles, handed Pru one, and slid the other toward Tommy just as Edie came back in. "Colin Baker, right?" Joe said. "Please?"

Tommy laughed. "Even one episode with that coat of his is enough to blind someone." He glanced at the pass-through where Edie had placed two vases. "I'm not saying you should forgive him anytime soon, if at all, but at least Shawn has better sense than to give you wilting flowers from the 7-Eleven up the street."

"Mmm-hmm." Edie's tone was flat. As she picked up the remote, she said, "Don't let yourself be bought." Then she pressed play.

CHAPTER FORTY

Pru shifted on the bed as Edie sprawled longways over her white, puffy quilt and picked at the loose thread of an embroidered daisy. "Maybe I need to reconsider my career." She flipped onto her back, picking at her cuticles with otherwise flawless, grass-green fingernails. It took a real funk for Edie to wear cotton shorts and an old pink-and-green Alpha Kappa Alpha T-shirt, and to not bother with makeup.

"It was one case, Edie. No one's fired you. You'll win the next one."

Over a week had gone by since Edie's big court case, and that had ended disastrously. Pru sat and propped herself on a few daisy-and-rose-printed throw pillows against the white wicker headboard. Then she patted Edie's leg and stood. She relished the plush white carpet that felt and almost looked like clouds under her bare feet.

"If they ever give me another one to take lead on. I still have a job, but all four partners made a point of telling me exactly how much money I'd lost the firm. I can't stop seeing the look on our clients' faces when the verdict was handed down." She propped herself on her forearms. Her bottom lip stuck out, and dark circles puffed under her eyes. "I was just too cocky for my own good. I thought I had a slam-dunk."

"It was also dumped into your lap at the last minute. You didn't have much time to prepare."

"Not an excuse," Edie said.

"Follow me." Pru stood at the bedroom threshold and looked over her shoulder to make sure Edie got up. She led her into the large kitchen with its milky green retro appliances and started rummaging through the refrigerator.

"Are you doing what I think you're about to do?" Edie slid into her small blond banquette to sit.

Pru pulled out bread, butter, cheese, and a tomato and set them on the counter. "I can make a milkshake too, if you want." She bent over and took out a frying pan, then started slicing up the tomato. "How many sandwiches do you think you can eat?"

"How many miles do you think I'll need to run to burn off all those calories even without a shake? I still want to do a half-marathon in September." Edie at least sounded amused now.

Pru laughed. "Two it is, then." She buttered the pan and started cooking the first grilled cheese. "You said it yourself: law offices are nonstop stress. They'll all get over it—you'll be back in everyone's good graces and you'll know better for next time." She sighed. "And there *will* be a next time. I guarantee it." She flipped the sandwich over and started constructing the next one. The phone chimed. She glanced down, hoping Edie hadn't seen the anticipation and probable guilt on her face.

"Back at you," Edie said. "I'm gonna take that phone and toss it in the garbage if Shawn keeps bothering you."

Pru set the first sandwich on a plate and moved to place it on the table. "Eat."

As she turned back to her cooking, she felt Edie still watching her. "You keep having nightmares and anxiety attacks, Pru. He's the reason why. He lied to you, he cheated on his girlfriend, and then he had the *cojones* to try to get back with you. Block his number."

"I can't help feeling like there's unfinished business, Edie." Pru's eyes burned, and she pretended it was from the stove. She scooped up the next sandwich with a spatula, slid it onto

Edie's plate, and got to work on one for herself. "Besides, I'm here to help *you* this time. If I don't, you'll stop eating, and then you'll lose weight, and you'll get even more depressed. We can't both feel this low at the same time." She licked some grease off her fingers and brought her lunch to the table.

Edie chewed on the first set of crusts. "Maybe I'll make you a key. You can come over, cook, and leave dinner ready for me every evening."

Pru sat across from her and pursed her lips. "You need to go back into work on Monday and show them you're unrattled."

Edie sat back and lifted her eyebrows. "If I get over myself, will you start trying to get over him?"

"If I try to get over him, will you start setting yourself instead of me up on dates?" Pru asked. They stared at each other. "That's what I thought. Eat your lunch, counselor."

That, at least, made Edie laugh.

Pru idled in Shawn's parking lot and stared out her window. Edie might have been right. Maybe he was the cause of her latest panic attacks. When she'd gotten back from Edie's yesterday, she'd found a small bouquet of lilacs in a vase with a note from Shawn that said *Please, let's talk about it.* Tommy must have brought it inside while she was out. As she climbed the stairs with Matilda, she rehearsed the scatterbrained speech she'd made up as she drove. Four hours or less of sleep over the course of a day and a half had muddled her thoughts, though. Her legs seemed to have doubled in weight as she made her way to the third floor, dragged herself to number 323 and knocked. There was no answer.

She leaned on the door and shut her eyes, too tired to feel dejected. She thought about sitting there waiting, the way Matilda would when Pru went out by herself. The dog leaned against her legs, propping her up.

"You looking for that cute guy? He moved out a few days ago." Pru turned her head and looked at a woman with weathered skin and long frizzy brown hair with white, wiry roots. She was dressed in a pair of bell-bottom jeans and a tank top, like a modern-day Janis Joplin. Her voice had that unmistakable gravelly smoker's edge to it.

The breath left Pru's body in a huff, as if she'd been sucker-punched. "What? Did he say where he was going?"

"Nah." The woman dug around in a fringed leather purse and fished out her keys. "Too bad. He was hot. Lots of fun to look at." She waved. "Have a blessed day." Then she let herself into her own apartment two doors down.

Pru didn't remember running down to her car. Nor did she remember pulling out of the parking lot and driving across town. Nor did she remember the security guy opening the gate to the retirement community to let her through. All she knew was that, as if transported there, she was on the front porch of Shawn's parents' house, staring at the swing where they'd sat. That seemed like an entire existence ago. She peered through the glass on the front door and through a window. All the lights were off. All the flooring had been laid and the walls were painted. There were no drop cloths, newspapers, or tools lying about.

Her vision blurred. He'd finished the house and gone back up North. She sank next to the front door and buried her head in her hands, heart and skull shattered. Their jagged pieces pierced and deflated her lungs. She'd blown it. It didn't matter who was more at fault—she'd run and hidden like a pathetic coward, just like Cliff said she was.

CHAPTER FORTY-ONE

Shawn turned the corner into the driveway too fast, only to see someone's dog sitting smack in its center. He hit the brakes, knocking his sandwich from its flimsy Sheetz bag onto the passenger floor. The car stopped within a few inches of the poor thing. He got out of the car and squatted.

"C'mere, boy."

The yellow lab wore a familiar-looking red collar. He glanced at the tag, jumped to his feet, and, not bothering to close the car door, hurried to the front door as Matilda trotted ahead of him.

Pru was sitting next to the door, her knees drawn to her chest, her head buried in her arms. She was wearing a pair of blue shorts and a white T-shirt with *UGA Hugh Hodgson School of Music* imprinted in red on the back. Her hair shielded her face as she bent forward, and her shoulders were shaking. He knelt in front of her. "Thank God."

She lifted her head. Her eyes were red and her face was wet and blotchy. "I was afraid you were gone." Her voice was like paper tearing.

He put his hands over hers and pulled her in for a hug. She slumped against him, and he scrunched her hair in his hand as he held onto her. She was lighter than he remembered. "I'm so sorry—for all of it." He kissed the top of her head. "Thank you for coming back." His voice cracked. "My monthly lease was up so I decided to hole up here now that there's floors and plumbing fixtures." Standing, he held his hand out to her. "Let's go inside and talk. Are you hungry?"

Taking his hand, she began to push herself up to stand, but her knees buckled. Purplish-gray circles stood out under her eyes. Her clothes were hanging off of her.

He took on her weight and helped her to stay upright. "Pru, when's the last time you ate or slept?"

She shrugged. "I'm sure I've done both at some point recently."

How did she even drive here?

"All right. Let me help you inside. You should eat my lunch." He headed toward the car to get it. The bag was on the ground and torn open. Matilda sat on the driveway with a piece of tomato hanging from her mouth. Scooping up the scraps, he dumped them back in the bag.

"I'll find you something to eat. C'mon in." He kept his arm around her waist as he let them inside.

Matilda followed them in and curled up on Shawn's yoga mat as he shut the door. "Hang on. I'll be right back." Shawn waited for Pru to lean on the granite island that separated the kitchen and the living room. Then he dragged the air mattress from the master bedroom. He set it longways against a wall, had her sit, and headed to the kitchen.

There was almost no protein in the fridge except for some pre-grilled chicken strips and three eggs. Sighing, he grabbed a water bottle, a hunk of smoked cheddar, and a bag of green grapes and brought them to her.

For a few minutes, they sat cross-legged next to each other against the wall. Pru nibbled on a grape, chewed it slowly, and made a gulping sound as she swallowed.

Shawn rested his hand over hers. She didn't pull away. "You should've told me," she said. "You let me think we . . . You said . . . I guess I shouldn't have assumed you wanted to stay here with me." Fresh tears made their way down her face.

After a few seconds, Shawn said, "I know, and I do want to stay here with you. I love you. I wanted to ignore Helena's existence. I wanted to ignore all the things in my life that were pulling me in different directions, and the person who got hurt was you." He waited for her to say something. "I don't deserve for you to forgive me, but I'd like to try to explain."

"I'm listening." She clasped her hands so tightly that her skin stretched until it was white, revealing a network of blue veins.

"When I graduated from college, I moved back home with my parents. I thought I was going to apply to grad school once I worked off my undergraduate debt. I started teaching more yoga classes and doing handyman work to save up some money. I met Helena when I was doing some carpentry for her parents. We sort of fell into a relationship. I didn't even think about it. It was just easy, I guess."

She took a small sip of water and stretched to put the bottle on the floor but couldn't reach. Before she could scoot away from him, Shawn took it from her and set it down.

"My father is a policy advisor for the New York Democratic Committee, and her father is the CEO of a small tech company based out of White Plains. Helena was already working her way up the corporate chain in her father's business. Our dads struck up a working relationship and my parents thought she was the answer to their prayers. They were sure she could talk me out of school and into gainful employment. And they thought that if we got serious, they could stop worrying about me and retire. So, for a few years on and off, we dated. I chose the path of least resistance, moved in with her, and figured that if we were attracted and got along, that was about as close to being in love as I was going to get."

Pru blinked a few times, shaking. "Why aren't you still up there then?"

Shawn leaned his head against the wall and turned it to her. "Because she was trying to push me into a mold that I didn't fit, and it became clear that she was more interested in the mold than in me."

They watched each other. Pru's eyes were wet, and he wondered what she was thinking. He swallowed hard and continued. "She expected me to disavow almost everything I wanted from life. I want a meaningful career. I want to write novels and scholarly papers. I want a white picket fence, kids, and the kind of loving household I grew up in."

Pru's eyes became wet again. "I want that too, but I can't. I had a perfect family before. That was taken from me and now I'm ruined." Her cheeks started to get blotchy and red.

Shawn pictured her in the scenario he'd just described, and a million variations on a reply bottlenecked in his brain.

I want to give all of that to you. I just need to figure out how. Let's just do it. Let's run away together.

Closing his eyes, he tried to wipe out all the promises he knew he couldn't keep. He didn't care about what he did for a living. He just needed Pru to be in his life, and to make her happy.

"I'll say it again." He leaned in and kissed her cheek. "You have no idea how perfect and whole you are to me."

"Tell me more about Helena."

"She doesn't want any of those things." He sighed. "We started arguing because I wanted to go back to school. My parents put pressure on me too. I pushed back by taking on more and more manual labor. She and my parents both insisted that I propose and settle down once and for all. I kept thinking I was going to but in my gut, I couldn't do it. I volunteered to fix up my folks' place here for them just to get some space to think about things. I knew I couldn't avoid Helena forever, though."

Pru looked down as a tear rolled down her cheek. "Why, Shawn? Why didn't you at least tell me nothing would come of us being together? I-I finally admitted to myself I wanted that, and maybe it could happen, and then . . . ." She took a shuddery breath.

"I know." Concern flooded him — Pru barely seemed able

to sit up straight. "I didn't want to get involved. And the fact that it happened so fast felt like whiplash." He peered around and caught her eyes. "Pru, as soon as you walked out, I realized it didn't matter how fast we were moving. I never feel like I'm resigning myself to something when you're around. But I knew I couldn't let things go any further until I settled things once and for all back home. I'd already been lying to myself. I wasn't going to lie to you anymore, not even by omission."

He squeezed her hand, and she gave a weak pulse back.

"I haven't been able to sleep or keep food down," she said. "I feel so stupid, Shawn." She looked him in the face, and he realized that behind that pain was another emotion. Pru's jaw was tight, and her eyes, though red and puffy, were narrow. "I trusted you." Her voice began to rise as the words came out faster. "You said I could trust you, and that you'd always be here, and then you went back on all of that. You said I was safe with you, and I wasn't."

Shawn shuddered as he started to cry. "I mean it when I say I love you, and I'm so, so sorry. Let me earn back your trust. I'm begging you." He took a quick breath before she could answer. "The main reason why I didn't renew my lease was because every time I closed my eyes, I saw that look on your face before you left. The whole place was poisonous."

There was a long stretch of silence as she seemed to think.

"You need more water." He slid off the mattress and picked up the empty bottles and half-finished food to put away.

She stood, steadied herself on the wall, and followed him. "Cliff hit you again, didn't he?" Pru said as he turned to her. She put her fingers near the edge of Shawn's lips, where the yellow vestiges showed where Cliff's punch had landed.

"I ran into him and told him to leave you alone."

Pru frowned. "I'm not a kid. And I'm not a piece of

property."

He looked away. "It wasn't that if I couldn't have you no one could, but I know what he's like. Even if you never forgive me, I won't let him get to you."

She almost smiled. "I can handle Cliff."

"I'll stand between you and him until I can't get up anymore." Shawn put a hand on her shoulder. "No one ever should be allowed to hurt you. Not me, not Cliff, not anybody."

Pru threw her arms around Shawn's neck and kissed him. He buried his head against her neck and without much warning, gravity lifted around him as a gigantic ball of regret dislodged from his stomach, wedged itself behind his eyes, and exploded into a sob. "Please, don't let go." His voice was muffled against her hair. "Don't ever let go."

CHAPTER FORTY-TWO

Pru wasn't sure who was rocking whom, or even which of them was crying anymore. When they quieted, Shawn pulled her closer, pressed his hand against the back of her head and covered her mouth with his. His lips were firm, and he sucked the breath out of her slowly. She tilted her head and closed her mouth over his jaw, tasting the salt and something subtle and sweet beneath it. His barely-there stubble scratched her lips.

He moved his head to find her mouth again. She held him more closely, moving her fingers down and around the dips and plateaus of his back and shoulders. Rounding his back, he held her face in his palms. Tears streamed past his cheeks. "I don't deserve you."

Pru placed her hands on his chest. His heart thudded against her palm. She managed a smile. "I come with a lot of baggage. Plus I'm really weird. No one deserves me."

He almost chuckled but new tears hovered along the rims of his eyes. "That's not what I meant," he half whispered.

Shawn held her against him and ran his hand up and down her back, making her spine tingle. "All I want is you," he said.

Tilting her head up, she lifted her hand and placed it over his cheek. "I really do like your accent."

He raised his eyebrows. "I don't have an accent."

Pru bit her lip. "What'd you say to me just before?"

"All I want is you." He kissed the crown of her head. It was subtle but unmistakable.

"Say that first word again?"

"All." It came out "awl." He chuckled. "You win. I love yours." He cupped her face and, mouth closed, touched his lips to hers. "I love everything about you, Pru."

Matilda's snores, the house, Pru's mixed-up life and his . . . it all dissolved. There were only their bodies together. He was hard. Pru slid her hand along Shawn's side, down the V of his torso, and rested her hand on his zipper. "Is it okay if I—"

He angled his hips so she could undo his shorts, and she slid them down his thighs. He wriggled the rest of the way out of them, toed off his shoes, and kicked everything away. She rested her palm between his legs and traced the outline of his cock through his boxer briefs. He took her hand away and she tensed. When she raised her head, he was watching her. "It's been a long time. Did I mess up already?"

He shook his head. "You came back to me." His hands ran over her shoulders and held her upper arms. "How can anything possibly be wrong?" Then he let go and touched her breasts, making slow spirals from the outsides toward her nipples. He stroked his thumbs over them and she shivered. "I moved your hand because I was going to last all of five seconds if you kept doing that."

She wrapped her arms around his neck again. They backed up until he was against the wall. It was almost a surprise that anything solid was around them. They touched their foreheads together, Pru standing on her tiptoes. Then she slid her forearms along his. His hair stood on end as he wrapped his arms around her waist and hooked his thumbs in the loops of her shorts. As he pushed her clothes off, a wet trail followed down her inner thigh. She pressed her hips against his, nearly pinning him. He tugged down his underwear and she kicked it away.

Taking a long breath, he kissed her more deeply. Pru grasped a fistful of his hair as she kissed him back and wound her calf around his. They were an arabesque—an arrangement of two melodies curling around one another. She worked her hands under the hem of his T-shirt, and he helped her pull it over his head.

Shawn slid a hand under her shirt but lingered when his fingers grazed a scar. "You're in charge here."

She raised her arms, and he pulled the shirt away. He undid her bra. Her skin flushed as he rested one hand along her waist and settled it over a swath of rough, bumpy skin. She held her breath.

"Look at how perfect you are."

Pru exhaled. She caged the tip of his penis with her fingers and spread pre-cum over it. He moved her hand away. "I'm clean, but I just realized I don't have anything to use," he said.

"I'm on birth control." She could barely speak.

He put his hand between her shoulder blades and guided her down and onto her back. The stubble on his neck was like damp sandpaper against her chin, but she didn't care. She pulled her shoulders off the mattress to keep her mouth on him when he shifted.

He pressed her back down. "Let me. Please." She'd never heard that tone of voice from him before. A combination of gratitude and pleading so quiet she inhaled the words more than heard him. They spread through her head and behind her eyes.

Shawn kissed his way downward. The light scrape of his teeth over her inner elbow sent warm shivers along her arm. He ran his tongue over her ruined, ugly side, and the sharp staccato of her skin seemed to soften. Then he slid his tongue around to her belly and the hinge of her hip.

Her muscles tensed. He lifted his head and met her eyes.

She propped herself onto her forearms. "No one's ever done that to me before — down there, I mean." She couldn't help stammering. "It's okay if you don't. I've never — um, I've never been able to come with someone before. I don't want you to feel like you have to try."

He made eye contact as a smile spread across his face. "Are you kidding? Now it's a challenge. Just tell me if you want me to stop." He lowered himself onto his belly.

"Shawn?"

He glanced up again, lips parted and nostrils flared.

"I . . ." She wasn't sure what she wanted to say. It suddenly occurred that she was stubbly down there. She was in between waxing. She tugged him up toward her and he sat back. "Never mind."

Her worries dissipated when he spread her thighs apart and gasped, "Wow." There was that strange expression in his voice again.

Reverence. He was worshipping her—deformities, rough places, and all. "So beautiful," he whispered. She believed him. She was beautiful. She was whole. His fingernail was feather-light just below her navel. His breath was like a whisper. His lips almost touched her clit, but then he reangled his head. She wanted to weep when the tip of his tongue slid along her labia, all the way around and back up the other side. She clenched her fists.

"It's okay. I've got you." She wasn't sure if he said anything else, but something like a phrase and a voice permeated along her hip hinge, followed by Shawn's fingertips ghosting along her waist. Slipping his hand behind her rib cage, goosebumps raised all over her. His mouth and nose glided over, around, and across each breast, a gradual quickening until his tongue flicked like a grace note over each nipple and he kissed his way back down.

"Please." Her voice was almost foreign. He found her clit with his tongue. Just as she lifted against it, he pulled away again. She hadn't noticed that her hips had begun to roll against him until he pressed his thumbs against her bones, kissed her belly, and murmured, "That's it."

"Shawn." She could barely breathe. He held her hips and moved his mouth, sucking and licking, darting his tongue in and out. Pru pressed her fingers hard against his scalp. Her heartbeat barely kept up with the rest of her body. A gasp followed by a low, throaty sound rose from her until everything seized. Her back arched and her nerve endings surged—a sudden crash and slow retreat of sensation.

He stayed there as the spinning in her head slowed, his touch lightening until she stopped moving. She didn't realize how hard she was gripping his hair until she began to pull him toward her. He balanced on his hands, looking down at her.

Pru reached between his legs and circled his cock with her fingers. He closed his eyes and his brow wrinkled as he smiled, then went smooth when he opened them back up. The dark brown of his irises was nearly black. She hadn't noticed the crooked dip of a wrinkle that branched like a tributary over his right eye and into his eyebrow until now. Thin, shallow lines extended almost to his temples.

Sweat beaded his forehead. His face was shiny with her, and her hips were already starting to lift again. Pru angled the head of his penis between her legs and he pushed in. She wasn't as ready as she thought. What felt like a light fist thudded inside her. She held her breath for a few seconds as the heavy pressure settled and expanded.

He pulled out, flushed. "Did that hurt?"

His lips were parted, and he was breathing hard, but his eyes were wide with concern. She shook her head. "Only a little." She smiled and touched his cheek. "I don't think anyone's ever stopped to check on me like that before."

He tilted his head.

"Let's try again," she said.

Shawn turned his face to kiss her hand. "You always matter." He slid in more slowly this time, watching her reactions as she watched his chest shudder and his jaw release. He shifted position by an inch and sensation burst through her. Her hips slammed against him, knocking their bones together over and over.

Something about his breathlessness, the low gruff tone of his voice when he said her name, and the way he clenched his teeth made her cry out. Her voice ranged from moans that started in her diaphragm and forced their way to her throat to high-pitched panting as he squeezed his eyes shut and thumped against her, abandoning rhythm until they were moving so fast her breath could hardly keep up. They held on tighter. They were in flight, each carrying the other higher and higher until a fugue of light and heat spread behind her lids. She went limp and he collapsed, catching himself on his forearms. He gazed at her, unmoving and glossy-eyed. His hair was drenched.

After a few seconds, he rolled onto his back and she started to scoot away. His eyes were shut, his arm draped over his abdomen as his breathing slowed. Pru tensed and swallowed, hard. He was done, and without his weight on her, the room cooled and expanded. There was nothing to anchor her. She was a helium balloon losing air fast.

He probably wouldn't mind if she pushed herself next to him and pressed her fingers into the hair on his chest, as if she could gather the musk and brine of him into her hands. She thought about how as a girl the stories of Circe and Calypso in *The Odyssey* upset her. Two magical women, children of Titans, couldn't keep Odysseus with them. He fell in love but couldn't stay there. He'd sailed away on a sea filled with his lovers' tears. Maybe Shawn secretly would rather she go home. She started to get up.

"Pru?" He rolled onto his side and propped his head on his elbow. "Where are you going?" His eyebrows knitted.

She stopped. "You want me to stay?"

"What? Of course I do." He touched her hand. "Why, do you want to leave?"

"No, I want to be here with you."

The worried tension in his jaw and brow released. "Stay. Please."

Lying back down, Pru draped a leg over his hips as he wrapped an arm around her. With her ear against his heart, she fell asleep.

CHAPTER FORTY-THREE

Shawn hadn't bothered to put his shirt back on before he started scouring the refrigerator for something to make for dinner. He shivered as the central air kicked in. As he balanced his phone between his chin and shoulder, he diced a bunch of spring onions, careful not to nick his fingers in the mostly dark room. "Is the house really finished?" his father asked.

"Yeah. I just have a few small things left to do. While I've got you on the phone, I want to talk about my plans from here." His stomach fluttered, and he slowed his chopping.

"Your mother and I do as well. But first, you need to come up here."

"Well, that's what I wanted to talk about, Dad. I'm planning to stay and—"

"We need you to get home. Come up, take whatever of yours you don't want us to get rid of, and we'll hash out what comes next in person with all of us present."

Shawn stopped chopping altogether. "Keep or toss what you want, it's fine. I'm staying in Georgia. We can talk when you're ready to move down."

"Shawn." He pictured the squaring of his father's shoulders that always accompanied that low, warning tone. "You cannot live with us. We're retiring. It's time to take responsibility for yourself."

Putting down the knife, Shawn walked to the refrigerator. He pulled out a bottle of fish sauce, some carrots, and a bell pepper, then tossed the vegetables toward the sink. "I know that." He tried not to sound annoyed. "What I mean is that I decided to—"

"I'm emailing you plane reservations right now. You'll fly up on Monday."

Why was it that whenever he made a decision about his life, he was suddenly twelve years old again? He turned on the faucet and began to scrub a carrot. "And stay for how long?"

"For as long as it takes. We'll see you in a week. Bye, son."

"For as long as what takes?"

His father had already hung up. Shawn put his phone next to the faucet. Back at home, it wasn't just his parents. His aunts, uncles, and cousins were spread throughout New England and Upstate New York. He reminded himself that Pru had no network of family at all. Maybe going up there wouldn't be so terrible.

He moved on to rinsing a pepper. He could make them all understand. He owed everyone that much. His insides heated. On the other hand, why should he have to justify himself to any of them? It wasn't as if he was asking them for anything—except, he supposed, permission to screw up.

Gathering up his washed vegetables, he brought them back to the cutting board. He couldn't tell in what measure his resistance was to his fear of being sucked into his family and Helena's undertow, or to how he'd literally just reconciled with Pru and now would have to leave her behind again.

He rinsed his hands and turned toward the mattress just as Pru stretched and yawned. One leg hung over the edge, and some of her hair was pinned beneath her shoulder. She held the blanket he'd lain over her to her chest as she sat up. "Hi."

"Hey there." The sky had darkened more. Pru's messy hair and bare shoulders were bright points among the shadows. He flipped on the lights and came around to sit next to her. "Hungry?"

She leaned her head on his arm. "Starved."

They propped themselves against the wall and extended their legs in front of them. "I don't have a lot in the house, but I figured I can throw together a halfway decent stir fry." He rested his hand over hers. She rotated her palm so they could lace their fingers together. "I took Matilda out to do her business and fed her the last of the chicken though, so it's going to be vegetarian." They both glanced at the yellow lab, who was snoring, lying on her back, belly exposed. "I also don't have chopsticks, so we'll be using forks."

Giggling, Pru threaded her arms under his and pulled him in for a kiss. Even sweaty, she smelled like rain-drenched wisteria. "Or this is also good." He cupped the back of her head and scrunched her hair as their lips parted open and he slid his tongue past hers. As they started to lie down, both their stomachs rumbled. He chuckled and sat up. "Maybe we should make sure we don't drop from exhaustion."

"Soon." She tugged him down with her. He lifted the sheet over them both and spooned around her. For a while, they just held each other. He'd been missing a piece of himself. Now he'd do literally almost anything as long as she didn't let him go.

"I just got off the phone with my dad. I have to go up to New York a week from today."

He sensed Pru tense and he kissed her shoulder. "Don't worry, I'm coming back. I'm going to sort out my life and end things once and for all with Helena." She rolled over and buried her head between his jaw and shoulder. He pulled her up and hugged her.

"I trust you," she said. Shawn hoped he was just imagining the hesitation in her voice.

By the time they'd finished dinner, made love again, gone out for ice cream and groceries and returned, Pru seemed calmer. Shawn watched as she kicked off part of the blanket in her sleep. The cover slid halfway down and he fought the temptation to run his palm over her exposed collarbone, the side of her breast, and the blue, lacelike scars on her side.

Even her breasts felt different from Helena's silicone-filled ones. Yes, they were squishier and not as symmetrical, but they were also softer. One nipple was more pigmented than the other. One side was more sensitive than the other. One was just about flawlessly white and on the other was a light constellation of freckles. He sighed. Just one last hurdle to get through before he could figure out how to stay here.

Shawn scrolled through his last few messages. "Christ," he mumbled. One was from Helena, saying she was glad he was finally coming home and coming to his senses. The other was from his mother, who basically said the same thing. Helena's father had sent him a Google calendar invitation to an interview at Jupitelligence, along with a rough starting salary to negotiate. The offered pay was good money. Excellent, actually. If he took the job and stayed a year or two, moving back here to be with Pru would be a lot easier. He'd have savings and work experience. He wouldn't have to bum off Pru for a place to live. She couldn't leave the orchestra—that wouldn't be fair to ask. But long-distance relationships could work. He just needed to convince her.

He'd also have to figure out how to accept the job and not the obligations to Helena that came with it. One problem at a time, though. He'd take the interview and then, if he got an offer, he could turn it down if Pru wasn't onboard with the idea or if it was contingent upon marrying Helena. Then he'd deal with whatever fallout resulted.

His parents would be disappointed and Helena would be hurt if he did that, though. Wouldn't she? The theme he'd grown up with—You owe it to the people who love you to do right by them—looped through his brain. Pru had given him all her love and trust—multiple times now. Didn't he owe her as well, then? Dizzy at the notion of all that decision-making, he rolled onto his back and ran his hands over his face, not looking forward to what might lie just beyond the horizon.

CHAPTER FORTY-FOUR

Shawn looked over at Pru in the driver's seat as she found a spot at the curb in front of the right airline terminal. Her jaw was taut. He put his hand on her cheek and nudged her around to look at him. "I'll text you as soon as I land. And when I get to my parents' house. And before I go to sleep. And first thing in the morning every morning."

Pru chuckled, but a tear dropped past her chin. "Come back soon." She sucked in her lips.

Shawn reached across the hand brake console and hugged her. "I'll be back before you know it." He smiled and wiggled a finger between her lips. "Why are you hiding your lips from me?" That made her smile for real and he kissed her.

Why the hell are you leaving just because your parents said to, putz? Why not send them an email if they won't let you get a word in edgewise on the phone? What are you thinking?

A security guard tapped on the passenger window and jerked his thumb. "We'll talk soon," he promised. She gave him a weak wave as he got out, grabbed his backpack from the back seat, and closed the car door. He waved back. Then he wove around the cars over to the sliding doors to the airport. When he looked around one more time, she was already gone.

Kennedy Airport was its usual crowded, confusing self. When he made it past the gate, Shawn glanced around, looking for his father. A chill went through him when it wasn't his dad's gray, thinning hair and slightly jowly face that he saw but Helena's tall, trim figure, her auburn braid draped past one shoulder. She smiled and waved. Shawn grumbled and made his way over, shrugging his backpack over both shoulders.

Helena threw herself at him, wrapped her arms around his neck, and kissed him on the mouth. He turned his face away. "You have no idea how much I missed you," she said. She balanced her hands on his shoulders to reach and kissed his cheek. "Let's get you home."

Shawn didn't catch much of what Helena was talking about during the hour or so drive. He picked up on some story about people in the office who he didn't know, her accomplishments so far in her new position, her latest workouts, some new throw pillows she picked out for her living room, and something about an itinerary.

He shook himself into reality in time to be surprised when she pulled into her own garage. "I thought I was supposed to stay with my folks."

Staring at him, Helena frowned. "Did you hear a word I said about the plans now that you're here?" She put on an obviously forced smile, all red lipstick and bleached teeth, and tousled his hair. "We also need to get you a haircut."

He smoothed it back and got out of the car. "No, I wasn't really listening."

"Well," she said, linking her arm in his as she led him inside. "It makes more sense for you to be here."

Before he could reply, she shut the door, pushed him against the wall and kissed him. She grabbed his hair in her fists and pushed her hips and breasts against him. He pushed her back. She didn't let go. Instead she pried his mouth open with her tongue and moved his hands under her shirt. Then she flicked open his jeans' button, unzipped him, and began to rub up and down his cock at the exact pace she knew she needed to make him hard within seconds, as if he were a machine to be switched on.

"Helena, we need to talk." She moaned and slid to her knees, taking his pants and shorts with her. "Helena, *stop.*" He tried to sound stern. She slid her tongue along his length, cupped his balls—again with just the right amount of pressure—and closed her mouth over him.

Oh, God. Oh, shit.

Shawn grabbed her shoulders and tried to push her away, but she dug her fingers against his ass, taking him in the rest of the way. His body rocked with her of its own volition. He glanced down and saw the way her cheeks hollowed as she moved up and down.

Are you out of your mind?

He took a big handful of her hair and yanked it up and backward. "I *said* to stop."

She yelped as she fell on her ass. "This is how you thank me for being nice to you?"

He didn't look at her as he zipped up and stepped away from the wall. "Only you would see it like that." He frowned and cleared his throat. "There's this little thing called consent. Have your secretary look up what it means and give you a report."

Reddening, she frowned as she stood. "How dare you speak to me like that?" She took a moment to compose herself and let her shoulders drop. "Shawn, baby, I missed you. You believe me, don't you? I couldn't wait to be close to you—to feel you against me." The corner of her mouth lifted and her eyes narrowed. "And inside me."

"We can't do this anymore, Helena. We have to talk." He headed for the living room and sat on the white leather sectional. He watched her approach.

Helena prodded his legs apart with her knee. "Why did you zip back up?" She unfastened her white slacks and unbuttoned her sky-blue, silky blouse, revealing a lacy, ice-pink bra. Cupping her breasts, she smirked. "You know what to do."

He frowned as glanced up and down her long torso, noted the tiny gold belly ring and the small incision scars from the implants and tummy tuck. "I'm not interested."

She buttoned up and laughed. "You're just cranky and tired from the trip. I'll make you a protein shake. I bet you must be sick of all that fried crap and grits they eat in the South."

"I'm cranky because I don't want to be here."

Helena put her hands on her hips. "What's the matter with you? I thought I'd be a sight for sore eyes after being surrounded by rednecks and yokels."

Shawn stood. "Excuse me?"

"You're going to need reprogramming," she said with a wink. "I'll make you some apple kale juice instead, but I'm throwing some protein powder in there." Helena turned and headed into the kitchen. Following her, Shawn squinted against the smart lights that flicked on as they passed the threshold.

"I don't need reprogramming. What the hell am I, your sex robot? For your information, there are plenty of colleges and universities in Georgia. And some of the kindest, smartest, and most generous human beings I've ever met are down there."

Helena ducked to grab the juicer from the cabinets under the granite center island, put it on the counter more emphatically than necessary, and twisted her sneer into a placid smile. "You need something to eat. Then we'll do some nude, restorative yoga, fuck until we're exhausted, and go to sleep. You have a job interview coming up soon. There's a new Prada suit for you in the first master closet—the smaller one. You need to try it on in case we have to get alterations."

He rolled his eyes. "I'm out of here." He grabbed his phone

from his pocket to call an Uber.

Helena hurried around the island and yanked on his sleeve. "Where do you think you're going to go? Your parents are just going to send you back here. And I know you can't afford to rent a hotel room. You belong at home with me."

Shawn pulled away from her and headed into the living room to grab his backpack, but she got to it faster and snatched it up.

"This is going upstairs into our bedroom." Her tone took on a clipped, authoritative quality and she raised her voice. "You're going to sleep in our bed. And you are going to fuck me like you missed me. This week, my dad and I are going to coach you for the interview, and then you'll see how much better everything is because we've made a commitment."

"I haven't committed to anything." He was almost shouting now. "If you could manage to think about someone other than yourself for a cha —"

"Don't." Helena's voice was firm even though he saw shock, maybe even hurt, in her face for just a second. She straightened and held his gaze. Her eyes appeared so hard that she could have been Medusa.

"I mean it, Helena. I don't want to stay here with you." Shawn took a step forward.

"Even if you don't know what's best, I do." Her voice was an icy knife. "On top of that, your family will be devastated if you back out now." She hoisted his bag over her shoulder and turned away. He took two steps to catch up, pulled it away from her, and tossed it toward the sectional. Helena glared at him, then headed up the circular staircase. "I'll be waiting for you," she said, looking over her shoulder.

Plopping onto the couch, he took his phone out of airplane mode. There were three messages from Pru. The first was that she missed him, followed by some kiss emoticons. The second was a question about whether he'd landed safely. The third asked if he was okay — clearly, she was getting concerned.

Sorry. I'm fine — the drive back didn't go exactly as I expected. I miss you too. You have no idea.

Pru replied right away with a selfie. Her hair was down, and she had on a brown *Life Is Good* shirt with a dog on it. She was smiling and kneeling next to Matilda, whose tongue lolled to one side in her usual silly grin.

Mattie misses you too. No one else gives her grilled chicken for dinner. She says to come home to us soon, or she's afraid she might starve.

Shawn's skin prickled as he glanced upstairs at the light coming from the bedroom. He toed off his shoes, stretched out on the couch, and shoved a stiff, textured throw pillow under his head. He typed in a heart emoji.

Tell her never fear, I plan to be back by the end of the week. I'll text in the morning. It's been a long day. I'll dream of you tonight.

CHAPTER FORTY-FIVE

Heading into his parent's kitchen, Shawn glanced around. He'd been up here for two days, and as many days of intense lectures and quizzing about the job interview by Helena and her father had him begging for a day off to spend time with his own family.

On the wall by the kitchen's threshold hung a yellow push-button phone with a twisty, roped cord next to a small wooden shelf that held a pen and a pad of paper with hooks beneath it for keys. On the other side of the phone was a column of dashes marking dates, sizes, and ages. He chuckled. His entire childhood was here in this little chart, marked sloppily in different colored pens and markers.

He picked up the pencil, stood straight against the wall, and made a hash mark at the top of his head. Then he labeled the date and wrote *twenty-nine, 5'10 1/2"."*

"You're making everyone so happy. It's so good to have you here where I can hug you." His mother turned from the opposite Formica counter with two mugs of coffee. The white one had *Aspen Valley Elementary Superstar* in large green letters. The other was dark blue with yellow crayon stars on it. He'd made that in the second grade as an art project.

She set the cups on the table, came around, and embraced him. "My little baby."

Shawn's mother was a head shorter than him. Her curly, shoulder-length hair was an even mix of silvery gray and dark brown. He hugged her tightly. The scent of Ivory soap and fresh challah enveloped him. Suddenly he wanted nothing more than to sit at the table with Chips Ahoy cookies and a glass of milk as he talked to her about life. "I've missed you too, Mom."

They sat across from each other at the table. He took in the deep crows' feet that extended from her big, light-brown eyes and into her cheeks. The skin around her mouth had begun to sag, and her neck was starting to look crepey. She was smiling and watching him.

"I'm so proud of you," she said.

How could he disappoint her so fundamentally by fighting everyone's hopes for him? How could he assert himself, knowing it would make her cry?

Shawn cleared his throat. "Mom, I want to talk to you about—"

"Son. I'm glad you're home."

Shawn stood and straightened at the sound of his father's voice, even though the words were spoken with obvious affection. "Hi, Dad." They hugged tightly, and Shawn noted differences in him as well. The arms that used to lift him up high and toss him around, making Shawn screech and laugh, were dry and thinner. They were the same height. Even though they'd just seen each other a couple of months ago, the notion that now he was grown up and stronger than his father, as if it were a surprise, suddenly struck Shawn. He blinked away a tear.

Sitting, he watched his father pour himself some coffee and settle in between him and his mom. "Shawn had something he wanted to discuss," she said. The creases around her eyes deepened as she widened her smile.

His dad's posture was relaxed and he was smiling as well. "We've got plenty of time for seriousness. I thought we'd bring in pizza from Manny's since Helena's busy tonight and we have you to ourselves. Was it something urgent?"

He briefly saw his father with a full head of light-brown

hair, still in his work clothes, tie loosened, his jacket draped over the chair. He envisioned his mother in her waist-high, dark blue jeans and yellow Skidmore College sweatshirt, her face unlined, dark hair pulled back in a ponytail. Shawn was eight years old. His father had been smiling, indulging one of Shawn's litanies of baseball trivia he'd gotten from a *Guinness Book of Sports* at the school library.

Shawn shook his head hard. He was almost thirty. His parents were aging. Mommy and Daddy were just people.

Taking a drink from his mug, he swallowed too much coffee. Its bitter aftertaste scorched his throat on the way down. "No, I guess it's not that important." His mind was on an affectionate, brief but somewhat explicit phone call with Pru that morning while he was hiding in the bathroom before he showered.

Coward.

The rest of the week passed by in a blur. Every time Shawn tried to have a serious conversation with his parents or Helena, he was met with wedding binders full of venues, menus, and color schemes from his mother. Or long speeches about what kind of job he was interviewing for from his father or Helena. He and Pru kept missing each other's calls, and he'd been too scattered to answer her texts right away most of the time. There was a follow-up interview scheduled in a couple of days. Even things with Helena had lost some of that frustrated, angry edge now that she was used to the idea of not sleeping together or having sex. Maybe taking some time to build up to this discussion was a better plan anyway.

This morning he'd looked in the mirror and asked himself, "Are you sure you're an adult?"

Every time he thought about how to break the news about his decision to his parents, he heard his mother's elated, relieved tone of voice. *You're making me so happy.* There had to be a way to at least make peace with his parents over this, if not Helena. He thought about his conversation about *Hamlet* with Joe at the beginning of the summer. He was, indeed, "One part wisdom and ever three parts coward." The difference was, arguably, that Hamlet had some modicum of nobility to him.

He could max the rest of his credit card and fly home tomorrow. Shawn thought about that as the second week dragged on. Today he'd found out that Helena's father had arranged to bump out the timetable by nearly two more weeks. In the meantime, he tried to sound hopeful as he texted Pru, swearing he couldn't wait to be with her again. He hadn't told her about how long the delay was going to be.

The plan was to go a week at a time, hoping he could change things.

CHAPTER FORTY-SIX

Shawn sat with Helena in her kitchen and waited for her dad to drive them to his next interview. Two and a half weeks had passed since he'd left Georgia. Last night, while he'd sat outside getting eaten by mosquitoes, Pru sounded like she was about to cry when he broke the news of the latest delay. She hadn't said it, but he knew she was afraid he'd changed his mind. He'd hinted at the idea of working up here just to get on his feet again and been met with several seconds of shuddery breathing on Pru's end. Promises meant nothing from him, given his track record, and he couldn't unhear the despondency in her voice when she'd said goodnight.

His first interview, which had been last week, had been with a couple of lower-level managers whose departments remained a mystery to him. He'd apparently made a good impression though. His mother, who had dropped by to make him a "proper breakfast," couldn't stop staring at him. He shifted and rolled his shoulders, trying to get used to the second uncomfortable designer suit Helena had bought him.

"What are you thinking about, Mom?"

His mother got up, kissed his cheek, and wiped away what must have been her signature rose-colored lipstick smear from his face. "You look so handsome." She smoothed back his hair. "Your hair looks so much nicer now that Doug took you to his stylist." Shawn hadn't even known that was where he and Doug had been headed yesterday. In truth, it looked good, but he hated it anyway. "I'm very proud of you." She adjusted his tie and gave him a tight hug.

Before Helena could add anything, a car horn beeped. Shawn kissed his mother and headed out the door, passing Helena and ignoring her. She followed him to the driveway, where her father's small black BMW was idling.

Helena sat in the front seat next to her father while Shawn twisted and wedged himself into the rear passenger seat. For the duration of the twenty-minute drive downtown, he tuned out the back-and-forth advice from the two of them. The space behind his eyes throbbed by the time the elevator landed at the sleek executive floor of Jupitelligence with its gleaming hardwood floors and modern, minimalist front desk. The receptionist was a middle-aged man in a suit that looked too expensive for what couldn't be a very high-paying job. He stood when the three of them set foot into the foyer. Doug and Helena each passed without saying a word. Shawn hung back and waved, saying, "Good morning. How's it going?" The receptionist frowned at him.

From there, Helena kept her arm threaded around his, her phony corporate smile glued to her face as she led him around the chief officers' suites. They all had big windows with views of the city's boutique- and café-lined sidewalks, framed photos on the walls of the offices' occupants shaking hands with celebrities like Elon Musk and Bill Gates, and solid, imposing desks with big leather chairs. The executives all shook Shawn's hand, bantered with Helena, and reiterated what wonderful things they knew he'd bring to their "little team." Every so often, Helena would cup her hand to his ear, and whisper, "Darling, you're frowning again."

As they rode down the elevator to the human resources offices, she started saying something about going shopping for a wardrobe of more suits. Shawn was half listening and half deciding how committed he was to this job trajectory. "You'll need at least four more." She then went on to another topic that he didn't catch right away.

Shawn hit the emergency stop button. "Sorry, what did you just say?"

She put her hands on her hips and hit the start button, and the elevator continued its descent. "I said you'll be starting in three weeks. We're having a party to celebrate. Everything's set up."

He reached over and hit *stop* again. The car jerked and they staggered against opposite walls. "I'm going back to Georgia at the end of this week."

Helena laughed. "What on earth for? Everything you could possibly want is right here." Her voice softened. "Including me." She hit the start button and moved to stand in front of the panel so he couldn't reach it.

Soon he was sitting in a small human resources office across from Stuart, a fortyish man with stylishly cut blond hair, wearing a vestless suit with the jacket undone. "Helena's said so many good things about you," he said. "Tell me more about what you can bring to the Jupitelligence team."

Shawn stared past him. Before the elevator incident, he'd meant to at least try to make a good impression. He'd be able to tell his parents he'd done his best. It was nearly lunchtime, though, and he was tired of smiling, tired of talking about absolutely nothing with people who were much too impressed with themselves. "I'm not sure. Probably not much, in all honesty."

I'm so sorry, Mom.

"I guess I can teach everyone yoga—I've been certified since college. And I can probably do some minor repair work on the premises." He offered the fake, friendly expression he'd learned while growing up around bigwigs. "What exactly does this company do, anyway, aside from generate millions of dollars for its executives and shareholders?"

Stuart's face colored, but he swiftly recovered and straightened his posture. "Here." He slid Shawn a folder with a picture of the office building with the planet Jupiter on its roof, styled to resemble Superman's *Daily Planet.* "I think all your questions should be answered with this." He cleared his throat. "What we're here for today is to discuss your starting salary. The bosses are, um, impressed with your stellar credentials."

Shawn tapped his fingers on the arm of the chair. *I can pick up more jobs to at least pay my part of the rent to Tommy, if that's an option.*

A few days had passed since he'd seen a text from Pru or heard her voice. He wondered if he'd said something to upset her. Worse, what if something had happened to her? He should contact Edie—he still had her number. If not that, Joe would know. He'd also probably let him sleep on the couch for a month or two.

He relaxed his posture and lifted a hand in an "I don't care" gesture. "Twenty, twenty-five maybe?" If he was going to shoot himself in the foot, he might as well make sure the bullet went clean through his shiny, uncomfortable wingtips.

Stuart sat back and chuckled. "I think given who you are, we can offer you much more than $25,000 a year. That's far less than even our most junior positions."

Shawn held his gaze and kept his purposefully asinine smile steady. "No, you don't understand. I mean per hour, part-time. I have no business skills whatsoever. I have a BA in English with a focus in creative writing. I'm an E-RYT 200 teacher with Yoga Alliance. At least I was until I couldn't afford dues anymore. I usually make thirty or thirty-five dollars a class, but given how utterly incompetent I am in a corporate setting, as well as how uninterested I am in being here, I think twenty-five dollars per hour-long yoga class a few times a week would be more than generous on the company's dime, don't you?"

Stuart squirmed in his chair. "How about this? I'll just let you take that folder home and look it over. I think we can give you more than a typical entry-level salary, and I'm sure you'll move up the chain of command in no time."

He stood and held out his hand. Shawn stood as well. Even if Pru was angry with him about something, he'd still rather be broke and almost a thousand miles away from Helena than work up here pulling down whatever insane salary either Helena or her father were dictating. Without offering his hand in return, Shawn turned and left the folder behind as he walked out.

"How did it go, honey?" Helena asked once they were alone in her house.

"You'll have to ask them," Shawn said. He plopped onto the couch and rested his sweaty feet on top of the glass coffee table.

Helena sat next to him and frowned at them. He picked up the remote and started flipping through channels. She grabbed one of his feet, pulled off a sock, and started massaging it, but Shawn pulled it away from her.

Getting up, she stood in front of him, blocking his view of the television. "Shawn, why have you been acting like this? Did I do something that awful? I've gone out of my way to make you happy since you've been up here." She squinted her eyes shut and sniffled and tears formed when she looked at him again. "I just want for us to be happy. I'm doing everything I can for us."

Shawn angled around and turned off the TV. "Okay. Let's finally have this conversation."

She perched on a nearby ottoman, folded her hands in her lap, and waited.

"I'm not happy. For that matter, I'm not entirely sure you are. And honestly, I can't even be certain we ever were all that happy together. Look how many times we've broken up. This isn't working. It hasn't been for years."

He watched a few emotions flicker across Helena's face as he waited for her to reply. She blinked and her tears fell faster. "How can you say that? We have all this history. If I didn't want to be with you, I would let you go."

"You mean like hand me my walking papers? Relieve me of boyfriend duties? I've been trying to quit. Has my contract finally expired? Is that the best kind of language to frame things in for you?"

She shot up again. "That is not what I said." Her voice rose. "You're talking crazy. Your parents are going away. This will be your one home." Shawn watched as she seemed, chameleon-like, to transform herself into a gentler persona. "Our lives together will finally begin for real." The sudden switch to a plaintive tone was on-pitch, but there was something hardened and cold in her pale blue eyes. She reached out and grabbed his hand. "You won't sleep next to me. You won't even touch me. You're hurting me, Shawn, and you're biting the hand that feeds you."

He wrested his hand back, stood, and walked around to the back of the couch. "No, I'm not. We both know this isn't working out. I'm asking you to be an emotional adult for a change." He cringed at the way he worded it. "You're too smart to pretend you want something that you really don't."

Helena lowered her chin and fixed him with a stare. "Don't tell me what I want."

Shawn grabbed his backpack from underneath a side table. "Do you hear how ironic you sound right now?"

As he opened the zipper to head to the downstairs bathroom and shove his things into it, Helena got in front of the door and grabbed his face in her hands. She tugged him forward and kissed him, shoving her tongue against his lips.

"The fuck, Helena?"

"That's exactly what I want," she said. She was practically snarling.

He pushed her away and headed back into the living room. "I don't. What are you doing? How much clearer can I be about this?"

Her face went blank. Then she cleared her throat and the tears fell again. "Why are you trying to ruin everything we have, baby?"

Maybe it was because she added that last word, or maybe it was the accusation. He straightened, took a step forward, and looked down at her. "You're acting like an entitled know-it-all. Nothing about this relationship is genuine." His body was cold and hollow. "Those tears you turn on and off are as fake as your expensive tits." He didn't recognize the callous tone coming out of him. Maybe cruelty was all he had left for her at this point. Maybe he'd be horrified about his behavior five minutes from now.

Helena blinked twice, walked to the staircase, and lifted her chin. "You don't give a shit about anyone who cares about you. All you need to do is keep your mouth closed, smile, and do what you're told. You're the one who's acting holier-than-thou. When you're ready to get off your spiritual high horse, you'll know where to find me." She stomped up the stairs.

Shawn pulled his phone from his pocket and sat on the edge of the couch.

I miss you so much, he typed.

There was no response from Pru.

I'm so sorry. I'm going to make this up to you as soon as I get home."

He spent the next hour alternating between scrolling on his phone and obsessively checking his texts and email. No word. He scrunched his eyes shut, willing a message from her to pop up on his screen. He fell asleep sitting up, his hand over the phone in case he felt it vibrate.

Chapter Forty-Seven

Putting down her bow, Pru checked her phone again. Nearly three weeks had already passed, and Shawn hadn't returned any of her calls or texts over the past several days.

Can we talk? I'd love to hear your voice. Is everything okay?

She waited, halfheartedly beginning her piece again as she waited for his reply. None came. After a few minutes and more false starts, Pru put her things away, went to her couch, and flipped through the Maplewood Summer Orchestra Intensive paperwork. She hadn't accepted the invitation to the prestigious weeklong program yet, despite Uncle Barney's encouragement.

"I'm home. I'm doing better. Go. I want you to enjoy yourself," he kept telling her.

Another week went by. Tommy, Joe, and Edie started voicing concern over her mood and lack of appetite. "Have you heard from him at all?" she'd asked Joe the day before.

He hadn't. "Go to Maplewood," he advised. "If I hear from Shawn, you'll be the first to know." He didn't sound especially hopeful.

Shawn, I'm getting worried, she wrote. *Did I say something I shouldn't have?*

There was no reply.

Two days later, she texted again.

I'm thinking about a music intensive up North. It's a big deal to be invited, but if you're coming home soon, I'd rather be here with you. When will you be back?

A day later, she sent *I miss you so much.*

Later that day, *I love you.*

Three days later *Okay. I understand.*

Pru's hand shook when she hit send on that final text.

"I'm sorry, Pru." Andrew sounded angry. He had three sisters and had told Pru she was the fourth and he would protect her like he did them.

Tommy gently took the phone from her and let her sob on his shoulder. A few minutes later, she signed her electronic acceptance to Maplewood. Then she turned and squeezed Tommy and Andrew's hands. "He's not coming back, is he?"

"I don't know, sweetie," Andrew said. They sandwiched her in a hug. She let them sway her from side to side for a little while. With Matilda curled up underneath her feet, they watched Torchy Blaine movies until the New York Super Fudge Chunk was gone, and Pru had fallen asleep with her head in Andrew's lap and her legs on Tommy's. They stayed that way with her all night.

A week's worth of practicums, concerts, and even composing went by fast. Maplewood, which was up in Chappaqua, New York, was gorgeous. There was almost no humidity. The entire town, as well as the sprawling campus, was surrounded by mountains and deciduous woods full of fat chipmunks and jewel-toned wildflowers.

Pru smiled as she put away her cello after the last official performance of the season and started to walk toward the concession stands. Terry, a soprano violinist, jogged to catch up with her. "I'm so sad we all have to go back home," he said, smiling.

She grinned as they fell into step. Terry was tall, at least six feet, with a full, blond beard and a giant barrel of a torso. It had amused her to watch and listen as such delicate high notes danced and twirled around his fingers when he played.

"I bet your wife and kids are missing you, though," she said.

She pointed toward the falafel truck and they headed toward it. "I've loved getting this far away and just focusing on music," she added. It had also been nice to use a professional-quality loaner cello for the duration of the stay rather than pay extra to fly with her personal instrument. Even traveling had been stress-free. Uncle Barney and the others had been right—she'd needed this. She estimated it had been nearly two weeks since she'd heard from Shawn. Every time she remembered that, she focused harder on how much she loved being up here.

Terry straightened and waved at someone in the distance. "That's an old friend from high school," he said as a tall, pretty woman with dark red hair approached, waving back. When they drew closer he said, "Long time, no see. What are you doing here?"

"Terry, oh, my God, it's good to see you," the woman said. She was several inches taller than Pru, looking elegant in a light blue sundress and matching espadrille heels. She glanced at Pru, looked her up and down, and turned to Terry again. "Guess what, I'm engaged! I'm here because my mom's friend is on the Maplewood board. She's putting together a trio for the engagement party."

"Congratulations," Terry said and leaned in to kiss her cheek. She air-kissed him back. "When did this happen?"

"Not long ago," she said. "I'm so excited he's ready to settle down, finally."

"Congratulations," Pru said.

"Who's the lucky guy?" Terry asked.

The woman winked. "You know exactly who."

Terry grinned. "About time." He turned to Pru. "This poor woman has been trying to pin her boyfriend down for literally years." His eyes widened. "Oh, sorry. Pru, this is my old friend—"

"Prudence Blum, we need you," someone called.

"I've got to go. Congratulations again," Pru said to Terry's friend. She turned to Terry. "See you on Sunday at the private party." He gave her a thumbs-up and waved as she left.

The renovated mansion was easily the largest home Pru had ever been inside. She'd been in plenty of plantation houses before, but never one that was actually used as a private residence rather than an event venue. There weren't any plantations in the North. But still, she'd never met a small family or single couple who lived in any kind of antique mansion before. Several families likely could live here and rarely see one another. She blinked and glanced around as she tried to make sense of her surroundings.

Out front, valet drivers in black uniforms drove wave after wave of English, Italian, and German cars offsite. A woman in a beige suit and wearing a headset walked Pru, Terry, and Elana, a violist, past the sparkling lights along the flagstone walkway. They passed the unnaturally green, expansive front lawn with a few small groupings of Adirondack chairs and a couple of croquet sets, inside through a black-and-white, art-deco tiled foyer full of people in suits and cocktail dresses, and out to the backyard. She saw round, white-linen-covered tables with floral arrangements and a small stage set up with a microphone. Behind the speakers' area were the instruments, chairs, and music stands where the trio would be playing.

Pru's plane would take off this evening. An already packed, prepaid Uber was going to be ready to take her straight from here to LaGuardia when she texted for it. Better still, since the trio was on a stage with a back entrance, she'd have no reason to have to mingle with the stuck-up crowd gathered here. She supposed those kinds of people didn't change regardless of where in the country they lived.

Pru smoothed her simple beige sheath dress as Candace and her husband Doug, the hosts, strode onto the stage. Candace's red hair was tied back in a fancy updo, and she wore a silver-and-white cocktail dress. She held herself tall, a picture of grace and elegance. Everyone grew quiet. "We are so grateful for all of our closest friends and family to join us for our anniversary party," Candace said into the microphone. "Doug and I welcome you and would like to propose a toast not just to us, and not just to our close, wonderful friends, but to our daughter's fiancé, the newest member of Jupitelligence—and even more importantly, of our happy family."

Pru focused on not rolling her eyes as she watched what had to be well over a hundred "closest friends" applaud. Candace and Doug turned and beckoned two more people onto the stage.

"We present to you our beautiful daughter Helena, and her fiancé, Shawn."

The red-haired woman Pru had seen at Maplewood a couple of days ago stepped out in an emerald-green, form-fitting dress and white stilettos. Pru didn't hear anything else that was said. Following Helena, sober-faced and dressed in a pair of jeans, an Oxford shirt, and a tan blazer, was Shawn. Pru stood, dropping her bow and knocking over all three music stands. Everyone onstage startled and spun around to stare.

"Pru." Shawn's mouth hung open.

She couldn't move for what felt like minutes as they stared wide-eyed at each other. Bile seared up her esophagus. She clenched her stomach, turned around, and hurried away, stopping herself from breaking into a run. The edge of the stage disappeared without warning. She was airborne, then landed on her ankle. Pulling off her shoes, she threw them in the bushes and half ran, half limped across the property toward the driveway. When she could support herself on a fancy lamppost, she texted for her car. It was only at that point that her heart and her ankle practically exploded with fiery pain.

CHAPTER FORTY-EIGHT

Shawn froze. "What is going on here?"

One minute he'd been standing in the stage wings, unclear about what he was supposed to be doing, and standing by Helena in stony silence. Then someone shoved him toward the stage as Helena dragged him behind her. Candace and Doug said a few more things, Pru was there for about ten seconds, and the next thing he knew, his own parents were standing by him. His mother's eyes were bright with tears and she was beaming at him.

"What are you thinking being dressed like that?" his father had hissed. "This is an important event. You need to step up." Before Shawn could reply, his mother urged him forward.

"Sorry about that. Our cellist had an emergency." Candace smiled at the audience. "We're so proud to be here on such a beautiful day for a beautiful reason." She stood aside as Helena tugged Shawn front and center. "And now, Shawn Levinson has something to say to our daughter."

Helena also smiled and waved at the audience, then held her hand out to Shawn. He blinked. "Why are you wearing my grandmother's engagement ring?"

Some nervous laughter rose from the audience.

Helena leaned in and whispered, "We got it resized ahead of time. I said I'd take care of everything. You don't have to do anything but get on your knee and pop the question."

Shawn tightened and released his fists a few times then spoke into the microphone. "I guess I know what everyone's here to see me do." He didn't bother faking happiness or even politeness.

There was light laughter and applause from the audience.

He adjusted the microphone stand so that people would still hear him and turned to Helena. "Helena, this ring is now yours. You can keep it or give it back to my parents. You can sell it on eBay. You can even flush it down the toilet if you want."

The entire yard was silent, except for the low gasps he heard from the others onstage with him.

"Do whatever you want. I'm not proposing. I never wanted or intended to propose at any point in time. I came up North to break things off definitively, but you ambushed me. I don't want to work at your company. I don't want you and you have refused to hear me." Bracing himself for a pang of guilt, he looked at his parents, who had gone white. "No one's been listening."

His mother's chin was shaking, and she clutched her husband's arm.

Shawn looked away from them. "So, feel free to plan a wedding. Plan a honeymoon, even—knock yourselves out, everyone. But kindly quit planning my life as if it isn't mine to live."

Helena and her parents stood still. Her mouth opened and shut a few times and then she chuckled. "His sense of humor, right?" she said into the microphone.

Uncomfortable murmurings and chuckles sounded from below.

Shawn turned to leave the stage. As he passed his parents, he saw his father's darkening face and tears in his mother's eyes. "Your house is done," he told them. "You can go down anytime. Sell my shit in the old place. I don't want it, and money's the most important thing anyway, right?"

He went down the stairs and looked around to see if he could spot Pru. She was half-running, half-limping toward the end of the driveway. He ran to catch up.

"Pru, wait."

She ignored him, stopping when she could support her weight on a filigreed lamppost while she fumbled for her phone.

"Pru, please. I need to explain."

The handful of people sitting on the front lawn all looked at them.

She whipped her head around. "I don't think you do," she said. Her face was red.

"You're hurt. At least sit and I can look at your ankle."

She straightened and winced. "Don't touch me. Go back to your engagement party. Just . . . just go. My ride will be here any minute. Then I'll never make an inconvenient appearance in front of your friends or family again."

"Pru—"

"Twice, Shawn. I trusted you *twice*. The first time was before I knew about your girlfriend, and this time . . ." Her body quaked as she took a breath. "I gave you every last part of me there was to give. And when I thought I'd given it all, I found more for you anyway."

"You don't understand." Shawn's chin was shaking, and his sentence came out almost as a sob.

"I do understand." Her voice rose. "Did I simply not measure up to your . . . your Barbie doll back there? You used me. Maybe you meant what you said to me at the time, but how long did it take for you to choose the upgrade? When did you decide to stay up here? You didn't even have the decency to return my messages and tell me."

Shawn's arms hung at his sides. "What are you talking about?" How was he not getting her calls or texts? "Please, Pru. Let me—"

Tears began to slide from the corners of her eyes.

He took a step forward. "It's not what you think."

A gold, older-model Kia pulled up and Pru hopped over. The driver, a middle-aged Asian man, came out and helped her get settled. They drove off, leaving Shawn standing in an exhaust cloud. He buried his face in his hands, then felt around for his keys, which included ones to Helena's car and house. He remembered they were in his backpack.

Screw it.

Helena had left hers with the valet. He'd use those to go get his stuff and leave town somehow, even if it meant asking Joe for a loan.

As he started to walk across the front lawn full of guests, many of whom had their phones out by now, toward the kiosk, Helena ran to catch up with him. "Shawn, wait."

He picked up his pace.

"Shawn, you can't just ignore me after embarrassing everyone like that."

He stopped. "Yes, I can walk away. And I'm pretty sure I'm not responsible for what any of you feel at this point." He started walking again.

"Shawn." Helena caught up and grabbed his shoulder. Turning, he lifted his hand and peeled her fingers off of him. "Your mother is sobbing in front of all those people."

"I'm sorry to hear that. Hopefully, she'll forgive me someday. I need to go after Pru."

Helena tossed her head back and laughed. "You can't be serious. She's ridiculous looking — like a college-aged Marilyn Monroe with bad hair and a stupid accent. She's probably never set foot in a real corporation or black-tie event in her life, save to provide the entertainment. She has nothing to offer you." She folded her arms. "I did you a huge favor — again — by blocking her number on your phone." Her smile reminded him of what a crocodile might look like if it could make its eyes narrow and look down its snout. "It's a good thing you haven't changed your password in three years. I changed her phone number in your contacts list by a digit so she wouldn't get the wrong idea if you tried to talk to her. You're free of her now." She put a hand on her hip. "Nothing's changed. We can go back and fix this right now." She reached for his hand.

"You what?" His head and chest were about to incinerate. "Here, I'll do you a favor too," he shouted. Shawn grasped her hand, yanked the ring off her finger, and threw it across the lawn and toward a row of large hydrangea bushes. It missed and bounced along the street. "Are we finally crystal clear?"

Helena turned bright red, lifted her hand, and moved to slap him.

He ducked out of the way. "Go back to your celebration. Or whatever the fuck is going on back there. Do your precious damage control."

He stormed past the shocked, now more extensive murmuring crowd who had gathered to watch the drama. The short walk from the lawn was a blur. Shawn started when a hand landed on his shoulder.

"Okay then." His father's voice was quiet but firm.

He stopped walking. "Dad, I don't want to hear it." He didn't shout, but he also didn't bother keeping the fury from his voice.

His father's shoulders rounded. "I know. I gathered that much." There was a note of contrition in his tone this time. They started walking toward the valets. "I hired an Uber for you." Dad took a wheezy breath. "Can you get into Helena's house?"

Shawn slowed his pace, and his father's breathing slowed. He was getting old. All of this was about making sure his and Mom's only child wouldn't be without a safety net once they were gone. "I have the keypad code," Shawn said.

Patting Shawn's back, his father said, "Good. You can go and get your stuff, then go home and take whatever stuff of yours you want. There should be a one-way Amtrak ticket in your email."

Shawn stared at him. "And that's that, then? Is it goodbye after this?"

"I don't know, son." His father put his hands in his pockets. "You've chosen your path in life. I don't like it, but you've made it clear that it's your life to live and you're right. I'll say the same thing now that I said when you were in college. Your mother and I love you. Do whatever you're going to do, but I'm not supporting it." He folded a few bills into Shawn's hand and walked away.

Just for a moment, Shawn remembered that untethered feeling when his parents had finished helping him unpack his freshman dorm in college and kissed him goodbye. It had been like standing on a rope bridge, where everything around him expanded to three times its size. There was a long drop below and nothing to catch him.

A green Accord pulled up and beeped.

Shawn pocketed the cash and headed toward his ride.

CHAPTER FORTY-NINE

"Motherfucker." Joe placed Pru's suitcase on the floor by her couch. He followed her into her kitchen, sat, and took a sip of his airport coffee while Pru filled the electric kettle and flipped the on switch. There was always something vaguely comforting about friends with similar Southern accents. Joe's accent was the most pronounced. "I know Shawn pretty well. This is some fucked-up shit, even for him." He furrowed his brow. "I'd ask how you were holding up, but that's pretty obvious."

Pru got up from the table and took out a mug for her tea. When she lifted the kettle and found it was still cold, she sighed and plugged it in. "I think I'm just numb."

Joe's phone buzzed. "Edie wants to know how many pints."

She managed to turn up the corners of her mouth, but that was more for show than anything she felt. She wasn't feeling much of anything beyond empty heaviness. "I don't think I can eat. Even the thought makes me queasy."

He typed in his reply, then spoke to her again. "You've got to eat. Have you had anything today?" He looked at another incoming text. His face clouded. "Shit."

Pru tested the water again and poured it over her teabag, then went to the table and sat. "I don't know." She thought about it. "I tried to eat some of the crackers they served on the flight."

He stared at his phone, cursed again, and ran his hand through his hair.

"What?"

Joe pursed his lips. "Maybe you should hang out at Andrew's place for a few days. Or maybe Edie can take you. I would, but I had a friend over last night, and the place still smells like rum and sex."

Pru looked up from her tea. "I haven't unpacked yet, so I guess I could ask. Why?"

"Shawn's taking a train back down. He'll get here in a couple of days. He asked how you were doing and if I could get you to hear him out."

"No." She stood and leaned against the refrigerator. "What could he possibly say to me?" Her voice cracked. "He didn't even have the courage to break up with me. Instead, he humiliated me in front of over a hundred strangers and a couple of colleagues." She pulled her braid over her shoulder and tugged it hard. "If he comes by, I have no idea whether I'll scream at him or fall apart."

From around the corner, Tommy opened the door. Pru waved as Matilda greeted him. He was frowning. "First things first. Come over here." She stepped into his arms and he rubbed her back. "We will get you through this."

"I am so done with him," she said as she hugged him, then pulled away. "What's the second thing?"

He let go of her. "I have no idea whether he's tracking your phone's GPS or stalking you old-school style, but I just saw Cliff's car turn down the street."

Joe stood and walked into the living room. "Let's go sit outside and wait for him." He pointed at Pru as she followed him. "You stay inside and close the window shade."

She did a quick body scan. She wasn't shaking *that* much and her eyes were dry. In fact, all she felt was hollow — like the insides of her head and torso had been burned away and reduced to ashes. "This isn't a Hatfield and McCoy showdown. *I* will deal with him." She pushed past both men, walked outside, and waited by the carport.

Cliff's powder-blue Lexus pulled behind her and Tommy's cars. He got out carrying a bouquet of pink roses. "Welcome home, babe." Pru imagined yanking the head off a life-sized Ken doll and skewering the body over an open flame. "I'm going to take you out, and you can tell me all about Maplewood."

When he got closer, Pru said, "Cliff, leave. Do not come here again." Her voice was monotone. "If you see me in public, don't look at me. When orchestral season starts up again, don't try to talk to me unless Sandy or Martin explicitly tells you to."

Cliff was still smiling, but his gaze hardened and he closed his fist around the stems. Pru smirked when he winced from the thorns.

The man stepped closer and lowered his voice. "You've had your little summer fun slumming it with that northerner. I forgive you. It's time to admit you need me." He reached around, flattened his hand between her shoulder blades and mid-back, and pushed her close to his chest.

Pru moved to knee him between the legs, but he swiveled and she missed. He walked her backward until she was pinned against Tommy's car.

Face darkening, he spun her around and pushed her cheek against the car with one hand while he pinned her arm behind her back and kneed her legs apart. "Be nice." His voice was a commanding growl. "I think we should grab some lunch and talk about this like adults."

The trembling began through Pru's torso. It originated somewhere deep in her belly and, almost in slow motion, expanded through her chest. Her stomach shook, then her shoulders. Tears bourgeoned. She shut her eyes as laughter burst through her. She could barely catch her breath. It took a few tries for her to say, in between gasps, "You're such an idiot. Let me go."

Behind them, the screen door opened and shut. A few feet in the other direction, Edie's red Prius slowed to park on the curb in front of Joe's Jeep. She jumped out, pulled off her heels, and held up her phone as she started to hurry toward them.

"I'm starting to lose my patience, Prudence." Cliff's voice echoed off the carport roof. "I don't want to end up sending you to the hospital again because you made me lose my temper."

"Get off of her, Cliff," Joe shouted.

Distracted, Cliff loosened the pressure on Pru's arm just enough for her to push off from the car and bump him back a couple of inches. She jabbed her elbow into his solar plexus with her free arm. He grunted in surprise as he let go of her. She squeezed between his body and the car and took a few steps away.

"Cliff, I am going to pull off your balls and impale them on the fence if you lay a hand on her again," Tommy yelled.

Pru took another step back, widened her stance, and put her hands on her hips. Her head and elbow ached from where Cliff had put pressure on them. He glowered and opened his mouth to speak.

"Not another word," Pru said. She was surprised at the low menace of her own voice, especially as the adrenaline rush ebbed. "A lawyer and two witnesses just saw you assault me and threaten me, and I guarantee that at least one of them got most of it on video." Her bravado and energy seemed to drain through her feet and into the ground, leaving her head woozy, her arms numb, and her legs wobbly.

Catching up and waving her phone around, Edie offered the smile Pru had seen Edie practice in the mirror for court. Her eyes narrowed a tiny bit. Her mouth began in a closed-lipped smile but gradually spread into a grin that Pru liked to compare to a ravenous lion baring its teeth. This was her "gotcha" face.

"I didn't get your good side," Edie said to Cliff.

"Anything you say is going to make your life a lot worse if I press charges," Pru continued, shocked at how calm her voice still was. "I don't even want to hear you try to apologize."

Cliff stood still. "It's just that I love you so much—"

"Shut up." Pru took a step closer. "Here's what's going to happen next. You are going to leave. Edie and I are going to discuss what the consequences of today should be. If you ever try to come near me again, I will send that footage to Martin. When our conductor brings it to the board of trustees, we'll see if you keep playing for the Lower Georgia Symphonic or anywhere else in the state."

Edie stood a few feet from Pru. "Prudence Blum, I am beyond impressed." She brightened. "I've already got a few other consequences in mind." She turned to Cliff. "Let's see how easily you can buy your way out of criminal charges now."

Before Cliff could respond, Tommy called out to Pru. He and Joe jogged over. She snapped her head in the men's direction. "I've got this, guys," Pru said, although she wasn't sure for how much longer.

"Pru." Tommy extended his hand. "You left your phone. You need to take this call," he said, softening his voice.

Edie looked from the two men to Pru and Cliff. "Leave. *Now.*" She pointed at Cliff's car.

Tommy and Joe flanked Pru as she took her phone. "Hello?"

"Ms. Blum, this is Lucille Patterson. I'm Barney Abramson's attending oncologist. We've met a couple of times."

Pru took a short breath and swayed. Tommy grabbed her waist to keep her from stumbling. "Hello, Dr. Patterson. Is my uncle okay?"

There was a pause. "Barney was admitted to the ICU two nights ago. He's being sent into hospice care today per his arrangements. You need to come down here right away."

Pru's joints loosened the rest of the way. The phone slid from her hand, and Tommy caught it. "Dr. Patterson? Hi, it's Thomas Holt again."

The rest was so much noise. An assortment of voices. Tommy on the phone, Edie and Cliff bickering, and Joe murmuring reassurances, hugging her as they sat on the grass. Pru didn't remember sitting. She heard her own voice making some sort of noise but she couldn't quite feel her body. Tommy squatted in front of them and looked up at Edie. "Edie, you're not blocked in by Captain Asshat. Can you afford to leave today and take some time to drive Pru down to Florida and help her out? If you need to get back, I'll drive down and switch places with you for as long as I can."

"I can take—" Cliff began.

Joe carefully transferred Pru to lean on Tommy then stood. "Cliff, so help me God, if you do not get off this property by the time I count backward from ten, we'll call the police for trespassing to add to your rapidly growing list of legal problems."

Edie was on her phone talking to someone. Cliff's car engine started. Joe and Tommy disappeared and returned with Pru's purse and still-packed case, Matilda on her leash, and a bag of dog food tucked under Tommy's arm.

Almost five hours later it was dark, and Pru was staring out the window of Edie's car as they crossed the Alabama state line into Florida.

CHAPTER FIFTY

Pru stood on the narrow porch of her uncle's house and watched the breeze sweep sand across the raised wooden walkway that led to the beach. Scraggly dune grass jutted in tall clumps around the exposed roots of half-dead palm trees. Brown, dried seaweed and shell shards from various mollusks littered the shoreline. The sun glinted off the waves of the Gulf, making the water sparkle.

She reached up and touched the faded wind chimes she'd made when she was ten. That had been a summer camp project with driftwood, green and brown beach glass, and some now very frail and chipped mussel shells. A few pieces of shell crumbled to the floor as they silently hit each other.

The front door squeaked open and the daytime nurse wheeled Barney outside. "Those are almost as old as the house." Barney looked toward Pru and the chimes.

She turned toward him. Her uncle's blue eyes looked almost as bleached white as the sand. "We'll be okay, Walter." Barney reached around to pat the nurse's hand. Walter, who had calloused, light-brown knuckles and hooded, dark green eyes that looked extremely tired, turned to Pru.

"It's fine. I'll keep an eye on him," Pru said. Walter braked the chair, nodded, and headed inside. "I remember you and Grandma helping me hang them up when you moved in here." She rested her hand on the deck railing and brushed some sand away.

Barney gestured at the chimes. "The shells were all painted pink and orange, your favorite colors."

262

Pru laughed. "It was so ugly. I don't know why you kept them up here all this time."

"You'll get splinters doing that. Take your hand off the wood and get Walter to sand that down for you," her uncle said.

Pru stepped back and pulled over a partially rusted, once-green metal chair. "That's not part of his job. His job is to take care of you. And I'll be fine."

Barney smiled. "I kept the chimes up because they belonged there. That way you always knew this was your house too, and you could come whenever you needed. You should take it with you when you go. It'll remind you that you belong wherever you want to belong."

"I was here all the time as a kid because of the beach, and because you made me egg creams." She put her hands on the back of the chair and leaned her weight in. "You said I was too skinny." She gestured over herself. "Not a problem anymore."

Barney started to laugh then turned red. He began to wheeze as he coughed. Pru hurried over and handed him the glass of water Walter had left for him. She held it up while he drank until he pushed her hand away. His hands were as gnarled and blue as the scars on her side — the ones he'd never found out about and never would. The difference was that his skin was thin and mottled and his finger joints were misshapen from arthritis. "My little baby niece. You're still skinny. You're just grown up now. I'm proud of who you turned out to be. Esther and your parents would've been too."

Pru took a few steps and put the glass on a recently painted white table under the front window. She sniffled and turned to compose herself for a few moments.

"Prudence Amelia, turn around." She turned. When she was younger, Barney seemed so much larger than life. He'd been five-foot-seven at his full height, but whether casually or professionally, he'd commanded any room he entered. "You've been standing there too long to find just the right spot for that water. Come sit with me."

She hurried over and adjusted the blanket that Walter had draped over him. "Are you cold? Do you want to go inside?"

He waved toward Pru's seat. "Sit." She circled around, pulled in her chair, and sat. "I have things to talk to you about. Tell me, are you happy?"

Pru widened her eyes. "Of course I am, but I'm worried about you."

Barney patted her hand. "Me, you shouldn't worry about. We both know how it ends from here." Pru shook her head and bit her lip. "You don't look happy. You haven't sounded at all happy lately, darling. Tell me what's happening."

She looked ahead at the grasses shifting in the light wind. "Nothing's happening. I'm good."

Barney tapped her hand, hard. "You were always terrible at lying. Tell me." She looked at him. "Whatever you have to say, I'll take it to the grave." He winked and Pru shuddered.

They sat in silence for a while, listening to the tide roll in and out. "Something happened, I can tell," he finally added. "You couldn't even hide that party you had here when I left you alone for a weekend business trip when you were in high school. I found red cups and liquor bottles all over the sand and under the porch when I came home."

Pru laughed and they were quiet again for a while.

"Okay, fine," he said, breaking the silence again. "I'll tell you some secrets if you tell me some."

Her eyes widened. "You have secrets?"

He grinned. "Sure. That business trip when you had your party? That ended Friday. I was with a lady friend the rest of the time."

Pru did a double take. "What?" She wasn't sure whether shock or amusement were in her voice.

"You think I lived like a monk after you came to stay? I must've been about sixty-five. I was a young man." He grinned. "I know that isn't young to you. One day you'll get to be even older than I am and you'll think back to your youthful seventies." He cleared his throat and pointed. Pru rose again, retrieved his water, and helped him take a few more sips.

"What about you? You have someone in your life?"

Pru swallowed hard and scrunched her eyes shut. Pretending sand had gotten into them, she rubbed them.

"Look at me, little girlie." He used to call her that when she was much younger — before her parents and brother had died. She shifted to face him. "You deserve to be happy. You deserve for someone to love you, and it's *not* that fella from the orchestra."

Her hand rose to her shirt, along her waist, without her thinking about it.

"He was no good. I heard it in your voice every time you talked about him. Is he out of the picture now?"

Pru nodded. "Yeah. For good."

Her uncle leaned closer. "You're not wearing Esther's chain."

She looked down. "It came undone while I was caught in a thunderstorm. I lost it. I'm sorry."

A wave from him dismissed that. "She would tell you it was just a thing. She's not in there."

Pru knew he was right. Esther wasn't especially sentimental. Still, aside from the cello and photographs, she didn't have much tangible to remember her grandmother by. She fought back some tears.

Barney touched her hand. "Prudence, I want you to hear a story."

"Okay."

"I let your Aunt Becca down because I spent more time

working than I did with her. She wanted kids. I wasn't ready. She wanted to travel together. I was too busy. She wanted me to be around more. I couldn't even make it home in time for dinner most nights. We were married for ten years and she divorced me because she was so lonely."

Pru leaned in. She hadn't heard much about her aunt before.

"You know why I was gone all the time? I was never unfaithful to her, but I didn't think I'd be good enough if I couldn't prove myself in the world. I had it backward. There was never anything to prove, not even to myself." His voice was like soft footfalls over a rocky dirt road. "Sweetheart, love is what's most important. Promise me you'll remember that. Don't let people push you around, but don't deny yourself a chance at happiness when it's there for the taking. Can you make me that promise?"

She stood, walked across the deck, and leaned on the railing to face him. His hair was thin and white. "You spent too much of your life taking care of me instead of loving someone." She took a shuddery breath and wiped away a tear.

"No, honey." His gaze was steady. "I spent my life loving you more than anything, even before you moved in. But you of all people know what it's like to miss someone and feel all alone. Don't let me be the last person to make you the center of their whole world. That's all I'm asking."

Pru rushed over and knelt at his lap. She put her hands on his frail thighs, which used to be so strong and stocky, and looked up at him. He ruffled her hair and said, "Okay, hon. I think I need to go take a nap."

Standing, she leaned over and hugged him. He kissed her cheek. Then she opened the door to call for Walter.

Barney's bed was set up in the living room. That night, Pru slept on the couch just a few feet away and watched his chest rise and fall until she fell asleep.

When she woke in the morning, Pru got up and leaned over him. "Uncle Barney," she whispered. "It's nearly seven. It's just about time for your pills." She touched his hand. It was cold.

No.

Pru dropped into a bridge chair next to his bed. She shook him. "You need to wake up now." Her voice raised nearly to a shout.

Walter rushed in, brow furrowed, and put his fingers to Barney's neck. He shook his head. "I'm sorry, Miss."

Matilda walked over to "hug" her. "Wake up, Uncle Barney." Her voice was a quiet squeak. Then she dropped her head on his chest and began to cry.

CHAPTER FIFTY-ONE

Shawn almost thought he was in the wrong neighborhood as he turned onto Pru and Tommy's street. From the time he'd returned to Georgia at the beginning of August, he'd spent every morning sitting on the front steps, closing his eyes, and inhaling the strong, cloying scent of wisteria. He would pretend Pru was just inside, about to come join him.

Now, at the end of September, the single-story homes had the same faded blue, yellow-, white-, or brown-painted brick, but they were separated by bare chain link fences.

He pulled in alongside Tommy's car, went to the porch, and sat on the duplex's concrete steps. They were still wet from last night's downpour. He shielded his eyes with his hand and looked across the street at squirrels running up and down a pine tree. At eight in the morning, the sun was already too bright. Its light bounced as it reflected off the small rain-filled potholes in the road. He wiped his brow with the back of his wrist, picked up his paper coffee cup, and set it down without drinking.

When Tommy's door opened and shut, he twisted around. Tommy was in a pair of faded green shorts and had a blue bandanna tied over his hair. He leaned between the duplex's doors, holding a white mug with musical notes on it. "Pru just got her uncle's ashes yesterday. She's going to scatter them on the beach and should be back not long after that. She needs to go to the closing on Barney's house."

"Don't suppose I can help her down there?" He suspended his breath and released it.

"Nice try. Joe and I are still under strict orders from Edie, and she terrifies us more than you do."

Shawn shifted a few inches to stay in the shade. "At least Cliff's not gonna bother her."

Tommy chuckled. "Good riddance. I heard he's moving out to California, where he can be someone else's problem." They silently stared ahead for a while. "What about you?" Tommy asked.

Shawn picked up his cup and stood to lean against the railing, facing him. "Are you asking how long I'm going to be her problem?" He'd thought about that. Pru had gotten a new phone with a new provider, and no one would give the number to him, nor would they send her links to the multiple YouTube videos of the blowup guests uploaded from the surprise engagement party. All the emails he sent had bounced back. "I want to at least explain what happened."

Tommy took a few sips. "Edie's been in mama bear mode, and I don't think Pru's ready to hear from you. She's just starting to snap out of her depression and act like herself again. She'll come back eventually."

"And then?"

He shrugged one shoulder. "I don't have a crystal ball."

Shawn scrunched his eyes shut and tensed. "I'm not that other guy, I swear."

Tommy pushed off the wall and leaned on the railing next to Shawn. They faced the street. "No, you're not. I believe you love her. Otherwise I wouldn't let you hang out in front of the house like a sad puppy." He looked at his watch. "I've gotta get ready for a day of parent conferences." He took a few steps and opened his door. "But my advice is to stop doing this."

"Okay." Shawn started heading for the steps. "I'll quit bothering you. Sorry about that."

The other man's voice softened. "What I mean is you can't wish her back here. You're doing all the right things. You've got a decent apartment and a steady income, and you're giving Pru space. Maybe make up with your parents if you can."

Shawn cleared his throat. "I don't see that happening. Between the scene and the replays on the Internet, they're still apoplectic."

"I'll tell you what. I'll try to convince Edie to text Pru the video links."

Shawn turned again and shook Tommy's hand. "That would be awesome. Thanks so much."

He opened the door. "Give yourself and her more time to heal."

"Tommy?"

Tommy turned around.

"What happened to the wisteria?"

He dropped his shoulders. "The city got someone in to remove all of it since it was choking out too many trees. It's too bad — it made the air smell like something other than melting rubber when it got hot out. They burned all of it down to the roots." He went inside.

A lump rose in Shawn's throat. He leaned over the railing for a few more minutes. He took a few deep breaths, hoping to catch the ghost of the flowers' scent, but there was nothing. Then he got into his car and drove away.

Chapter Fifty-Two

Sliding off his sandals as he walked into the front studio room of Harmony Yoga, Shawn squinted against the bright sunlight through the storefront window and lowered the blinds. Will, the owner, liked them to stay open. But even in the air conditioning, it was too hot for comfort.

Walking over to the thermostat, he lowered it. The class before the one he was about to teach had been hot yoga, so the temperature was almost as unbearable in here as it was outside. Posters of Ganesha and Shiva curled at the edges on the robin's-egg-blue wall opposite the window.

He unrolled his mat at the front of the room and closed his eyes, enjoying the quiet. The door opened and he heard footsteps. Shawn opened his eyes.

"It's cold in here." The newcomer was Julie, another teacher who was working at the desk. She raised the thermostat, then walked across the room to turn on the New Age music.

"Change the temperature back and don't turn on the music." Shawn forced himself to stay relaxed and leaned back on his hands. "Most of the students who take standard yoga classes can't stand the heat and neither can I." He kept his opinion of hot yoga and other, trendier practices to himself. He wanted to keep his job as head teacher.

Julie faced him. "It can't be all the way down to seventy-five. Your students will freeze. They won't be able to do their asanas safely."

Almost all of the women teachers he'd met were painfully

271

thin, with sharp features and airy "the universe wants to support me" vibes. The women who packed their classes looked similar, and the men wore tanks that showed off their tanned abs and lean biceps. Hot yoga was essentially a dating meet and greet.

Julie turned to go. "Seventy-five," Shawn said.

She rolled her eyes and adjusted the temperature. "Remember, turn on the music fifteen minutes ahead of class," she reminded him before she closed the door. He reached around to turn on the ambient music as low as he thought he could get away with. Will liked for the teachers to play it as part of the "atmosphere," but Shawn preferred quiet.

His students—primarily middle-aged and older women, but also a few younger people—filed in and set up their mats by the blocks and straps he'd laid out for them.

Most of the students, at least the more mature ones, quietly greeted one another as they situated themselves. A few of the younger adults, however, immediately began to twist themselves into advanced balances or inversions. As usual, most of the young women were fully made up and wore spandex pants with sports bras. Even the guys looked like a Lululemon store threw up on them.

Shawn smoothed out his plain T-shirt and shorts and smiled. "Welcome. For those of you who are new to class, my name is Shawn Levinson. Thanks for joining me today. Let's warm up with some sun salutations."

Shawn touched his palms together, lifted them to the sky, and arched back as he began to lead the class through the first set. "By all means, find your own pace and modifications that meet you where you are today." Some of the students started to slow down while a few tried different variations of Cobra or Upward Facing Dog. The show-offs in the back began to add full backbends and arm balances into the routine.

Shawn walked around the room. A woman with curly

steel-gray hair who had been coming to class every day winced as she held Downward Facing Dog. Shawn knelt in front of her and pressed his hands over hers. "Try lifting through your tailbone." She did as he suggested, and Shawn stood. She exhaled and smiled up at him.

He made his way around the room, assisting people, until he got to the younger group. "I'd like you to stay clear of those deeper poses," he said. A couple of them rolled up their mats and wove around the other students to leave. The other three resumed the basic sequence. Shawn gave them a thumbs-up. "Thanks, guys. I appreciate it."

He made his way back to the front. They moved into their standing poses and balances. "The whole point is to pause in each pose," he said. "Notice where you feel sensation, and let it happen without judging it."

He led the class through savasana, and the worry lines on all thirty students' faces smoothed. Their arms splayed palms up and their feet flopped. A couple of people were snoring. Sitting on the mat, Shawn couldn't remember the last time he'd slept peacefully instead of lying awake, excoriating himself.

Physician, heal thyself.

After everyone had left and he'd cleaned up, Shawn put his hand on the doorknob and glanced at the clock above the front desk. Maybe he'd pick up some Thai takeout before heading home. He grabbed his keys and headed for the front of the building. The lobby had a wall full of mostly superfluous stuff for sale—crystals, dubious dietary supplements, little figurines of various Hindu deities, and books about everything from fasting cleanses to the *Bhagavad Gita*. He remembered Krishna's argument to Arjuna about taking action when warranted. It was time.

Shawn looked up from the year-old *People Magazine* he'd been flipping through in the reception area of Donaldson, Waters, Maxwell, and Edison, Attorneys at Law. As Edie rounded the corner, the receptionist, a thirty-something woman whose dark brown hair was cut in a severe bob, said, "Your three o'clock is here."

Edie locked eyes with him, stopped in her tracks, and frowned. She folded her arms. "Really? There are lawyers all over town you can use. Go home."

Shawn picked up his file folder and stood. "I need to talk to you and this was the best way I could think of. Just five minutes."

The receptionist adjusted her round wire glasses and looked from one to the other. "Is there a problem?"

Edie exaggerated a sigh. "No. Right this way, Mr. Levinson." She led him down a hallway of offices and opened a door. "After you." They were in a plain meeting room with a large table and swivel-back chairs. They sat across from each other. "My time is valuable." There was a warning edge to her tone.

Shawn opened the folder and pushed it toward Edie. "I spent the last week combing through Panama City obituaries and cross-referencing them with address searches. There are eight possible houses where Pru's uncle lived. I'm heading down there tomorrow and plan to knock on the doors of every single one of them until I find Pru. If that doesn't work, I'll go to City Hall and figure out where she is. I was hoping to just cut to the chase and you could tell me where to go."

Edie smirked. "Oh, I would love to tell you where to go."

"I know," Shawn said. "Please."

She grabbed a legal pad and scribbled something down. "He's unlisted, but I admire your resolve."

Shawn reached for the paper, and she flattened her hand over it. "You have no idea how angry I am at you for hurting her over and over. If I give this to you, you need to promise to make it up to her with interest. If I hear you do anything other than that, I will make your life hell."

Shawn leaned in with his forearms on the table. "I love her, Edie."

She relaxed her posture and slid the address to him. "Go then. Go make her happy."

Chapter Fifty-Three

Pru planned to have a meltdown later in the day.

She sat in a folding chair at a card table in her uncle's kitchen and opened her laptop. This table and chair, and the full-sized bed in what had been her bedroom, were all the furniture left in the house. The kitchen was stark and blank with cream-colored walls, light blue cabinets, and clay Mexican tile. The rest of the place had the same flooring and color scheme except for her old bedroom, which she'd painted sage green when she moved in as a teenager. It was the end of September. In two days, she'd be home. She wondered how much longer she could stretch out her bereavement leave without the LGSO firing her.

When she pulled up her email, her eyes widened. The Georgia Philharmonic Orchestra — the big, more well-known, major orchestra in Atlanta, had reviewed her video audition and was impressed with her live Zoom interview from the month before. The email welcomed her to join them in January for a midseason start once another cellist moved on. Several attachments were contracts, legal documents, and a list of sheet music to expect at her home address, assuming she accepted the higher-prestige, higher-paying job.

She couldn't stop smiling as she signed everything and hit *send*.

The house was mostly packed. The small cardboard box containing a few sentimental items sat by the front door, ready for her drive home tomorrow. The realtor had been right. Selling the house hadn't been a problem. Her phone rang.

Speaking of realtors.

"Hey, Rhoda, how are things?"

"Not bad at all, sweetie." Rhoda had a strong New Jersey accent, and "all" sounded like "awl." She'd been recommended by Barney, who had left explicit instructions for Pru about how to settle his affairs. His gift to her in this sense was knowing she'd be overwhelmed if things weren't spelled out for her in order. "I'm coming over with some papers for us to review before closing tomorrow." Rhoda dropped her r's in some words and pronounced "property" more like "prahpudy." The accent was similar to Shawn's except more exaggerated.

Pru clutched the back of the kitchen chair. Her knuckles were already white. "I wasn't expecting company. Can't I just look them over tomorrow?"

"I'm nearby with my daughter and son-in-law — they're down here visiting for one more day. They're looking for someplace similar and I thought it couldn't do any harm, could it? So I'll bring the papers with me. It'll be one-two-three quick. We'll be by in half an hour."

"No."

There was silence on the other end of the phone. That was a word Pru had gotten used to saying more and more often, and doing so rarely nauseated her anymore. When she'd first arrived, Edie had had to do just about everything for her by proxy.

"I need at least a few hours before you get here." Living by herself with no friends around had taught her that adding "please" when she in no uncertain terms meant "no" was an invitation for people to try to wear her down, and they usually did.

Rhoda laughed. "Honey, what did you do, throw a big party last night? You're neat as a pin. I'm grabbing my keys and the papers now." Pru heard the click of the realtor's heels across the light wood floor of her office.

"Rhoda, I mean it. Y'all can come, but I need that extra time. You can stop by late this afternoon, maybe around four." She kept her voice calm and firm.

There was more silence on the other end. "Okay, sweetheart. I'll take all the kids out to breakfast and do some shopping first. It's eight in the morning. I bet you just rolled out of bed. Take your time."

"Thanks, Rhoda." They hung up.

Pru had already made the bed and showered, but she needed the mental space before more strangers and a gregarious, bright-pink-lipsticked realtor with dark, teased-out hair descended on her. The therapist she'd been seeing had focused on helping her work with her anxiety rather than try to tamp things down. Matilda hadn't had to come to her rescue very often over the last couple of weeks.

But this was the morning she was going to let herself fall apart completely. That would leave her the rest of the day to pull herself together before closing tomorrow and driving back to Georgia the following morning.

She rose and did a happy dance, then called Tommy. "I did it. They're hiring me."

"Baby girl, that's amazing news. We can have a combination engagement party, new job party, and promotion party for Edie when you get your butt back up here."

"Edie was promoted?"

Tommy laughed. "Don't you ever read your texts?"

She chuckled. "I've been turning my phone off at night." A few seconds of silence went by. "It's going to be strange coming home after all this time. It was bad enough when I got back from New York. I sure hope he's happy with his decision." She imagined Shawn and Helena at a wedding altar, her in a tight doily of a dress and him in a tuxedo. "I hope he enjoys strangling in the silk neckties he'll be wearing for the rest of his life."

"Remind me never to piss you off."

Pru laughed. "I've warned you enough times."

"Oh, don't I know it." Tommy chuckled. There was a long pause. Eventually, the ten-weeks-long adrenaline high from anger was going to wear off. A fresh start in a new job in a new city could not have presented itself at a better time, probably. Tommy let out a long sigh. "Scroll back through your texts."

She switched to speakerphone and looked. "There are two from Edie from yesterday. One is about her promotion. I'll call her tonight when she's less likely to be busy. The other has some links and just says *It's time you saw this*. I bet that's spam. Maybe she's been hacked. I'll email her and delete that as soon as I'm off—"

"It isn't spam, and she hasn't been hacked. Don't delete anything. Just follow the links after we hang up. I've gotta run, anyway. Keep an open mind and forgive her for not showing you sooner."

"I will. Love you."

"Love you too."

She hung up and turned to Matilda. "What do you think, Mattie?" Matilda was sitting next to the door, thumping her tail against the wall. Pru got up and retrieved the plain, stainless-steel urn on the counter. It, her new job and inheritance, and Edie's messages reminded her of the large tile she had on her wall at home—*To Everything There Is a Season*. She thought about the deep, bright colors of the tree and the red bird in its branches. Still, things were changing at breakneck speed. She wondered whether she'd be able to keep up for long. "Let's go outside."

Matilda bounded out the door as soon as Pru opened it and made a beeline for the water. Tall clumps of grass and cattails swayed in the breeze. They had the entire expanse of sand and clear, green ocean all to themselves. Pru spread a blanket, placed some rocks on the corners to keep it from blowing away, and set down the canister. She threw a stick for Mattie to chase a few times. Matilda's low-tide swims had done wonders for her arthritis. She wasn't limping anymore and she'd lost a little extra weight.

She picked up the urn again, opened the lid and started to pour Barney's ashes along the shoreline, far enough away from where Matilda was swimming to keep her from rolling in them. When she came to the last of them, Pru took a shuddery breath and watched them disappear into the Gulf of Mexico. "I love you, Uncle Barney. Thank you for, well, all of it. For all my life."

She returned to sit on the blanket with the empty jar. Finally, after so many weeks, she let the breakdown begin, as if a clawed, fanged beast had torn off a door inside her and broken through. Pru wrapped her arms around her bare shins as she shook. She allowed all that pressure to erupt through her chest, bottleneck at her throat, and push out the first few tears. The sobs built up speed. Bubble after bubble of loss, loneliness, and fear rose through her and burst, causing her to cry so hard that Matilda ran from the water to lie next to her.

Pru choked and gasped over each new wave of sobs. She cried for her parents, her brother, and for Grandma Esther and Uncle Barney. She grieved her upcoming loss of having Tommy next door all the time and worried over leaving a job she didn't love, anyway, in favor of the unknowns involved in a new job in a new place. She cried for the boyfriend she'd loved so much. Most of all though, she finally let herself cry because there was nothing left that she could do.

When she was out of tears, the heaviness that had nearly shoved her into fetal position lifted enough for her to sit straighter and scratch Mattie's head. "Okay, girl. Go play."

Matilda stood and galloped to jump into the water again, then ran out and rolled around on the sand until it covered her head-to-tail and stomach-to-back.

Pru laughed. Everything would be okay. She'd proven to herself that she could be alone.

She pulled her phone from her pocket. Over an hour had gone by. Then she remembered Edie's texts.

Wide-eyed and gobsmacked, she watched videos of Shawn standing onstage in Helena's parents' backyard and reaming everyone standing there with him. She gaped at Helena admitting to having tampered with Shawn's phone, and Shawn throwing away a family heirloom just because it had been on Helena's hand. Pru shuddered. She'd jumped to the wrong conclusion and pushed him away.

The tide crept along the shoreline and sank into the sand. For most of her life, she'd believed the world was conspiring against her. That wasn't true. Losing Shawn was her own fault. Her friends always said she was too forgiving and trusted people too easily. They were wrong — she was too pig-headed and jumped to paranoid, cynical conclusions too hastily. On top of that, she'd made a promise, and she'd blown it to smithereens.

"I'm sorry, Uncle Barney." She looked at the empty canister and envisioned her life as a broken clay urn, imagined the gaping holes there would still be as she pieced it together again. Shawn had once quoted a Yeats poem to her:

Things fall apart; the center cannot hold . . .
everywhere the ceremony of innocence is drowned . . .
The best lack all conviction.

She wasn't the best of anything, though. She'd taken a hammer to her own heart.

CHAPTER FIFTY-FOUR

Maybe it wasn't too late. Pru opened her contacts list and remembered she didn't have Shawn's number or email programmed into her phone. Panic squeezed around her ribs.

Joe will have it.

Pru was just starting to scroll for Joe's number when Matilda jumped to her feet, barked once, and sped toward the house, wagging her tail. Pru stood, wiped the sand off herself, and looked over her shoulder. "Matilda, get back here."

The dog ran back into the water, spun around, and did a puppy bow. Pru turned in the direction that Matilda was so excited about. She had to shield her eyes against the sun and saw the dark outline of a man.

"I'll go if you say to." The man held his palms out. She recognized his voice immediately. "But please, let me at least talk to you. Let me look you in the face one more time and you'll never have to see me again if that's what you want."

Pru blinked as he walked forward. He was wearing the same faded gray SUNY Buffalo T-shirt and shorts as on the first day they'd met.

She couldn't move for a few seconds as he approached. When he touched her hand, she grabbed his face and kissed him. "You're really here."

He folded her against him. "I never stopped loving you. I can't, and I don't want to." His voice broke.

She pulled far enough away to look at him again. He'd grown back his short beard, and his messy hair was a little too long. His eyes were wet and turning red as he bit his lip. "I should have listened to you," she said. She wrapped her arms around his waist and pressed her ear to his chest. His heart was racing.

Shawn's posture relaxed. "Oh, thank God." He lowered his head and kissed her, first tentatively, barely touching his lips to hers. Then they softened their mouths and she grabbed the back of his shirt.

He pushed his tongue between her lips. She half-sucked, half-inhaled him in. They could consume each other. They'd pull one another's skin and skeletons into their mouths until he was her and she was him. She slid her hands under his shirt and dug her fingertips between his ribs and he pulled it the rest of the way off. Their hips struck against each other like a match swiping along its striker.

Pru backed up, pulling him along until they were standing on the blanket. He held her breasts and trailed kisses along her collarbones then found his way back to her mouth. His beard scraped against her skin. She leaned up and caught his lower lip between her teeth. They fell to their knees and grabbed fistfuls of each other's hair. He pulled her forward as he sat and then tensed. "Ow."

She pulled away. "Are you okay?"

"Yeah," he replied. "I brought you something. I just jabbed a sensitive spot with it."

"You brought yourself. That's all I want."

He lifted a hip and dug around his front pocket until he produced a small box. Pru stiffened. "Don't panic. It's not what you think."

Pru took the box from him and opened it. The small Star of David he'd shown her while they waited out the rain in his car—the gift from his grandparents—glinted in the light. It was attached to a thin gold chain.

"I wanted you to have something meaningful from me. Every time I saw this on my keys, I remembered that first day we met, and how I couldn't find your grandmother's *chai*."

Her eyes teared. "Thank you." She handed him the box. "Will you put it on me?"

Shawn pushed her mess of a braid aside and fastened the clasp behind her neck.

As she sat between his legs, he wrapped his arms around her and they watched the water. Periodically, Matilda trotted over with a stick and Shawn leaned around to toss it into the small waves. He kissed behind Pru's ear. "I will never, ever do anything to hurt you again."

She leaned her head back. "I hurt you too. I jumped to conclusions when I should've trusted you."

Shawn wrapped his arms around her more tightly and she twisted around to kiss his jaw. Then he pulled her on top of him, working his hand up a leg of her shorts.

"We can't have makeup sex out here. It's not as fun as it looks in the movies. Sand literally gets everywhere." Pru rolled off him and pulled him to stand.

The corner of his mouth lifted. "Is that right? And you know this how?"

She grinned. "Trust me."

Shawn sucked in his lower lip. "Implicitly." Matilda ran up and shook herself out, sending water, sand, and dog hair all over their legs. Threading her fingers between his, Pru led him into the house.

CHAPTER FIFTY-FIVE

Shawn opened his eyes, rolled over, and peered past the edge of the bed to check the clock on his phone. It was a few minutes after twelve. Pru was still curled against him, hair splayed over her face. He carefully extricated himself, threw his shorts back on, and softly whistled for Matilda who, having been dozing by the foot of the bed, trotted over. She smelled like dead fish.

"Oh, man." He wrinkled his nose and turned his head. "Okay, let's get you cleaned up."

Two towels hung in the tiny bathroom on a couple of hooks. He recognized the color scheme as French Vanilla and Amazonian Green. Shawn was certain that every possible color of paint in Home Depot and Lowes would be forever burned into his consciousness.

The dog followed him to the bathroom, saw him pull back the sea foam green curtain, and started to back away. "I don't think so. C'mon, in you go." He snapped his fingers and pointed. Matilda stepped into the tub, head down and tail between her legs. Shawn turned on the water, looked around, grabbed some of Pru's coconut-scented shampoo, and started to lather her up.

"I see you've decided to play bad cop," Pru said from behind them a few minutes later, just as Shawn was finishing Matilda's last rinse. The dog made a few pathetic whining noises. "She acts like she's headed for the gallows every time she needs a bath." He turned around to find Pru still undressed and smiling. "But thank you for doing this."

He leaned on the counter and couldn't help smiling back. A few months ago, she'd covered up her midsection whenever possible. The hard relief on one side of her small waist was as beautiful as the smooth other side. That was the side that reminded anyone she allowed to see it of what she'd overcome.

Pru covered her mouth to yawn. She'd stopped waxing, her teardrop-shaped breasts swung slightly, and with her sleep-tousled hair and noticeable tan lines, he couldn't tear his gaze away until Matilda whined again. He let go of the dog's collar. Matilda bolted from the room, rubbing herself along the walls and leaving wet streaks before he had a chance to dry her. The mattress squeaked as she grunted loudly.

"The sheets are going to smell like wet dog and sex," he said.

Pru laughed. "Wash me next." Stepping forward, she crossed her wrists behind his neck.

"We should probably both get clean." Shawn put the showerhead back in its cradle, let his shorts drop, and helped her into the shower. He'd wanted to linger there with her but the water turned cold too quickly. So he wrapped a towel around his waist, got behind her, and kissed her shoulder as she dried off.

Pru leaned back against his chest and sighed. "Too bad about the sheets. I'll have to do laundry before we go back to bed."

Lifting her heavy, wet hair to one side, he kissed between her shoulder blades and their towels fell away. Even with only an inch or two of space between her clean, wet skin and his, she was too far away from him. He pulled her closer.

"Shawn." She reached around and grabbed the back of his head.

"How about this instead?" Without waiting for an answer, he stepped her forward until she was against the wall. He supported her as she stood on tiptoes.

"Walls are good. Counters are probably good. The floor might be uncomfortable, but we could put down the pillows and towels and —"

He kissed the back of her neck, licked behind her jaw, and bit her earlobe. Then he bent a little and his cock pressed between her thighs.

"Oh." She pushed back against him. That was the end of the discussion.

At 7:00 a.m. two mornings later, Shawn waited for Pru to drop her rental car keys in the building slot. She slid into the passenger seat and they started driving north. They hadn't discussed Pru's new job in detail yet, or whether he was supposed to follow her to Atlanta eventually, or if she wanted him to get his own place if he was moving.

They still hadn't said much by the time they stopped for breakfast after driving for a couple of hours. As they picked at their egg burritos at a rest area picnic table, the unspoken conversation was somehow louder and more confusing than the silence. "What happens from here?" he asked.

Pru folded her arms on the table and looked at him. "Well, I thought we'd go back to my place if that's okay."

He shook his head. "No, I mean, when you start up with the Georgia Philharmonic. How did you want to work things? I figure you have enough from the house sale to get settled, but as far as moving . . ." He wasn't sure how to word the next part of the question.

She dabbed her mouth with her napkin and balled up it with her paper wrapper. "We need to talk about that. Between the house and Uncle Barney's assets, we can find a place together easily, even if we're out of work for a while." She looked down. "I mean, if you want to do that." Their eyes met.

"I'd like that, but if you don't, I understand."

"*We'll* be okay if we're not working?" he asked. "I don't want you to spend whatever inheritance you have on me. I want to be with you more than anything, but not if it's at your expense."

She bit her lip. "About that. When I mean *we*, I mean that even though Atlanta and its suburbs are more expensive than where we are now, we still won't run out of money."

For a moment, Shawn remained quiet. "Pru, I just got back on my feet financially. I'm not comfortable with being dependent again." He considered asking how much she was talking about. Maybe if they had some kind of agreement to pay her back eventually, he'd feel better about things.

"I've been thinking about it." She got up and sat next to him. He took one last bite of his food before shifting toward her. "What if instead of living somewhere that's just my place, we bought something together? Sure, the money would come from me, but we could open a joint bank account and put the house in both our names. If it belongs to us equally, then you're responsible for it too. It'd be ours instead of mine. And then I'd start working, and so could you, but I also had another idea."

He bit the inside of his cheek and nodded once. "I guess that sounds possible, but I don't have the credit for a mortgage, even if you took care of the down payment. The whole thing still sounds lopsided."

The corners of her mouth lifted by a fraction. "No, you don't understand. If we get a fairly modest-sized house we won't need a mortgage. It would just be ours outright."

She stood. Shawn grabbed his garbage in one hand and Matilda's leash in the other, and they headed back to the car. Neither of them spoke before he got into the driver's seat and started the engine. He let it idle. "That's all right with you? I just—"

"Yes, and I'm not her. I could never demand what you do or keep you as, um, a consort, I guess?"

Shawn laughed. "That's an interesting way to think about it."

"We've got plenty of time to find a place and figure out the details, for you to find another job, and all of that. But I thought maybe you might want to do something other than full-time teaching and physical labor. Georgia State and a couple of other universities are about twenty minutes from the nicer suburbs of Atlanta and they have MFA programs. Most graduate programs won't take you unless they mean to fund you as well—that's how it was when I was in school anyway—so it's not like I'd be paying for it. I would, of course, but I figured if you applied, you'd rather—"

He bit his lip, unsure of how to ask the question he was dying to ask. "Um, just out of curiosity, when you say you—or we—don't have to worry about finances, how much of an inheritance were you left with, if you don't mind my asking?"

Pru looked down, then at him. "About $500,000 in investments and a little under $100,000 in savings. The house sold for about $250,000 too."

Shawn blinked, unsure of how to process that.

She took a breath. "I don't want you to think that I think I own you. I'd never tell you what to do with your life. I want you to be happy, and I hope that means living with me. I was planning on donating a lot of it and using some for Tommy and Andrew's wedding gift. I'm still planning to keep working." She started to shake. "I'm not going to be like her, I promise. I—"

Shawn took up her hand and kissed her palm. "I can't lose you again. It took a few tries, but I think I'm over being stupid about that." He pulled her halfway over the console and kissed her. "Have I told you that I love you today?"

She grinned. "Yes, but I sometimes forget things. It's best

if you keep reminding me."

"I love you like crazy."

Sitting back, she looked at him. "I love you too. Let's go start our life together."

EPILOGUE

Two and a half years later

"A re you ready, Master Levinson?" Pru stood by the front door and waited as Shawn emerged from the bedroom. He'd changed into a pair of tan slacks and a light green button-down shirt that wasn't quite as wrinkled as his other clean clothes. His face was still pink and damp after shaving.

The corner of his mouth hitched up. "Don't call me that or it'll go to my head." Then he grinned. "Unless it's in the bedroom. We can definitely experiment with that."

Pru frowned. "Really? I didn't know you'd been thinking about that. I mean, I trust you and all, so I guess it's okay." She dug her nails into her palms and wondered what, exactly, he had in mind.

Shawn laughed. "I'm kidding." He closed the distance between them and hugged her.

Wrapping her arms around his waist, she looked up at him. "An MFA, a tenure-track job offer, and a pending book contract with a major university press for your novel all seem like reasons to let you have your way with me if that's how you want to celebrate." He'd worked so hard doing odd handyman jobs and teaching yoga, not to mention some of the original carpentry on their own house, all while he TA'd for the English department at the University of Georgia until he finished his degree. The novel had been his graduate project.

He squinted at her. "I'll take that under advisement." He let go, took his keys and wallet from the table by the door, and turned the light off. "Be good, Mattie." Matilda got up from in front of the tiny brick fireplace, stretched, and plunked onto the dog bed in the corner. Shawn held his arm around Pru's shoulders as they headed down the flagstones that led to his old Subaru, which was parked in the white concrete driveway.

He walked her to the passenger door. "Are you nervous?"

She smoothed out her dress—the same one, she suddenly realized, she'd worn that awful day in New York—and hunched her shoulders. "Kind of."

"They'll love you. I promise." He held her by the upper arms and kissed her. Shawn and his parents had been on regular speaking terms since a few months after they'd moved down, but this was the first time they'd agreed to see him in person. Pru had never been properly introduced. They had dinner reservations to mark Shawn's graduation, which had been just over a week ago. His parents finally were satisfied, as he put it, that he wasn't as much of a slacker as they'd assumed.

He lifted Pru's hand to his mouth. Her small sapphire engagement ring, which he'd given her the day he'd graduated, caught the last vestiges of twilight. The fact that they were getting married probably had a lot to do with this reconciliation. She threaded her arms around his waist and he gently bit her bottom lip. "Maybe we can be late to dinner."

Chuckling, she put her hands against his chest. "No, we can't."

He closed the distance between them and ran his hand down her waist. "I'll tell them we were practicing for when we're ready to give them grandchildren."

She feigned shock and laughed. "Oh my God, Shawn, you will not."

Shawn winked and opened the door for her.

As he pulled out of the driveway, he stopped before they

headed down the road. The pillar lights around the large pink azaleas blinked on in front of their white Craftsman bungalow with its sky-blue trim. "You never did tell me," Pru said. "You were keeping the title of your novel a surprise. Can I know it before you tell your parents?"

He rubbed her thigh, leaned in, and kissed her. She smiled against his mouth. "*This Is the House that Love Built*," he said. She rested a hand behind his head and they lingered over one more kiss. Then he shifted into drive and they were on their way.

The End

ABOUT THE AUTHOR

Karen Janowsky received a master's degree in English with a concentration in creative writing from Florida State University in 1994. Her poetry and short stories have received several awards and have been published in literary journals since 1990. Currently, she lives in Maryland with her husband, teenage son, and six cats. She teaches writing at the College of Southern Maryland and The University of Maryland Global Campus.

Printed in Great Britain
by Amazon